Praise for *The Umbrella Country*

"Bino A. Realuyo proves that the telling of a novelist's heart and country is contained in the smallest movement of moments. Word upon lyrical word, his novel is beauty that dwells like a beloved's lingering ache, a beloved's familiar voice."

—Lois Ann Yamanaka
Winner of the Lannan Award
Author of *Blu's Hanging*

"Heartbreaking . . . Poet Realuyo assembles a powerful array of characters for this coming-of-age story."

—*Publishers Weekly*

THE UMBRELLA COUNTRY

BINO A. REALUYO

BALLANTINE BOOKS

NEW YORK

A Ballantine Book
Published by The Ballantine Publishing Group

"Miss Unibers" appeared in *Special Edition Press: The Philippine American Quarterly*, vol. 2, no. 4, Fall 1994.
"States of Being" appeared in *Caliban*, Issue 15, 1995.
"Hallowed Be Thy Name" appeared in *The Asian Pacific American Journal*, vol. 4, no. 4, Fall/Winter 1995.
"Querida Means 'Dear' " appeared in *Manoa: Pacific Journal of International Literature*, Winter 1998.

http://www.randomhouse.com/BB/

Library of Congress Cataloging-in-Publication Data
Realuyo, Bino A.
The umbrella country / Bino A. Realuyo.—1st ed.
p. cm.
ISBN 0-345-42888-9 (alk. paper)
I. Title.
IN PROCESS PS3569.E U
813'.54—dc21 98-11668
CIP

Cover design by Ruth Ross

Cover photo by Rick Rocamora

Manufactured in the United States of America

First Edition: March 1999

10 9 8 7 6 5 4 3

For "Genie" Sintos Almonte

THE UMBRELLA COUNTRY

GUTTERS OF A HOUSE

It was the season of sun.

I was balancing myself on a foot-wide unfinished concrete-block fence across the street, watching this steady parade of dust, dirt, and people. In the sky were thin, overlapping patterns of yellow against blue, hovering over boys walking barefoot, pushing carts and belching out words in different tunes, a good day for the countless vendors who passed through our street every morning with their livelihoods placed on their heads and shoulders: mothers and daughters with laundry wrapped in huge sheets, older *Taho* men with thick soybean drinks in big cylinders, newspaper boys. They were so preoccupied that they hardly noticed me, except for this one newspaper boy—Boy Spit—who always and tirelessly gave me his five-second sideways stare and made faces about the Johnson's Baby Powder collecting thickly around my neck, my protection against sweat and heat, making a V-shape down my chest.

Then he would spit so loud and thick, I could only imagine a flood of sickness coming out of his mouth. Watching him, I knew somehow that he and I were one, as much as he despised my powdered neck and I, the thin dark rings of dry sweat around his. I knew I could spit just as loud, just as thick, and just as powerful, so that everybody here, even the hang-around-do-nothing *sangganos*, would wake up from their drunken stupor.

I could squat on this fence all day until Mommy noticed me and stuck her head out our window to make her long, spitless whistle. There was always something here to see. At noon, there would be a totally different set of characters, mostly bill collectors wearing their double-knit pants so wide they covered their three-inch-high elevator shoes. We all hid from these evil-worshipping, Brut-smelling pomade men, shutting our windows on them after lunch. Early in the evenings, the food women would pass—dried fish, *tinapa,* vinegared milkfish, fermented vegetables. Their voices were songs to these dimly lit streets, a reminder that only a few hours after the burst of dark, nobody would be allowed outside.

"Oy, curfew. Curfew *na*. Go inside," mothers would scream out their windows once the sun had gone down. Nobody would tell me what really happened at midnight, some big secret the whole world conspired in. Nobody ever explained why this was so. All I was told—police roamed the streets to catch anyone still outside. The jeepney streets were dead quiet, enveloped in darkness. Something about "Martial Law," two words everybody used to explain everything. "Oy curfew *na.*" So we had better stay in bed if we didn't want to end up in jail, or on the front cover of the *Bulletin*. All the children would scuttle inside. A series of shouts slowly followed and lights would turn off, in one house after the other, as if it was all planned, as if the houses themselves needed to sleep.

But they never slept, those houses. Ears, eyes, mouths, always awake, alert, watching everything, anything. Listening.

Piso. Diario. Piso per bote. Lata.

The wind brought me Boy Spit's voice.

Our house, where everything happened, a house of wooden shingles connected to our neighbors', ours in the middle of three, with aluminum gutters wrapped around the rim of the roof, like some cheap crown Boy Spit would wear if he joined our *Miss Unibers*, our house holding on to the others like a close-knit family. The gutters on each house were in different states of rust, bent and tilting on certain areas, marked by holes, holes on all of them, by years of seasonal typhoons. Other houses were connected to each other as well, all of them similar, some of them very old, some new. Only the color and age of the doors set them apart. The wooden doors were the first to go once the flood had sat still for weeks. One could easily tell by looking at the bottom, at the floodline across, the color of mud-softened wood. Most of our neighbors painted their doors immediately after the flood. Our door had the same color for years, a certain shade of brown, like that of a tamarind leaf days before it fell off a twig. Two long rows of houses facing each other created our street, ours to the east, where all the cats gathered, lying in our aluminum gutters to sun themselves.

They were always up there, those gutters; you wouldn't notice until you looked closely. That's why it came as a surprise when one day Daddy Groovie decided that it was time to change them to plastic. *Plastic,* the way he said that word, so forceful. *What's gotten into him?* I could see the question in everybody's faces. It was one of those rare moments when he actually planned to do something for the house that had anything to do with his construction job. The following morning, they were there: plastic gutters lined up inside our house.

Plastic. Women always used that word to describe men. *Ang plastic-plastic mo, so fake.*

"No more aluminum gutters," Daddy Groovie exclaimed, his face so dark his teeth gleamed. "Look at this plastic, made in the States *yan.*" Whenever he said the word *States,* he would raise his chin. He repeated it many times, staring at the plastic gutters that were just like his name—Groovie—made in the States, a name he had given himself while he was drunk.

The gutters were long. They would touch our ceiling if I stood them up against the wall of our living room. They looked soft, unlike the aluminum ones, whose edges were as sharp as Gillette's. I thought I could probably twist the plastic gutters the way I did my rubber slippers until I ripped them in half. They were clear, and I imagined the rain flowing through with everything the cats had left, or perhaps with the cats themselves, as they sat there lazily for days.

"Ready?" Daddy Groovie asked, as we all waited for his instructions on how to bring the gutters outside. "You take those." He told Mommy and my godmother, Ninang Rola, to hold the ends of one, while he and I took another.

Outside, a multitude of eyes were waiting.

The children of our street. Most of them felt special when they could boast about their houses being painted, their windows being replaced, or their rooftops rebuilt. They would run and tell everybody, as if we couldn't see what was going on or hear the noises of hammers and nails. But I didn't tell anyone about our new gutters, although I knew it was the first time Daddy Groovie had done something like this. I simply waited for the children to come and watch, watch me carry plastic gutters out of the house, watch me gather them on one side so we wouldn't trip over them. And there they were—English-speaking Titay and Sergio Putita—sitting on the unfinished concrete-block fence, throwing questions into the air—what are you doing, wow, what's this, plastic, wow, from where, wowow—and all I could tell them was: *I'm too busy to talk.*

Plastic, the way they said that word, only because they had never seen Stateside gutters before.

"Where is Pipo?" Mommy stood by the gutters, wiping her head with the back of her hand. I could tell she was playing along with Daddy Groovie. She had long given up on asking him to fix anything in our house. Seeing her with a hammer in her hand was a familiar sight. I had often found her with Daddy Groovie's tool belt dangling around her waist, fixing pipe leaks in the back patio, pounding the walls with nails, changing our fluorescent lightbulbs on the ceiling while Ninang Rola stood by to hold the small rickety chair for additional support. *Dahan-dahan. Dahan-dahan.* Be careful.

"Pipo's upstairs. That's okay. We can manage," was Ninang Rola's answer to her.

Mommy looked at me, unconsciously shaking a Gerber jar full of wood nails.

"He's studying," I said quickly, pretending I was looking at the gutters beside her.

Suddenly there was a ladder against the wall, a narrow and tall one from the ground to the roof. Daddy Groovie's footsteps on the ladder, then on the roof, could be heard from inside our house. Whenever I heard him make a big step, I would cover my eyes, quickly look at the window as if my own body would fall by. Somehow I felt it was me who was on the roof, balancing myself on the edges of the gutters, discovering toys we had lost after flinging them up into the air. But I had always been afraid of heights, unlike many of the boys here who climbed the roofs of their houses without hesitation as if the ground were a mattress they could land on should they accidentally fall. But Daddy Groovie wouldn't need a mattress, his body being as hard and thick as the asphalt ground itself.

Pipo, on the other hand, only listened to it all, in our bedroom, where the noise of footsteps was louder and clearer.

"Is he done yet?" he asked Ninang Rola each time she

came in. He stayed inside the whole time at his favorite spot on the floor, squatting and surrounded by newspaper and magazine cutouts. He gathered them toward him as soon as he saw me.

"What's this?" I managed to pick up one of the pictures without having to sit down. Between us was a box, half-filled with pictures. Taped on its side was a cutout picture of the world.

Miss Unibers, it said, in Pipo's chicken-scratch handwriting.

Pipo gave me a sharp look that reminded me of the stray dog that bit me when I was much younger, of the manner it stared into my eyes for a long time before it leapt at me, piercing its teeth deep into my hand. Whenever Pipo looked at me, it was always as if he was about to leap and bite, a stray dog, squatting on the floor, rib-thin and savage.

"Mommy is looking for you—" I almost didn't hear myself.

He snatched the picture out of my hand and threw it into his Miss Unibers box, without saying anything. Looking at the box made my skin crawl. I inhaled air a few times, blocking thoughts out of my mind.

That was Pipo. One quick look at his longer legs, you could tell he was older than me, you could see it in the eleven-year-old veins on his arms.

A week later, the plastic gutter melted in the summer heat. Sgt. Dimaculangan's wife came from across the street late that morning, screaming that our gutter was on fire.

Pipo was the first one outside. When he ran back to the house, he screamed, "Fire!" He stampeded to our bedroom, looked out the window, managed to sit on the sill, and pointed his fingers at the gutters.

When I came out, our neighbors were already there, their necks bent backward as they stared at the gutters on our roof. Standing beside me was Mr. Sing-sing from Tarina All-Around store. He commented that Daddy Groovie had not returned his ladder. He was talking to another man whose name I didn't know. I could only remember the faces of the neighbors who lived beyond ten houses from us because I had seen their faces looking out their windows, or I had seen them painting their doors. There were too many people in our street for me to know who lived in each house. If we didn't know them, we usually just said, "The old man from the yellow door . . . the fat woman from the green one . . . that ugly man from the dirty-color-of-his-face door."

Daddy Groovie took out the ladder and leaned it against the wall of our house. From the window upstairs, Mommy and Ninang Rola tied the ladder to the window with thin hemp and straws. "Steady," Ninang Rola announced. Both of them were wearing colorful sundresses with shoulder straps. Ninang Rola's straps were held together by safety pins that glistened in the sun. Her clothes had always been as old as her. She had never wanted anything more than what she called "God-given gifts." That day, her God-given gift had little rips at the bottom, parts of it bleached white, blown by the wind.

"That's what happens," repeated Mr. Sing-sing. "If he

knows how to return what he borrows, nothing like this will happen. *Dios ko,* it's been a week. Punishment. The Lord knows. *He* knows."

"What punishment? Things like this happen all the time. It's too hot to use those. What are those? Imported gutters? They will never last in this heat," said the elderly Mrs.-from-across-the-street. I gulped when I heard her but I didn't say anything. We always inhaled every word said by anyone older.

"What a waste! Stateside gutters? What a waste! Good thing Groovie didn't buy them," retorted Mr. Sing-sing.

"How do you know?" The Mrs.-from-across-the-street looked at him, slammed his back with her palm. "You know too much, don't you? You should keep your eyes to yourself, mind your own business a little bit more or *you* are the one who's going to be punished. You think you are all-knowing, like God-Jesus-the-Savior-Almigh-teee?"

The man snapped his jaws shut, his cheeks sank into his rugged face. He looked back to Daddy Groovie, the same look he always had behind his counter at Tarina All-Around store while waiting for the next person to walk by and buy something.

Mommy and Ninang Rola came running back out, one after the other.

"Not fire. Just smoke." Mommy stood beside Sgt. Dimaculangan's wife, arms swinging. "Just smoke." Mommy's face knotted as she watched Daddy Groovie struggle to go up. The corners of her lips pointed down.

Daddy Groovie grabbed the sides of the ladder and shook them slightly for balance. He also knocked on the bottom steps and tested his weight on the first step. He looked up while pulling the ladder toward him. "Sturdy," he said. The woman behind me let out a deep sigh, "Ayy." Then he went up. I couldn't help but stare at the two holes on Daddy Groovie's loose shorts as he moved up. *Where were his Jockeys?*

"Stupid Groovie," said a hoarse voice above me. "Thank goodness I didn't ask him to put my gutters up!"

I had gotten used to hearing his name mentioned by unknown people though it took me a while to get used to saying it myself. Groovie was not an easy word to say; I wasn't even sure if I could write it correctly. Most Stateside words were hard to say.

"Stupid Groovie," the voice said again.

When I looked behind me to search for the voice, I realized how big the crowd had grown. Families in the block who seldom got together were all out for this one. They even held each other's hands. Some were carrying umbrellas, hiding themselves from the sun, mostly women; men never carried umbrellas in the sun, they weren't supposed to. My playmates gathered around an empty corner, behind the group of hang-around-do-nothing men.

Even Boy Manicure, the owner of a beauty parlor about five houses away, was there, holding an umbrella decorated with little yellow butterflies. Our eyes met when I turned around. I quickly looked away. I noticed how everybody was fanning themselves with bamboo leaves woven and shaped like upside-down hearts. I suddenly started feeling the heat myself.

Daddy Groovie's weight rocked the ladder. He raised his

left foot but before he could put it on another step, one of the ropes snapped. The torn piece landed on his face and he quickly flung it into the crowd. *"Putang-ina,"* he cursed, then looked down, as if searching for it. A bird quickly flew across to snatch the torn piece, mistaking it for a worm.

We all held our breath. Mommy ran inside again. In a few minutes, her face was at the window, worriedly tying the rope. "Keep steady." She sighed and curled her lips to a wrinkly circle, puffing air, so embarrassed perhaps at all these eyes watching her. "Careful, now." She pulled the ladder slightly toward her. It started to shake again.

"Bamboo ladders usually don't break," said the Mrs.-from-across-the-street, after seeing me gasp a few times. She ruffled my hair with her hand. Her fingers felt soft, as if parts of them were being shed on my head.

I wasn't thinking about the ladder. Or Daddy Groovie falling. I was afraid that his shorts might fall off. At home, he was famous for his giant boils. I was sure he had one at the time since he had been complaining about how he couldn't sit very well. He also had been boiling hot water in the morning before he bathed. Mommy said boils were better taken care of by sitting on a bucketful of hot water. "Everything we need is around us. We have leaves and roots for all kinds of diseases," she would say. "Or above us," Ninang Rola would respond, while telling Daddy Groovie how God's wrath showed up in many different forms in the human body. Boils, just one of them.

His crack got longer and longer the higher he went. I wanted to pull his shorts up, these khaki cutoffs he wore in the house every day, old and seamless, with bulging pockets on the sides, where he put some of his tools. He seldom wore belts because they left marks on his skin. "But at least wear Jockeys," Ninang Rola always told him. When a screwdriver fell out of his pocket as he climbed up, everybody screamed. His shorts went down, exposing his buttocks. Pipo ran out of the house, screaming, "Who fell?" I realized that he wasn't outside the whole time when the back of his head was suddenly in front of my face. Some laughed, embarrassed. *Dios mío. Dios ko.* Mothers covered their children's eyes with the bamboo leaf fans.

My mouth opened. Thanking God.

No boils. No boils. Just a pair of what looked like dark, cratered moons in the middle of the day.

Daddy Groovie gathered his shorts up and rushed back down. I followed him when he ran inside our house. Ninang Rola showed up with safety pins. Mommy brought a belt, telling him, "Here, put this on." Although Ninang Rola was controlling her laughter, there was no sign of that on Mommy's face as she helped Daddy Groovie stick the belt through the loops.

"What do I do with these?" Ninang Rola asked Daddy Groovie, showing him the safety pins on her palm.

"Wear them on your lips," he said.

Ninang Rola burst into laughter as he walked out of our house again, yanking his shorts up, so tight around his waist his belly stuck up. "Ay, my God, that man, that poor man." She followed him with her eyes, gingerly putting her hands around Mommy's nape.

Soon, Daddy Groovie was climbing the ladder again. The silence of the neighbors followed him up. He replaced the plastic gutters with the same aluminum ones he had saved on the back patio. He had Pipo and me catching the plastic gutters he lowered from the ladder. Up close, I noticed how the burned holes were a little bit bigger than the termite holes on the walls of our house. Children younger than me gathered around us but I couldn't look at anybody while I helped, didn't even answer the questions they repeatedly asked—where is the fire, where is the fire? But Pipo, of course, with his arms full of guts, got them to surround him as soon as we finished, and explained to them what had happened, creating stories that made them nod their heads.

Ninang Rola used to say that Pipo inherited Daddy Groovie's thick green veins, what she called "guts." Daddy Groovie indeed had no shame. Full of veins. Climbing the ladder right back as if nothing had happened. He wasn't the only one. To live in our street was to have a skin as thick as rubber slippers. Shame, I was told by Ninang Rola, had only made people miserable, hungry, but it didn't mean one had to have no shame at all, maybe a little bit, because what was important was that we did what we had to do to fill our empty stomachs with food, to keep our lives going. Shame, after all, was inherited, like many things around us were, and there was no running away from it; one of those things that she always referred to as "Something in your blood. Nothing you can do about it." Ninang Rola was the godmother of words. Sentences, long and short, took a special meaning in her mouth. Nobody here could grab my attention as quickly as she could. She was Pipo's godmother first, and when they couldn't find one for me, she became mine as well.

Mommy stood at the door, arms crossed against her chest, jaws tight. Her eyes focused on Daddy Groovie without blinking as if they were holding him, pushing him to the ground, slamming him with plastic gutters. It wasn't the first time I saw her like that: staring at him when he wasn't looking, and thinking of so many, many things I could only guess. Ninang Rola was standing beside her, kissing her scapular necklace, reciting the names of the saints perhaps whenever Daddy Groovie pulled out a nail from the wood.

The crowd slowly disbanded. They mumbled and shook their heads while they walked back to their houses.

"No use." Daddy Groovie descended the steps and dropped the last plastic gutter. "Who needs this house when I go to the States?"

"Hay, *Naku*!" Ninang Rola walked back inside, shaking her shoulders. Mommy let out a big gasp, then followed her in. I shook my head and first looked up to what he had just fixed, then at Daddy Groovie while he went to the street toward Tarina All-Around store to return the ladder he balanced on his shoulder like a cross. He ran into his construction friends and laughed with them, hitting one of them with the ladder when he turned around. It was between his laughter and when he looked away from his construction friends that I caught Daddy Groovie catching a glimpse of the old gutters on the roof. I bowed my head when I saw his face, his constant swallow of spit and air that made me feel that somehow he had known, as much as he wanted to cover it up, that shame was very much in his blood, even if his guts spread all over his arms of veins.

When Daddy Groovie came home that night, he had shopping bags of food—fish, *ampalaya*, *kangkong* leaves, sacks of rice. He took off the shirt he wore on his daily visits to the window and handed it to Mommy to hang outside on our back patio. He put on a flowery shirt that reflected his mood. His thick pomade hair was the only thing that stayed the same, with little ridges that showed his scalp.

"Hurry." My cousin Maricon ran to me while I stood outside, my head tilting backward, mouth open, staring at birds hovering above. "Daddy Groovie got a package from the embassy!" she added, aware of what would interest me.

"Application forms." Daddy Groovie pulled out documents from an envelope.

We sat around the table, all seven of us, listening to him attentively.

"This is one step to go abroad. Important step," he continued, waving the forms pompously, showing them to us one by one: white forms, yellow forms, more white forms.

I couldn't help but hear the chorus of women selling dried and vinegared milkfish outside: *Bangus. Bangus kay-ooo.* The milkfish song at night.

There were already two fried milkfish on the serving

plate and little saucers full of vinegar and mashed peppers. The steam of white rice covered Daddy Groovie's face from where I was.

I waited for someone to answer him, maybe bring up the gutters again, so I would know what we were going to do with the plastic ones left lying in the back. I froze my spoon and fork and looked toward Mommy as if I knew that she was going to say something.

"Good news, huh?" she asked. Mommy asked the same question all the time. I always felt she was never interested in the idea of going to the States. Even when Auntie Dolares sent letters and Christmas cards from Nuyork, Mommy would only ask if there was good news, good news meaning exact dates, time, and place.

"Yes, according to Dolares, in possibly two years or less, the petition will be approved. Then there will be an interview at the embassy. Then, of course, I can leave."

So he can leave. Mommy's eyelids fell. "Why don't you take the stomach of the fish, isn't that what you like?" she asked me nervously.

"Y-yes," I said softly.

"Finally. Nuyork. Tall buildings. Good food. Better learn my English," Daddy Groovie said. Then he continued in English, "Spokening Inglis there all the time unlike here, in Manila." Humming while he scooped his rice. "Even Dolares speaks it so well now, huh?"

"Dolores, Do-LO-res, *not* Do-LA-res. LO, not LA. LO like Loko-loko, like you!" Ninang Rola pointed her lips while she scolded him. "That's all you think about, States, *dolares,* that you even change your sister's name. Not everybody's like you, you know?" Ninang Rola pounded her fork with her spoon to release the rice grain caught in it. She often told me that *dolor* meant "pain," that my Auntie's name meant pain, and that was what she was all about. I asked her to explain but she wouldn't. She always expected me to understand what she said the first time.

Daddy Groovie ignored what Ninang Rola said as if he didn't hear her. He was once again in a reverie, his eyeballs popping like his boils in summer heat.

"So what happened with the gutters again?" asked Jean, while her twin sister, Jane, said *Yes, yes.*

"I don't know. I was at the market all morning. I always miss these things, too, Ninang Rola," responded Maricon.

"Maria Consuelo?" Ninang Rola looked at Maricon steadily, which meant that conversation was finished before it even began.

"What happened, Ninang?" repeated the twins. Our boarders, Jean and Jane Lacsamana who weren't wearing the same clothes for a change, occupied the other room upstairs. They both looked so alike, bangs on their foreheads, thin straight hair down to their waists, so ugly that when they were born in the late fifties, the earth shook, killing over ten thousand people in the north. They lost their mother at birth. I always wondered whether the mother actually died at the moment the midwife placed the twin Lacsamanas beside her. Frightened to death. Her eyes open. But the twins claimed that their mother was swallowed by the earth. I thought that the earth had swallowed them, too, except they were immediately spat out, and spared, to bring more suffering to the world.

Jean took out her rattan fan and started fanning herself because the steam of the food made our house even warmer. "So what happened to the gutters again?"

Everybody ignored her, except for Maricon who opened her mouth every chance she got.

Mommy was quiet as well. Suddenly, both she and Daddy Groovie were not in the space where we were. Daddy Groovie: I knew he was somewhere else, in the States, working at his new job, the job he had been proudly talking about for years while he condemned his inability to maintain a construction job, blaming it on Martial Law, on the president, and on curfew because nobody could work at night anymore. And Mommy: she wasn't in the States, I knew that. She never spoke of a country other than our own. She rarely left the house, making dresses at home at her Singer Machine; I have five orders, she'd say, two dress shirts and three gabardines, orders, orders. The whole week, she'd be stuck at her corner in the dining room.

The worlds of this house. Everybody was always engaged in a world of deep thoughts. At dinner, Daddy Groovie was in his own—the world of the States—murmuring words that didn't make sense while he swallowed fish without chewing, grinning at the same time. Mommy's world was apart, her own; a world where nobody had ever been, or could ever go, not even Daddy Groovie. Especially not him.

A sudden burst of laughter brought Mommy back. Jean was spitting rice, trying to catch her breath. Jane was picking rice caught between her front teeth. Everybody was laughing but me. I had been watching Mommy the whole time, so I hadn't heard what the twins had joked about.

Mommy stood up and started clearing the table, taking Daddy Groovie's plate first. She put the plates on top of each other.

"Stop daydreaming," Ninang Rola said to Daddy Groovie. "Do that on your bed."

We all looked at Ninang Rola. Mommy continued cleaning without a word. Daddy Groovie put down his glass of water after emptying it, then stood up. Water dripped down his neck.

So quickly the laughter was replaced by silence. Jean and Jane helped clean the table by shaking the rattan placemats, dropping fish bones on the table. Mommy piled another handful of plates and went to the kitchen.

So did Mommy love him?

It was a question I had always asked myself. I didn't know what love meant then but I was certain Mommy knew. Love might be the wrinkles on her forehead whenever Daddy Groovie came home drunk. She would tell Pipo and me to get a pail of warm water and a face towel, then dab his face while we stood around. All four of us never said a word to each other, except for Daddy Groovie who recited words and names nobody knew and understood. Pipo and I had been part of this ceremony all our lives, the ceremony of circles: Daddy Groovie on Mommy's lap; a pail of warm water on the floor; the dabbing circles Mommy made on his face; the dizzying smell of San Miguel beer; both Pipo and I close by. All our worlds were somehow so connected and somehow so far apart, they made me wonder what brought us together in the first place.

The sound of a crying bird.

My eyes opened in the middle of the night, then my lips. *No,* I whispered to myself. I felt I could float through the ceiling with my nightmares clutched in my hands so I could hurl them into the aluminum gutters for the stray cats to eat at night. There it was again, that low, muffled noise. It might be cats meowing and scratching the roof, hungry and in heat, or the rain trickling on the shingles. I wished it would stop but it went on, just like it had many times before, except tonight it wouldn't go away. I closed my eyes, held my pillow, and waited for the sound to disappear, for the morning to come so I could forget, but it continued. Slowly, I moved my hand to wipe my sweaty face, hoping somehow that this was just another dream. Putting my fingers into my mouth, I tasted my sweat. I was wide awake.

The sound was in the room.

Our room was too small for four people and rows of cabinets but it expanded in the dark. The partitions of cabinets simply vanished with the walls. Mommy arranged the cabinets in such a way that Pipo and I would be separated from her and Daddy Groovie. They had the side facing the window. Our side was next to the stairs, closer to the lingering smell of food. We always slept with noises of the streets—yells of boys selling salted eggs and fried pork rinds in wicker baskets they carried over their heads—but at curfew time, voices disappeared, and it became so quiet sometimes that the snapping of leaves from tamarind trees could easily be heard.

I stepped out of my top bunk and made sure I didn't make a creaking sound. I landed on the floor, after using Pipo's bed as a step. I was the expert on soundless movements. I had done this many times. I used to get up late at night, when everybody had fallen asleep, to check if they were still breathing. I would stand in my favorite spot, by the dresser with the big mirror, where I could see all of them as the lamp post outside shone on their bodies: Daddy Groovie and Mommy in the bed at the center of our bedroom; yes, they were still breathing. Then I would go back to bed. In Pipo's case, I usually just moved sharply on the bunk and if my brother responded, by changing his sleeping position, I knew he was still alive. Then and only then could I sleep well. Eventually Mommy caught me and said a few words, as if she had read my mind and my fears, something about her dying in the middle of the night while I was wide awake to witness it. She didn't say anything else. That was all I needed. Ever since, I always wake up in the morning with an even greater fear that somebody will not be waking up with me.

Down on floor level now, the sound was even more apparent. The big eye of the window stared at me, flickering with lamp post light. The room had so many corners, I could hide anywhere. I went behind a huge cabinet and looked toward where Daddy Groovie and Mommy slept. In the dark, I thought of a cockfight, the way they looked, naked like that, two smoked, trained cockfighters except that their motions were totally hushed, and they weren't leaping in the air and scattering their feathers. I didn't know what they were doing except that Daddy Groovie was in control of whatever it was, his hands on Mommy's mouth as her voice passed through the holes between his fingers. The crying bird. The sound of cats. The rain. Mommy was pushing him away but he wouldn't budge. He seemed to be some kind of powerful giant who managed to pin her down on the bed, as if he had so many hands. I stood watching, still wondering if this were all a nightmare.

"So what are you going to do when I'm in the States, huh?" Daddy Groovie whispered. He sounded angry, although anger always came side by side a knotted face and pointed stares. It was too dark to see what was on his face. His voice got deeper. "Find another husband, huh? Huh? Huh? The way you always wanted. Just waiting for me to leave, huh?"

And no, she wasn't crying. I had never seen Mommy cry in my life.

"Groovie, stop—"

I saw Daddy Groovie lift something from the floor, what looked like a piece of wood and move it toward Mommy, grabbing her neck tightly with his left hand.

"Why don't you just use this, huh? How 'bout this for your new husband?"

"Stop, Groovie, don't."

I slowly walked away from them, sideways, not knowing whether witnessing all this was better than waking in the middle of the night to make sure they were breathing still. *Groo-vie.* A faint begging sound led me to my bed.

Bird, I said to myself, face up to the darkness of the ceiling, my body feeling the heaviness of its weight on the thin mattress.

We all slipped into the morning as if the night had its hands on our backs, pushing us. I woke up to an empty room. Ninang Rola had already left for church. She had a lot of walking on her knees to do. Daddy Groovie wasn't there either, probably at the piers with his construction friends, something I could tell by looking at the hanger by the door where his favorite hang-around pants were kept. Pipo was probably convinced to go to church with Ninang Rola so that he could watch her, make sure nobody took her bag. She spent her Sundays walking on her knees in Iglesia de San Pedro, hands postured as if begging for life or perhaps an early death, eyes at a steady gaze at the front altar, rosary hanging around her fingers. Her knees were darker than the rest of her skin as if they were permanently dirty. She joined hundreds of parishioners every Sunday to do this, atoning for their sins which she herself might have enough of. When I went to the Iglesia one time, I noticed how clean and shiny the marble floor was, then I saw Ninang Rola on her knees. How I wished they could all come to our house so I didn't have to polish the floor with red Johnson's Wax every other day.

Mommy walked in and opened the cabinet door. I went to the other side, so that I wouldn't see her undressing. I didn't leave the room. I looked away, pretending I wasn't watching, something I had been doing for as long as I could remember. I had seen her naked many times. I had carefully examined the contours of her body, delighted by the way her round breasts hung like curtains to her chest, her nipples mounting to marble-shaped tips. How different her body was from Daddy Groovie's rugged and muscular one. Her skin was very light, even lighter when the sun shone on her back; her stomach was very flat and smooth, unlike Ninang Rola's scarred one.

"Gringo. *Lumabas ka,*" Mommy said. She never asked me to leave the room before. Her voice came from deep, deep inside. Even if her back was turned to me, I could see the way she opened her lips when she said my name. It wasn't a panicky voice like when Daddy Groovie was fixing the gutters on the roof. It wasn't her calm voice whenever she sat at her Singer Machine.

"Gringo," she called me again. It was the voice between.

"Yes, Ma," I answered politely. But I stayed there, long enough to watch her drop her nightgown. Seeing her, I thought about the night when I got up from my bed: the silent screams muffled by Daddy Groovie's hands. The night full of placid drops of noises.

I nervously tiptoed out of the room, down the stairs, out of the house, but Mommy's body kept on appearing on my mind.

Bruise spots on her back, so fresh, so soft. Light lines of old scars, perhaps taking the shape of Daddy Groovie's hands.

I stood out in the street, in the middle, by the old Mustang across our house. There was a flock of birds on the street, picking on leftovers of bread. I always wondered about becoming a bird so I could fly away whenever I wished to, so I could watch our whole street from above. I chased them away until they all hovered around me and lined the sky, creating a cross, before disappearing behind the clouds.

Ninang Rola said that we all carried crosses on our backs, the crosses getting bigger as we grow old. Life is a trip to Calvary, and there are no easy ways to get there, she told me, over and over again, especially before she left for Iglesia de San Pedro for her Station of the Cross, which she made even more difficult by doing it on her knees.

Except for the newspaper boys who wouldn't miss a day of work, Sunday mornings brought empty and quiet streets. When I was about to go back in, I heard a familiar yell. I saw somebody who looked like me coming, although he was wearing a threadbare T-shirt and his feet were muddy.

Bulletin, the boy yelled again. He looked at me. I thought I was looking into my own eyes. He jerked his bundle of newspapers up his right arm. As soon as he walked in front of me, I realized he was his own kind. If the birds were to come together and form a human figure, they would look like him. Burnt face. Forehead with a long scar about his eyebrow. Heavy jaws. Bird lips.

Squaawwkkk. Boy Spit, I said to myself, this name I gave him in my mind. His thick phlegm landed between my feet. He continued to stroll away.

Bulletin. Diario.

"Pssssst," whistled a voice above me. I looked up to where it was coming from and saw Mommy behind the window. At first, I looked at the eyes of aluminum gutters and they looked back at me. My eyes descended to the big window grill, black and rusty, then behind it, to meet Mommy's eyes as she leaned against the windowsill, waving at me to go back inside, whistling a long spitless sound.

MISS UNIBERS

A bird died at the first sign of flooding.

From our second-story window, I could connect all forms of destruction with a seasonal song while I watched our neighbors fill up Tupperware, buckets, and drums with rain to be carried inside, but still, we quietly resisted the rain. The higher the flood rose, the more lives it took, sometimes animals—rats, dogs, frogs—floated in the flood and sometimes people and homes, which I had not seen myself but heard so much about. It was only this time of the year when I felt that there was more than enough of anything for everybody. As long as I could remember, water has always been scarce; it often got cut off or dripped out of the faucets. Not that I looked forward to floods because most of that type of water we couldn't use anyway, but the sight of water gushing out of nowhere always reminded me that somebody up there understood what was lacking down here.

A quick slam of wind pushed me away from the window, closer to Pipo who was on the floor beside his Miss Unibers box.

"What are you going to wear this time?" I asked, when I saw him cutting little crescent-moon-shaped pictures out of magazines. No answer. I could only hear the gush of humming rain outside and murmurs of little children as they playfully chanted over the death of the little Maya bird, slowly being whirled into the sewer.

Meanwhile, Pipo studied a black-and-white picture he had taken from Mommy a while back. Although he never asked me to watch the door or listen to approaching voices and footsteps, I would always stand guard whenever he did this, so nobody could suddenly walk up the stairs and catch him.

"Are you wearing *that*?"

Miss Unibers, our game of the season.

Games appeared and disappeared in our street. When they came back, if they ever did, they would usually take another form, like soft drink bottle caps: gambled with one year, shot up into the gutters the next, and flattened to become caroling instruments at Christmas. It happened every few months to accommodate the changing weather, but no one could really tell what we would come up with next. Unpredictable as typhoons, *pabago-bago ng isip,* the elders would say about us because our temperaments changed quickly, sometimes long after a flood or before all our rubber slippers were made into boats.

While all the other boys gambled with marbles, play-cards, and rubber bands to know who would be ruling our street next, the rest of us busied ourselves with Miss Unibers in those last days of the sun. I remember it clearly: I was standing at the back of the red cement steps of English-speaking Titay's verandah, watching with dismay the two contestants left in front of us. Plants in big terracotta pots made leafy walls on either side of the stairs and the big, old wooden doors carved with the letter *R.* We were hidden from outside, from other children like Big Boy Jun and his marble-gambling friends who would surely taunt us upon seeing us in costumes. The tall plants absorbed our voices, even English-speaking Titay's loud, cracking one.

"Secon-runnerup, Miss Germanee!" Her voice was an out-of-tune song.

I clapped my hands to a succession of questions, overlapping like the rat-ta-tat yells of newspaper boys in the morning: Why was everybody so quiet when I sang? Would I ever make it to the top three? Did I have to sneak out in my mother's clothes to win this? Wasn't a wraparound of bedsheets and curtains enough for a gown?

"Firs-runnerup, Miss Ha-why."

English-speaking Titay gingerly pinned the sequined sash around Ling-ling who was wearing her first holy communion dress, layered with lace. English-speaking Titay was known for harassing boys with her big, flabby arms and her English in such a way that nobody would engage her in an altercation, mistaking the thickness of her skin for English proficiency. "What chu want?" she yelled at a boy one time, and the boy ran away, frightened not by

English-speaking Titay, who was shorter than him, but by words he couldn't understand.

I fingered the edge of my glittering sash as I gawked at the plastic table roses stuck across Ling-ling's chest, the green stems visible from afar. I had thought about wearing something similar but I couldn't find any in our house. We had only kept real plants; cutting parts of them would probably kill them. Ninang Rola would certainly get upset, especially after having patiently spent a great deal of time applying egg white on the leaves for them to glimmer. I grabbed my falling wraparound, wondering what had happened to the big safety pin that kept my costume in place. "Stop wiggling." Ling-ling turned to me with huge eyes and a whisper while she faked a smile on her face. Born a duck, she grew up into a girl. But even at the age of nine, she still possessed all the characteristics of a duck: her toes were so spread open that pebbles would always get caught between them; she lifted one leg to rest; her tongue was too small, she squeaked when she spoke.

"Tenk chu. Tenk chu. Eeek."

The winner stood there, towering over all of us. Unlike me, he hardly had a spot of sweat on his face. His costume was an island spice, flavored with candle-wax fruits on his head and a very, very tight nightgown, the one Mommy had been looking for for over a month. For days, she attached *puñeta* to all the names of our closest relatives—*puñeta* Mrs.-from-across-the-street, *puñeta* Sgt. Dragon Dimaculangan, *puñeta* Baby Cherry Pie—blaming the neighbors for stealing our clothesline with fishhooks. I never said a word. I wasn't even surprised to see Mommy's nightgown appear again as a gown with heart-shaped pieces of velvet fabric pasted all over it, shoulder straps replaced by a plastic vine of sequined multicolored leaves, a lace table runner on his back like a cape. All of them looking familiar. Even him. Pipo. Miss Unibers.

For the third time.

The rain swooshed so heavily that the sliding window shutters almost shook out of their grooves. I held them firmly to keep them from falling over. Behind me was Pipo. Behind me, our room. Pipo. This room layered with wallpaper over the years. Mommy said I was born here. In this very space, a few months after Pipo was born, I was conceived. It could have been raining outside, too; that was when couples like Sgt. and Mrs. Dimaculangan had nothing better to do but make babies. It could have been during the summer, during one of the brownout nights, when the city tried to conserve energy and turned everybody's lights off. Those nights, when mosquitoes haloed people's heads, they slid the shutters closed. Then I was conceived. Then I was born.

There was one big bed in the middle of our room.

Mommy and Daddy Groovie slept there, where I could have been conceived but no one would say. They never spoke to me about things that happened before my birth as if our lives only began thereafter. When I looked at the bed, I always imagined Mommy and Daddy Groovie's cockfight at night, thinking I could have been conceived immediately after what they did. That same bed was where I spent mornings as a small child waking up in my own wetness. Mommy covered the mattress with a multifold of blankets because of the stains I left. She decided one day to stuff my Jockeys with thick pieces of carefully folded cloth so that when I wet at night, I wouldn't wet the bed. I would go to sleep with a huge bulge in my shorts. Every morning when I woke up, the cloth was soaking wet. And so was the bed. A bigger wet spot overlapping with the other stains. Mommy said I would ruin the bed by peeing on it all the time, so she decided to move us into a bunk, me on top, Pipo on the bottom. The mattresses were thin. In a few months, they were thinner. The following year, I stopped wetting myself. I dreamt that I was inside an empty drum that we used to fill with rainwater. Somehow, being inside, the drum was taller than me. The paint inside peeled. It began to rain. Not until the rain reached my neck did I realize it was my own pee. Boy Manicure, from the beauty parlor five houses away, was there. Although I couldn't see him, I knew he was watching and laughing away. It could have been the sound of his laughter that reverberated inside the drum that woke me up, or the sudden flash of his Technicolor Revlon face in front of me. But I knew when I woke up I was dry, and I had been waking up dry since. I told everybody that a dream of rain healed me. Ninang Rola attributed the change to God's blessings, which for her, and many of us, came through rain from above.

A window in a house. A big open eye that never slept.

The same window where Daddy Groovie spent his days sitting, watching the movement of life outside while he chewed on his peanuts. He would wilt like guava leaves on a hot summer day, collecting his dreams of the States, putting them in little heaps the way he would peanut shells. Sometimes, the wind would blow his peanut shells and Pipo and I would catch them like falling yellow leaves. Once, he created paper boats that never sank in the flood. He must have seen Pipo and me struggling with little boats made of paper, cardboard, or rubber slippers. He taught us how to make them. I was seven then. Another moment with Daddy Groovie worth putting in a picture album because it was never to happen again. While it rained outside, Daddy Groovie taught us how to fold the paper differently, what edges to cut, and once the boat was done, where to prop it up with a Popsicle stick so that it wouldn't sink. He would say over and over again how lucky we were to learn this from him since his own father never taught him anything, how there were certain things we had to discover ourselves. While Pipo built the paper boat himself, I was imagining how many black ants I could put in the boat. I lost one of the paper boats one day; when I found it again, it was still floating on the flood, resting on a stone, the ants very safe inside. At times, we would put black and red ants together in one boat and see what they would do to each other while floating on the flood. Nothing. They just made little holes in the paper.

Little windows on a boat.

Pipo would never give up. "Could paper planes fly better?" He once handed Daddy Groovie a plane he had just made. Daddy Groovie took it from his hands, watched it fly into a curve, go into the back of the cabinet and disappear. "Now you know," was Daddy Groovie's response while he walked away laughing. "What do you think of that, *PanAm*?" Pipo attempted again a few times—a house made of Popsicle sticks, a sword made of bamboo, the proper way to turn slippers into boats. Each time Daddy Groovie ignored him, saying, "About time for you to learn this yourself." Since then, Pipo learned to discover all on his own houses in shoe boxes, paint in nail polish, dresses in curtains. He learned to use his hands, sometimes acquiring Daddy Groovie's heavy hands, chasing me with them, hitting me right on the head, my back, or using them to throw things that he could never improve: a tilting cardboard that was supposed to be a choo-choo train, a worn-out slipper sliced in half to be a boat, a shoe box dripping with nail polish that could have been a newly polished doll house, and a Miss Unibers nightgown ripped in the middle.

Soon rain became the rhythm of humming, creating so many different sounds, so many songs for this flooded city. The thickness of the season lay on the ground, at least ankle-high. People sang or whistled while they plodded through the flood. I could hear little children singing for the sun to come back. Radios were on, alternating between early morning love songs and weather news updates.

Inside our bedroom, I repeatedly hummed a song I sang at our Miss Unibers. I could still hear the enveloping silence when I delivered my bathroom-rehearsed talent. Nobody looked at me. It would have been better if they laughed or expressed some form of emotion so that I could know how bad I was. I knew I couldn't sing and didn't have any other talent. Just this round, owl-eyed face. Twin balloons for cheeks as if I were always keeping air inside my mouth, about to blow Juicy Fruit. Lower lips protruding so that one could see the soft flesh inside, a mouth of pouting, a mouth that always seemed to cry. Gaps between chipped teeth, so that whenever I saw a Colgate commercial I felt that everybody was looking at me, up and down, my mouth getting smaller and smaller, this giant toothbrush attacking me.

My face was similar to the dark, except night became day and my face stayed the same. Many times, I had attempted to transform it by smiling differently, masking it behind daydreams of beauty queens in the black-and-white pictures Mommy kept from the sixties. Long glittering gowns. Mesmerizing bouffant hairdos. Arms and fingers, bent and spread out like mannequins in eternal postures of display, or like Virgen Maria on church pedestals, rings of flowers curling around her fingers, every week a new one. I imagined I was the mannequin at Aling Tina's tailor shop at the end of our street, whose dress changed every week. I would have the long and light-colored hair of Delilah de Samsona, the mannequin at Boy Manicure's beauty parlor. The perfect angular face of Sonja Carolina Santa Cruz, the head of a mannequin that mysteriously appeared and disappeared on Mommy's decade-old Singer Machine. But somehow I always ended up looking plain and flat, and my costumes like the old blankets that Mommy dressed the ironing board with.

And the one who managed to come up with the best

costumes was the same one who secretly stole Sonja Carolina Santa Cruz's mannequin head to use for fitting his hairpieces, kept his Miss Unibers box under the bunk bed. But deep inside me, I knew that he was born with the ability to turn towels and bedsheets into the most decorative gowns, and to walk with grace on his long legs without bending his back or losing his balance. *That* I could never quite get right. I didn't have the gift of long legs. Towels hung lifeless around my neck. I never thought about wrapping them around my head, the way Pipo did all the time, even at home. At our first Miss Unibers, he capped his head with Mommy's floral towel, a huge hairpiece, with all the flowers decoratively showing, and so high, twice the size of his head! He became Miss Kodak. Miss Swimsuit. Miss Long Gown. And eventually, Miss Unibers.

The flood left a layer of mud on the ground. Rubber slipper prints just about everywhere. Our neighbors were talking about how the streets were cleared of beggars, how walls were built to hide the slum areas not far away from here, this way the foreigners couldn't tell they even existed, how men and women were hired to clean the streets in red-and-white uniforms and to flash welcoming smiles, how we should all keep clean and stay around the block because somebody might come and pick us up thinking that we were children of the streets. It was a rare occasion—Miss Universe—in our country for the first time. You could tell the excitement in people's faces. Everybody was betting on either Miss Finland or Miss Spain to win it. *O, I'd bet my prize cockfighter for MisPain, O?*

Amid the thrill and confusion, my playmates gathered at English-speaking Titay's house to watch the Miss Universe show on TV.

Sergio Putita babbled about how so many Stateside people were arriving, as if they would come near here. We only saw them on TV. He added that since people were asked to smile at foreign visitors to the city that he was smiling every day. Everybody was acting unusual, too, especially Pipo, who couldn't wait to see the show so he was being extra friendly to English-speaking Titay for a whole week.

"What's that?" English-speaking Titay asked, turning to the window.

"Sounds like our General Electric fan," Pipo said, getting up from the floor that was so polished we could see ourselves in it.

We all ran to the window to see what the sound was. The window was not like ours; it was new, white, and made of metal, the glass thicker and rougher. Outside, the newspaper boys yelled and pointed at the skies. A helicopter roared above us. I knew that helicopters had been regularly circling the skies that month. Before I looked above, I noticed Boy Spit, standing in front of the procession of newspaper boys, as if leading them.

Sergio Putita squeezed in between Pipo and me. "You know what they're doing?" He began another one of his made-up stories that no one ever paid attention to. "Those are government helicopters trying to blow away the clouds so it won't rain again, especially during Miss Universe. We talked about this over dinner at home. Papa said it was embarrassing for the beauty queens to get wet in the rain because it never rained where most of them came from. So while it was raining here, they all traveled to the south somewhere. The president wouldn't allow it to rain again tonight so he sent off his helicopters." Sergio Putita spoke so proudly of what he knew. I stared at the ground, wondering how the government could hide the mud.

Putita. Little Whore. Sergio Putita claimed he invented Miss Unibers. It wasn't rare to see him singing "Sunrise, Sunset," his favorite song, and walking up and down the verandah steps and posing on the threshold, eyes flushed with an appetite for dreaming, spit drying in the corner of his lips. Pipo usually followed to show him how he should keep his back straight and tilt backward a little bit. They held each other up on the landing, cheek to cheek, smiles so big and fake, flashing missing teeth. It was English-speaking Titay who shouted, "Miss Unibers," but Sergio Putita screamed, his high-pitched voice sending summer birds back south.

"Look!" Sergio Putita pointed toward someone who was pulling his shorts up. "Big Boy Jun. He's so ugly. Even from up here, he's so ugly."

They all laughed. I continued watching Boy Spit.

"Ugly. Ugly." Sergio Putita started yelling at him so that they all ducked under the window. I hid behind the curtains.

Sergio Putita came from the most religious family in

our street. They ran all the Virgen Maria processions on Sunday nights. Anything that had anything to do with prayers, their family name was connected to: his mother sang at the church on Sundays; his father played the piano; his brother SWAT was an altar boy before he took odd jobs. Their house was full of tall wooden statues of saints with shiny faces and lifelike eyes, clothed with beads and lace that Sergio Putita hid in rice sacks and wore to Miss Unibers many times.

"Shhh. *La Madre Patria* is back," screamed English-speaking Titay's maid while staring at Miss Spain, although nobody understood what she meant. They all started walking back to sit on the floor. The newspaper boys began their parade, Boy Spit still ahead. While he walked past, I focused on his voice, ignoring the roaring sound above.

When I sat back down on the wooden floor, Miss Aruba was gracing the screen. Everybody thought she was from the province up north. Dark. Big eyes. Thick curly hair.

English-speaking Titay's maid remarked, "She's so dark. Must be Ilocana!" When the wrinkly old emcee whose name we could never say called Miss Aruba as second runner-up, the maid walked out, her face looking like she just dipped a slice of raw mango in vinegar and ate it.

"Aruba Ilocana beauty. *España Puta-Puta*. Pwehh."

She had no concept of countries but I had memorized all of them. But I also never thought Miss Aruba could be so dark. I looked at my skin when I looked at her. She was darker than I, although on TV, they all came in different shades of gray.

Miss Finland's name was announced. English-speaking

Titay panicked, pointing to the TV. "Oh, oh, oh, look, oh, oh."

"What? What's wrong?" asked Pipo.

English-speaking Titay stood up and ran off. When she came back, she was holding her doll. "Look." She put it next to the TV. "Look at MissFinlan, she looks like my doll! Oh, oh, oh, look!" She started jumping on the floor so hard that the rubber bands on her ponytail snapped off. The doll *was* a smaller version of Miss Finland—even on the black-and-white TV, it was easy to tell that she had blue, sunken eyes. "MissFinlan, that's your name."

Finally Miss Spain ran away with the glittering crown. We all watched attentively and nervously, wanting more than anything to fall all over her knees. Ling-ling, as dark as Miss Aruba, had that big-teeth smile on her face. The beak of a duck. Sergio Putita watched so closely that his mouth began to bubble. And my brother—he sat in the back in suspicious silence—I knew what he had on his mind. This reigning queen. Thinking he could do it again. Copying Miss Spain's big-teeth smile as well, studying her walk, her hairdos, her glowing eyes, her gait. Contemplating my death, my embarrassment. His skin glowed even more, getting lighter and lighter.

A whole city of children held in her spell.

"Where is Pipo?" Mommy asked before she sat down for dinner. I had removed the empty chair hoping that nobody would notice he wasn't there.

"Studying, perhaps?" replied Maricon. Her tone was one of disappointment because nobody touched her *bifstek*.

"*Viernes? Viernes? Qué se joda,* Maricon!" Ninang Rola had bellowed earlier in the kitchen, seeing the slices of beef floating in sautéed soy sauce and onions. "*Qué se joda,* Maria Consuelo Buenaventura. *Viernes.* Friday. No meat. Don't you know what's forbidden anymore? Enough to be with you in a lifetime! Don't drag me to hell. *Santíssimo* Rosario!" Of course, I knew she overreacted, as always, especially once she began saying someone's whole name. Maria Consuelo. *Consuelo de Bobo.* Good for nothing, Maricon.

"I saw him with books earlier." Maricon poured peppered vinegar into a bowl of fish sauce.

"On a Friday?" said Jean and Jane Lacsamana, the twin sinners, feasting on the *bifstek* that everybody ignored. We called them *Protestants,* another English word that was hard to say. Whoever they were, they had their own rules.

I knew where Pipo was, of course. This wasn't the first time he had missed dinner.

"Gringo. Where is Pipo?" Mommy read my mind.

"I don't know." I wanted to cover for him. English. Math. Religion. I wanted to say. Art. P.E. I wanted to add. But seeing their wide-eyed gazes made me realize it was perhaps too late; certain decisions were already made in their minds. But what was left to say? It *was* Friday. I quickly spooned rice into my mouth, and said in a low voice, "Studying . . ."

"On a Friday?" hollered Jean and Jane Lacsamana.

"Yes, I think," I said, locking my jaw and staring at the twins. These boarders, I thought, you never know whose side they're on! Although I told everybody in our street they were my cousins, they were as unrelated to me as English-speaking Titay's blue-eyed dolls. Even though we were all as dark as the soy sauce in the *bifstek*, I never felt close to the twins, knowing that they weren't here to stay, just like the rest of our boarders in the past. They occupied the other big room in our house; just the two of them while the rest of us either lumped together in one bedroom like an Eveready matchbox, or like Ninang Rola and Maricon, on a cot or on reed mats on a cold floor downstairs.

Daddy Groovie pushed his chair back, grabbing the edge of the table for support. I could see the rush of blood to his head. We had sat facing each other for years, the oldest and the youngest at opposite ends. I knew that blood. I knew when it went up to his brain. I had seen it with a San Miguel beer in his hand. The Spanish temperament Ninang Rola warned us about: Run away, when you see it, you must!

His steps on the stairs were as heavy as my whole body sinking into my seat. There was quiet at the table, as if everybody had lost control of their hands and couldn't lift their spoons. They couldn't swallow anymore. With head bowed and lips pursed, Jean and Jane Lacsamana got up and went to the kitchen. The rest waited. I stood up.

"Where are you going?" asked Mommy.

I pretended I didn't hear. I knew where Pipo was. That was where I was going. I knew what he was doing as well.

I sat on the landing of the steps upstairs. The door to our bedroom was closed. I could hear low voices downstairs, Ninang Rola advising Mommy not to follow. "When he's like that he doesn't see anyone," she was saying, "not even you and you know it."

Mommy listened to her in silence.

I wanted to go back down and tell her to stop Daddy Groovie but she probably already thought about it and decided to stay.

The long *yantok* was slicing the air. I could feel it land on Pipo's skin. This was always the way with Daddy Groovie. There was the need to hurt Pipo, whip him with his long, smooth, rounded bamboo stick that he had kept for us before we were even born. A dialogue with his first-born son, he called it. I could hear him cursing. *Puta ka. Lalaki ka ba o ano?* Huh? Huh? Are you a man? Who do you think you are, Boy Manicure?

Another whip landed on Pipo, another landed inside me. Boy Manicure, I repeated. Daddy Groovie always mentioned that name to Pipo as if it was one of his curses. I sat there knowing I could have done something; I could have said he's sick, he's in bed. They always believed me. I imagined Pipo cringing in one corner, hiding, as if the *yantok* couldn't go into the deepest corners of our room.

Daddy Groovie trudged out, still cursing. I bowed while he walked past and hid my head for cover, putting it between my knees and wrapping it with my hands. In darkness, as I closed my eyes, I saw Daddy Groovie's eyes, those angry squinty eyes, hurting Pipo, staring at me.

The door slammed behind him and opened. As soon as I stood up, Pipo came out of the room, dirt shaped by his fingers on his wet face. The red lines on his legs looked like long, squinty little eyes. Pipo looked at me with Daddy

Groovie's eyes, the squint of revenge. He grabbed my hair and banged my head against the wall and then ran away. My head almost hit the nail where we hung the broom. A spot of blood was left on the wall. I was too frightened to be hurt. There were quick exchanges of words downstairs. I walked into the room and shut the noise out.

Pipo's Miss Unibers box was on the floor.

For several nights, he skipped dinner to prepare for our next Miss Unibers. I always found a way to make sure he could do that, although he never knew I covered for him. His Miss Unibers box was lying on its side, wide open. Strings of fabrics were all over the floor. Scissors, Mommy's black-and-white pictures, a Miss Spain sash and all the other reasons why he won the contest three times in a row. Little hills of sequins separated me from the box. *Don't touch.* His voice appeared in my mind. *Don't you ever, ever touch this.* I thought about how many times I snatched bedsheets two hours before Miss Unibers and blanketed them around my body only to be laughed at. How I never had a chance to be one of the three finalists so I could at least announce the best interview answer I had prepared in my head for so long.

I walked past the box. *No touch. No touch.* The sliced air whispered softly.

Jeepney smoke swirled into the room the following morning, filled with signs of a good day. I was awakened by noises of people cleaning the street. I looked out the window and saw a few men throwing rainwater on the mud while complaining about the possible casualties of another big typhoon. *Thank goodness the flood went down fast.* Some had already started mixing paint for their doors. A group of women argued about what color to use next, if yellow or orange or anything bright would bring luck. "How about mud," one woman joked, "the color of his face." She pointed at an old man with a rooster who was maliciously gawking at them.

I wandered about in the room only to see Pipo's Miss Unibers box in the corner. He wasn't on his bed. I ran to the open door and heard morning voices downstairs. I slowly closed it and pushed their voices out.

I walked closer to the box. I tried to forget about what happened the night before. The yelling. The sound of air being sliced. The cursing. The smell of blood. Although I could feel the cardboard Jesus with the glowing heart on the wall observing me, my curiosity dug into the box. The feel of fabric rolled around my fingers. The fact that Pipo kept it from everybody thrilled me even more. The secrets in the box. Every minute, I cherished my discovery. Heart-shaped velvet fabrics. Jewelry made of tin cans. The curtain embroidery he wore the first time he won. Coconut husks. Even Sonja Carolina Santa Cruz, the mannequin head. And what was this—?

Long, smooth, black fabric. It clung like a cape with a hood on the top. Immediately, I thought of funerals, the blackness of brownouts. I wore it, touching its mystery, caressing its possibilities.

I was going to be the last one called. Miss Unibers at English-speaking Titay's verandah started very late. There were ten of us, double the usual number. I could already hear the names of countries: Aruba, Finland, at least three Miss Spains. Other kids from the neighborhood heard about it and came, a diversion they couldn't miss. From the applause down the verandah, I could tell there were at least a dozen people watching. The flood had connected the houses, linking secrets we had kept so long, the reason why we have never done it again since.

English-speaking Titay called Ling-ling. She was the third Miss Spain and number eight in a row. She copied Miss Spain's hair by wearing her mother's wig that smelled of mothballs. The redness of her cheeks was uneven, with remnants of the lipstick she had accidentally broken on her face earlier. She wore her older sister's yellow sweet-sixteen dress, a plastic lollipop in her hand. When she opened the door to the steps, I caught a glimpse of the children squatting on the verandah clearing, ten steps below us, giggling, covering their mouths with awe. They sat close to the walls of dwarf trees and thick pots of plants, leaving a huge opening in the middle for us to walk around.

Sergio Putita was number nine. I peeked through the crack in the door. His shoes made cloc-cloc noises on the steps. There were screams as he showed his costume: star-shaped aluminum foil cutouts glued to his skin with flour paste, enough to cover his private parts. He had stars on the exposed cheeks of his buttocks. He raised his hands up in the air, spreading his fingers, like a fan. He turned to his side. Pushed his shoulder back. Lifted his chin. Bent his knee. Walked down sideways. Rested the knuckles of both hands on his forehead. Then threw the blanket that he covered himself with. *Putita. Putita,* they cheered. "Misssss Finlann," he screamed, matching the loudness of their voices.

I found myself shaking down to my knees. I could see ten steps down and my head bouncing on each and every one of them. The door opened, the breeze came running toward me, and with it, silence. Eyes examined me from head to toe. My hood covered part of my face so that all they could see were my big eyes. The sides covered my cheeks so perfectly that they couldn't see my entire face, which was heavily covered with Johnson's Baby Powder. I thought of Pipo as I took my first step into the verandah clearing. As my clogs touched the tread, the wind blew again, into my outfit, inside, gently pushing my cape as if dancing with it, so naturally.

The silence was even deeper now, but I knew it wasn't the sound of shame. They all looked at me and I didn't see the shame of Daddy Groovie's eyes in them. I imagined how Miss Spain–Miss Universe would have handled this situation, so while delicately taking my third and fourth step down, I pulled the string around my neck, releasing my cape to roll down the steps. So magically. I could hear their hearts jump.

Now they could only see the nightgown that Pipo stole. Except this time, it was loaded with glittering beads and sequins shaped into stripes and stars. I slowly lifted my hands from my side as if spreading my wings, then put them together above my head to curl around each other.

While flirtatiously sliding one hand down to my head, I leaned backward and pointed my clogs against the edge of the step.

Halfway down, I stopped, holding still. I thought of Pipo again, the way he looked through me when he won Miss Unibers the last time, as if our blood was not connected. I thought of how he should have been here, how he could have easily won this, with his legs so long, skin so light, he would have beaten all the other Miss Spains. Suddenly I saw squinty eyes of blood, heard sounds of whipping and the loud banging of my head against the wall, a sound that has since stayed at the tips of my ears.

Pulling my shoulders back, I lifted my head to taste the embracing breeze. No more typhoon, I thought, no more typhoon.

And I took one last step down, hands resting on my waist. I examined each and every one of them, realizing how much their silence meant to me, capturing them with one blank stare.

"My name is—Sonja Carolina Santa Cruz viuda de Amparo Muñoz Pilipiniana . . . SMITH . . . I'm Miss Woodside–Miss Nuyork . . . I'm Miss USA."

HALLOWED BE THY NAME

Oy, Pipo, straighten your back . . . like that, no, don't bend your back, your hands, don't swish, keep your blood flowing through your wrist, uh-huh, like that, no, don't bend your arm, keep it down, like this, see? that's the way men are, always ready to blow, and your head, don't move it too much, keep it up, chin up, up, Pipo, up, as if always looking at the sky waiting for the rain, yes, that's the way to walk, don't wiggle your behind, wait, wait, where are you going? what are you doing? come back here, start again, again, now, that behind, keep it tight all the time, girls like it tight like that, you see? they're looking better now, now don't forget your chin, your hands, think about all of them, they're part of your body, think of them as one, your chin, back, behind, all one, that's it, you got it, that's the way, yes, yes, that is the way men are!

Daddy Groovie wanted Pipo to be like Big Boy Jun. At first I didn't understand, because when Daddy Groovie caught Big Boy Jun sneaking into our house and picking the stuffing out of the hole in our sofa, he chased him out, yelling, *Tarantado!* Big Boy Jun left a trail of cotton and little sponges in the street that I had to pick up and put back into the sofa. Then Daddy Groovie told Pipo not to associate with him at all, but I knew Daddy Groovie still wanted my brother to be like Big Boy Jun, act like him, not to put up with his embarrassing ways of calling him Pipo Pedicure—what could be worse? Daddy Groovie probably heard him call Pipo that name so he threw something at Big Boy Jun from the window. Could have been peanut shells, his weapon. Big Boy Jun dashed with the hot breeze. But Daddy Groovie hit him, right where it mattered, on his huge bald head. Big Boy Jun. Yes, Daddy Groovie wanted Pipo to emulate him. His idea of a son—big, boy, and a Jun—just like all the Juniors in our street. Two out of ten were Juniors: Apolinario Junior, Sing-sing Junior, MacArthur Junior, Junior Maria, Junior Junior, Junior the Third. And they all acted the same somehow, and had the same nickname: Jun. Must have been the water priests poured on their heads. I just couldn't understand why they walked with that same macho strut, as if their balls were hanging too low, too heavy; why they talked the same, in a way that never really made sense; and ran the same way, legs spread so far apart that they went in opposite directions. And the ability they had to make us shrink in the sun out of shame, because they had a way of coming up with names so quickly that they went straight through our ears, stayed inside our frightened bodies. Names that we wished they would never again remember. Could it be because they were all born with the same name? Junior. Jun. Big. Boy. Jun.

"Pipo Pedicure," Big Boy Jun snarled from the middle of the street. His face was a block of dark asphalt, always hot, and hotter while it melted in the sun. He took Pipo's ball of rubber bands and wouldn't give it back. Pipo tried to take it, managed to pull one rubber band only to snap and hit Big Boy Jun on the head. His head, how could anything miss his head? Big Boy Jun caught the ball and threw it over to his marble-gambling friends. Soon they had formed a circle around Pipo, forcing him to run from one boy to another as they threw his ball of rubber bands around. I watched them from inside the gate, my head going round and round until I found enough balance to grab a handful of little rocks for the little pouch I made out of my T-shirt. I scuttled to our bedroom. "Concentrate," I muttered to myself, "concentrate." From our window, I threw a rock at Big Boy Jun and his marble-gambling friends, and quickly ducked and looked through little termite holes that dotted the half-inch plywood wall. I missed. I threw a rock again and hit Big Boy Jun on the head. I ducked and waited to see if they could figure out where the rock came from, hoping that Pipo would remember what we used to do when we were much younger. Big Boy Jun looked around and cursed more. *Tarantado! Pipo Pedicure!* So did his marble-gambling friends: *Pipo-pipo-pipo-pe-di-cure*. Then Pipo began narrating to them the Parable of the Rocks: When Jesus ascended into the heavens, the clouds parted. Suddenly, there was a hole in the sky. Light came shining through, then it rained, it rained *rocks* on people who made it a habit to pick on the imperfections of others! I continued throwing rocks and ducking under the window until Big Boy Jun and his marble-gambling friends ran home in search of Band-Aids for their bleeding heads. They threw the ball of rubber bands at Pipo, hitting his knee. Pipo picked it up and looked toward me. It was as if he could see me hiding behind one of the holes in the wall. He was probably thinking about the day we had made up the Parable of the Rocks, when we used to take each other's side in all kinds of arguments and fights with other children. How easy it was to make enemies then, and how hard to make friends, because the children we saved actually believed that the rocks came from heaven. It became impossible to tell them that Pipo and I made it all up, to help them, to ultimately win over the marble-gambling boys. But they didn't believe us; they said God was on their side, raining rocks on their enemies. Much had changed since those days when Pipo and I would laugh just from looking at each other. Maybe that's why when Pipo came back into the house and saw me, he only gave a five-second stare into my eyes.

W*hen you look at people, make sure you look at them straight in the eye, when you look at girls, especially girls, don't twitch, don't wrinkle like a plant that hasn't been watered for weeks, keep your backbone straight all the time, your backbone, that's the key, you should drink raw eggs and Sarsi every day, it will keep your bones strong, come let me show you, pour Sarsi into a glass, then crack an egg into it, don't* *stir, drink it straight, swallow the whole egg, feel it splatter in your throat, like that, soon you will not be a boy anymore, with age comes the responsibility of men, and uh, girls, look at them in the eye and they wither, ha-ha-ha, when I met your mother, I gave her one look, that Groovie look, you see? I didn't have to work hard at all, I knew with that one look, I had her, wasn't I right? huh? huh? huh? I didn't even have to sing her songs at night to make her fall for me, unlike everybody else, serenading and all that shit, Groovie's not into that singing crap, see? that's the way to think, think to win, by looking at girls straight in the eye, straight, not crooked like your eyes are about to fall to the ground, no, don't bow your head, your eyes don't belong to the ground, up, chin up, look at the heavens, that sky that always looked down on all of us, what-da-hell, keep your back straight ayan, ayan, keep the stare firm, like the heat in your balls when you see girls with big tits, like that, Pipo, exactly like that!*

Sergio Putita's older brother, SWAT. The pig slop delivery boy. Named after a GI show on Tuesday nights. I caught Pipo looking at SWAT many times. Every Sunday night, during the Virgen Maria procession in our street, when she and other statues were moved from one house to another, I would wait at the window for the procession's twinkling lights. Every window in our street would be filled with curious people watching and smelling the sweet candlelight that approached with singing voices. Sergio Putita would be there marching. He would wave at me from afar and I would wave back but it was SWAT that my eyes followed: every step he made, his little leaps over puddles almost dropping the candle in his firm hand cupped underneath a cardboard to catch the melting wax. I could actually hear his voice singing "Ave Maria," so that I started singing myself, but when I looked down from the window, Pipo was there, waiting as well, his hands clawing the gate's grill until he could join Sergio Putita and SWAT. I watched Pipo laugh with SWAT, scratch his neck shyly with his left hand, play with the wax on SWAT's cardboard. *Ou-ou-ou,* he pretended he burned himself so SWAT could tousle his hair like a dog. They laughed so much they started coughing out words. The smell of candles was all that was left when they passed. And Pipo's laughter echoing in the room at night.

Every morning before I left for school, SWAT delivered a small drum of pig slop to Sgt. Dimaculangan's house across the street. I hated that smell, but I waited for it every day because I knew it would bring SWAT along with it. I would rest my head on the windowsill and watch. He worked for the city hospital nearby, where he stole frozen chickens, sealed them carefully in plastic bags, and buried them in pig slop. Every morning he took the carefully wrapped chickens out of the pig slop, splattering some of it on his chest. Shirtless, he would stretch with a look of disgust on his face that made me look even closer. An early yawn. His rib cage expanded. His stomach slightly protruded when he exhaled. His arms were shaped by years of pushing carts of pig slop. Sometimes, I would close the shutters so nobody would notice me watching, each time wanting to get as close as I could get. Once, I sat on the unfinished concrete-block fence across the street while Sergio Putita ran away from me, screaming because of the approaching smell. *Kaning-baboy, ang baho!* I found a reason to stay—I'm tired, need to rest a little bit, I'll catch up with you. SWAT pushed the cart in my direction, dripping with sweat, his shirt swinging around his waist. I bowed my head, raising my eyes from time to time to take a glimpse, to study the slope of his skin, the thickness of his shoulders, of his forearms. And if I missed him, I would think of the Virgen Maria procession, hum "Ave Maria," imagine the scent of melting candles and me, not Pipo, poking SWAT's wax on the cardboard sheet, burning myself.

Y*ou will never change, will you? just like Boy Manicure, aren't you? just like your Lolo Pino, embarrassment to our family, you want to know what happened to him? you want to know? he didn't live long enough to see you, to know that his blood would appear again,* impaktong lolo mo*! he died, eyes open, embarrassed, paying for everything he did on his deathbed, he probably paid everybody to attend his funeral, too,* baklang patay, *my father's poor brother, dead, like that? huh? so you want to grow old like that? huh? look around you, see who people make fun of around here? look at your father,* lalaking-lalaki, *real man, real man, look at these arms, see those, scars, scars, only a man would have those, look at you, you're growing up to be a girl, you know? Miss Unibers? Miss Unibers? that's for girls! boys don't dress up and become Miss Unibers! you* idioto*!* nasisiraan ka na ba? tarantado? *are you out of your little mind? maybe that's what it is—your mind so little, it doesn't work right, you want to be* *sent to Boys Town? there they'll discipline you, huh?* bubugbugin ka 'don, *maybe because you're not circumcised, that's what it is, chop that thing off, but listen to your name— PIPO, PIPO, so strong this name, when you say it, everybody keeps quiet, doesn't that say something to you,* damuho, gago, tonto, *that's not the way to walk, how many times should I tell you, you wilted* kang-kong, *dead plant, look at you, soon you'll be all grown up, what are you going to be, huh? beautician? might as well apprentice with Boy Manicure now while you're still young and make some money, make yourself useful, huh, huh? boys who think they're girls, they burn them in hell, every day a dozen, like your Lolo Pino, God-bless-his-soul, someday Boy Manicure will be burned in hell, too, his life is hell now, you want that? huh, huh?*

Boy Manicure had been watching me all these years. His eyes were the same eyes of our window, always open, curious. When I played outside in the rain, his eyes would play with me. When I walked in the street to school, he would walk there with me; my shadow became his sight. In our hide-and-seek game under the heat of the sun, I avoided being around his beauty parlor completely, but wherever I hid, it was as if he was there with me, telling the other kids where I was by his mere stare, behind a huge glass window, underneath the blue BOY'S BEAUTY PARLOR sign that swung with his gasps. I ran away from him. All I would hear was the laughter of my playmates, especially of Big Boy Jun, whenever he compared Pipo with Boy Manicure, swishing his hands, going "Oy, oy, oy," suddenly making me stiffen my muscles, straighten my back, and squat as if I was about to gamble marbles with the boys, my elbows carelessly resting on my knees. This way he would skip me from his teasing, so he would stay with Pipo while he limped his way out. I never wanted to act like Big Boy Jun. Never wanted to be macho like him. Never wanted to hurt anybody. But I didn't want to be like Boy Manicure either. "Beautiful eyes," Boy Manicure would sing from his beauty parlor while changing Delilah de Samsona's hair and dressing her up with clothes that glittered in the sun. "Butterfly eyes." I ignored him and ran away, although I wanted to watch him change the mannequin's dress. My shame ran away from him. But it wasn't because I disliked him but because all the other children ran away from him, their fantasies of disgust and fear voiced in whispers as they said, "He's dangerous." Nobody was really afraid of him. No. Because if they were, they wouldn't have found so much glee in ridiculing him. "The one who acts like a woman," they called him. The woman trapped in a body of a man that all fathers warned their sons not to become. Daddy Groovie's biggest fear about Pipo. My biggest fear about Pipo. About myself. *Pintada bruja.* They only saw the beast in Boy Manicure: thick makeup, dyed brown hair. Lipstick redder than fresh chicken blood. I ran away from him, too, even if sometimes I felt I wanted to talk to him. "Butterfly eyes," he would call to me. Sometimes I stopped and thought—maybe he really meant it—but the thought of children running overcame me and I found myself running away again. The children called him names. *Bakla.* A curse in every way. A word so permissible even a seven-year-old could use it. *"Bakla,"* Pipo said once. I choked. My throat full of words I would never say.

You see? if you listen listen to me, good things come to to to you, you see? like father, like son tayo, diba? *they didn't say that for nothing, me just like Papa, my Papa, he doesn't talk to me anymore, but I was once* el Favorito, *he likes me I know he does, he won't talk to me but I know he likes me, and why not? I was the one who looked most like him, acted like him, too, he-man, GI Joe, all the girls liked him, he didn't blink without girls staring at his crotch, s-spit spit coming out of their mouth. ha-ha-ha-ha, you're smiling, you think that's funny? huh? well, that's very funny, my papa is a very funny man, suddenly just stopped talking to me like that, like I was never born, how could a father just stop talking to his son . . . it's your mother you know? it's her! what? what do you say, huh? like father like son* tayo, *right? when you get to my age, Pipo, you will thank me for every . . . thing, for everything I taught you, the way you walk, the way you keep keep you you-ur backbone straight, chin up, your raw eggs and Sarsi every morning, all that Papa taught me, now you have it, you carry my blood, m-m-my name, it's yours, hic, and when hic you look at people in the eyes straight, always straight, that's right, Pipo, do do do it again, ha-ha-ha-ha, we will get along, along, I know.*

He came home late one night. Drunk. Wet with rain. Glassy eyes. No beer bottle in his hand. Slippery palms. He babbled about losing his construction job again, about rich people who always stepped on poor workers like him. About Martial Law. "If not for *putang-inang* Martial-martial this and Martial-martial that, I wouldn't lose my job!" He took off his tool belt, threw it on the floor, found Pipo playing with the pliers and screwdrivers later, found a reason to whip him on the legs with his *yantok*. He said Pipo was disobedient. Daddy Groovie couldn't see well so he missed and, instead, whipped his own shadow. His voice thudded in rhythm with the sheets of rain outside. Pipo was there staring at him when Daddy Groovie came out of the room and fell on the sofa. The wind blew the shutters, rocking them on the grooves. Rocking him on the sofa. They called me Groovie, he said, Grooooooo-vie, liked it! Stateside name, he said. He wanted everybody to call him Groovie. "Peace, man, peace man," he said, "no jobs here, but peace, too much fuckin' Martial Law peace." He made a peace sign with his fingers. "Fuckin' no one is building anything in this country because of the fuckin' Martial Peace . . . Law." He laughed. "Groovie, nice name, huh, Estrella, whatchathink?" Mommy and I looked at him, wondering why he suddenly wanted to change his name. "Nothing, nothing in this country, nothing!" Mommy and I began the ceremony of circles—Gringo, get a basin of warm water—Mommy dabbed Daddy Groovie's face with a warm face towel while holding him down with one hand. Round and round her hand moved on his face, each cycle erasing the smell of beer he brought in. I always called him Daddy. Everybody called him Daddy, even the ones who weren't his sons. They thought Daddy was his real name. But now he wanted Groovie, too. His arms lay on the sofa. Mommy took them and folded them on his stomach, which looked like a breathing mound of mud from afar. We didn't take him seriously until he fell asleep, but the following day, he remembered. The first word he said. And we have called him Daddy Groovie ever since. It was a hard word to say but we all managed to say it. *Groovie.* The sound his construction friends made when they strutted around for a good time after work, keys and tools clanging around their waists, only to find out later that they all lost their jobs again, finally finding themselves staring at crates of empty San Miguel beer bottles.

L*isten to me . . . always all always listen to me, you're my firstborn, never ne-ne-never, ever look away when you listen to me, you g-g-g-goddam . . . only girls look look away. . . .*

How I wanted to change Pipo myself, turn him into what Daddy Groovie wanted him to be, tell him how his backbone must always be straight, his chin, up, his wrists, firm, maybe this way Daddy Groovie would stop dragging him into the room to hide him from me. To make noises. He was the firstborn. Firstborns were supposed to act like that. They were supposed to be just like their fathers. Wasn't that why they came out first? They had to spend many hours in their fathers' hands to be shown the way to be grown up like them. Not under their belts. Secondborns like me would get our chance, but somebody had to show us the way. That wouldn't happen if Pipo continued to be like the way he was. Because even if Pipo didn't change inside, deep, deep inside, as long as his chin was up, backbone up, wrists straight, he could at least make Daddy Groovie believe that he had, and Daddy Groovie would slowly forget his *yantok*, that he ever had one. This way, Daddy Groovie would notice that I also needed to know how to act, how to walk, how to look at people in the eye, how to forget about SWAT and Boy Spit, especially forget how I felt whenever I watched them from our window, as if they would freeze right there, a picture that I could always look at, a wrong picture, at least according to Daddy Groovie, all wrong. And Daddy Groovie himself could teach me how to grow thick green veins on my arms, how to crack eggs to mix with Sarsi without breaking the yolk.

QUERIDA MEANS "DEAR"

WANTED: FEMALE BOARDERS.

Pipo thumbtacked a sign outside on a wall beside the door, written with a thick black marker that ran out of ink before Mommy could finish so that the last three letters of the word *Boarders* were almost not there. Our neighbor had posted the same from time to time: WANTED: FEMALE BEDSPACERS, if they had an extra bed in a room, BOARD AND LODGING or ROOM FOR RENT. Our street always had strange faces walking around, but while some of these boarders stuck around for years, most left as soon as they found a better place to stay. Mommy wanted only women to stay in our other room upstairs because according to her they were easier to deal with. Two women came and looked at the room but they left before I saw them. That evening, Mommy said we had found new boarders. Nice women, she said, they wouldn't have visitors. Pipo asked why. Mommy and Ninang looked at each other.

"They're *queridas*," they both said, in different tones.

"Que-rrrida?" Pipo's eyes widened.

I didn't ask anything, just continued eating a half-peeled banana that Ninang Rola divided between Pipo and me, wondering whether *querida* was what I thought it meant.

"Mistress. You know what that is? The *other* woman. You're too young for these things." But Mommy went on to talk about them anyway, mentioning English-speaking Titay's mother and Sgt. Dimaculangan's real wife.

Real wife? I thought. The other woman? I had never seen English-speaking Titay's father, at least not as often as I saw the other fathers of our street. We never really bothered to ask her where her father was. We assumed he was abroad because she had all these toys from the States. Now that I thought about it, abroad might mean something else. And Sgt. Dimaculangan? Who would ever think that all those children were his second set of family, all five of them, dog-thin and dirty, always running around naked and pissing at everybody? Besides, he was *always* there.

"We just don't say anything, let them do what they want. Home wreckers that they are. But do we have a choice? They're good boarders, quiet, don't complain like Jean and Jane." Mommy always remembered the names of the women who lived in the other room upstairs, and brought them up as needed. "They'll keep to themselves."

"Because they're in hiding, always running from the real wives. Woman are so different these days. In my time, there were *queridas*, too. *Queridas* of the Spanish priests. We weren't supposed to talk about them. Everybody knew those priests had children. Ahh, the children were beautiful. *Meztizos.* That's how all these *meztizos* were bred, you know? Through the Church, huh? *Santíssimo!* God forgive!" Ninang Rola paused and raised her head. "But now, just about everyone is a *querida*, so sad. And they talk about it, too. *Dios ko!* I would not say anything to anybody if I were them. Shame-shame. *Sin Verguenza.* Let's go back to the old times when we don't say anything at all. No more morals in this country. No fear in the Lord. Estrella, you're lucky you got married. Thank God *you* got married."

Mommy sat down on the sofa hands first, as if the sofa wasn't there and she had to feel for it. "Thank God I'm married?" She knotted her eyebrows and asked quietly, but loudly enough for Pipo and me to hear: "Rola?"

Ninang Rola bit her lower lip trying to take back something she wasn't supposed to say. Many words had slipped out of her mouth, but most of them didn't have to be given another thought. Nobody had ever given her a stern look or a long *Pssssst* because something had slipped from her tongue that should have stayed there.

"Well, the mistresses . . ." Mommy changed her tone, one finger pressed over lips. "They don't eat too much. They have to keep their figures. Slender. *Chiquitita.* That will save us money on food." She forced a smile on her face.

"Haa. *Chiquitita.*" Ninang Rola caught Mommy's smile and added her own wheezing laugh. "Having a slim body is the only way they can keep these married men. *Qué se Joda!*"

With her, Mommy became a different person. When Daddy Groovie wasn't home, they talked about many things, mostly their lives, and I listened. I had been waiting for Mommy to tell Ninang Rola about what Daddy Groovie did to her at night but she seemed to keep that to herself. Sometimes I wanted to ask her about it, but like Ninang Rola always said, certain things were better kept inside. And I had kept many, many things inside. *So quiet, this little one,* they always said about me. But I was a part of every conversation, although nobody knew, since, most of the time, I never said anything. I had always known that time had a way of answering questions. Somehow, one day, in one of their conversations, an answer or two would come up, perhaps Mommy would bring it up herself, or Ninang Rola, as she might have known what happened in the dark as soon as we shut our doors to sleep.

"Money, that's what it's all about. It is so important these days, not that it has never been important. And the fact there never seems to be enough men to go around, huh? Hah! Women. What we have to deal with is too much. The only good thing about being a *querida* is that they are so thick-skinned. Thick-faced. How can any sane woman choose this kind of life, huh? So much going against them—God, people. But do they care? Not at all. Oh, women, what we have to go through." Ninang Rola took a mirror out of her big pocket and looked at herself. "*Qué Chiquitita.* La-la-la-la. I can still be a *querida*, huh?" She slapped her face lightly, her saggy cheeks shook.

Mommy laughed. "Not you, Rola."

"Look at you. You should appreciate older women."

Ninang Rola lifted the mirror to look at her hair. She had a lot of white hair sticking out of the middle of her head. Her fingers reached to bury the white strands under the darker ones, picking them carefully as if they would fall out. "Getting old is not such a bad thing, you know? Old without a man. But at least I will die with dignity. Never in my life did I have an interest in a married man!"

There was a long pause between the two of them. Silence had a way of creeping into our house. It was in those quiet moments when the noise of people selling things outside was the only thing heard that I wondered about the past and what had happened before I was born. Even if I always listened in on their conversations, I knew there was so much they were keeping from me, especially when they both suddenly stopped talking. I could tell they were gone, on a trip back to their pasts, when the world had much morals, as Ninang Rola said, when there were no *queridas* except for those of the Spanish priests. Her life was religion, then and now. She always acted as if she knew everything. She knew when and where to talk. When Ninang Rola was quiet, you'd better not say anything to her. When she talked, you'd better listen. There's a right time for everything, she would say; sometimes it is better to speak with your eyes.

So I watched them with my eyes while they quietly continued whatever they were doing with their hands, while their faces remained blank, their lips shut, tongue in between like a third lip. As soon as they came back, one of them would notice me; or Pipo, who would be sitting nearby, trimming his nails or anything else to pretend he wasn't listening, either.

Mommy turned to me first, words running through her mind, then through her mouth. "Gringo," she began by saying my name with a full voice, "get me a glass of water."

"Water?" I asked, repulsed by the thought that their conversation ended right then and there.

Before she said Pipo's name, she took a long pause. She looked around as if he wasn't there and she had to find him. "Pipo, why don't you clean your mess upstairs. All your shoe boxes are all over the floor again." She ordered him without turning her head to him.

"PIPO," a familiar yell made us all look to the window.

Sergio Putita stuck his head and hands through the window grill, surprising everyone. "PIPO," he called again. His high-pitched voice made me get up from the chair. When Pipo saw him, he laughed and ran outside.

Ninang Rola watched Pipo walk out the door, slapping his buttocks as soon as he passed her.

"*Queridas. Queridas.* You're just lucky you have boys." Ninang Rola turned to Mommy. "Girls. Born to a world without luck."

She looked at herself in the mirror again.

Malasuerte.

Firsmistress was tall, thin, and had curly hair. When she smiled, her lower lip covered her upper teeth, only her gums showed. According to Ninang Rola, this one would never get caught by the real wife. Why? *She looked like she could act very well, you know, pretend.* Seconmistress, on the other hand, was short. “Hayy! So hot outside. Where’s the room? Ah, upstairs, I forgot.” She looked as if she always got what she wanted. “Has the other boarder moved in yet? What’s her name? Oh you, what’s your name? Oh these boxes, so hard to pack. My whole life is in there. . . .” She couldn’t seem to stop talking. She pushed her boxes into the house. Before she could ask for help, I disappeared upstairs. “This one is in danger,” commented Ninang Rola, “her mouth, all over the place, her life, along with it. Keep your eyes on her at all times.” Like Ninang Rola and the thousands of parishioners at Iglesia de San Pedro, they both had scapulars hanging around their necks, these little brown square things that looked so old and holy that anybody who wore them was instantly blessed.

I could tell why Mommy lumped them together, labeled them *queridas*, and spoke about them with a mixture of scorn and glee. They both ate the same way, very proper. Their spoons left their plates, stopped into their mouths and back to the plates at the same time. Because they ate very little, they always left their plates clean. They woke up early in the morning and made sure they had a pail of water ready for bathing. They ironed their clothes once every Sunday after Mass. They lit their altars every day, hung rosaries on their beds, decorated their walls with pictures of Jesus. And soon they joined in the Virgen Maria procession in our street without Ninang Rola asking them to. All three of them marched on Sunday nights. I would watch them from the window, one eye on them, the other searching for SWAT.

"Have they no shame?" Ninang Rola ran to Mommy who was at her Singer Machine. "How can they just join the procession like that as if God is so quick to forgive women like them? Estrella, do you think it's a mistake having them here? I feel for them but *Dios mío*, I don't want to have to march with them while people are gossiping about what kind of women they are!"

"There are thousands of them in the city, Rola," Mommy answered. "Besides, prayers are the only protection they have." She was right. The smell of candles always lingered in their room. At night, the mistresses were reduced to tiny voices, reciting names of the saints they spoke with about their secrets and of silent wishes to God to hide them more.

Had I been a mistress, I would also know the exact beginning and end of the day. I would know when and where I was every minute and who was around me. Like in those black-and-white Stateside movies, I would wait for him all the time. "Be with me," I would beg him, and like in the best part of the movie, I would say it in English, so he would know I was serious. "Please, please, SWAT, please . . ." I wouldn't let him go. I wouldn't let him hang around at the pier like Daddy Groovie. I would feed him milkfish in many different ways: fried, stuffed relleno, in soupy *Sinigang*. Anything to outcook his wife. I would also pray to Jesus for forgiveness every chance I got for the fear of one day dying as someone who claimed another woman's husband, and for the courage to hide it from the world.

I imagined the real wives coming to our house, screaming their names outside while all the neighbors gathered and watched. Pipo and I would squat under the windowsill to watch what was happening through the termite holes. Meanwhile, the mistresses would be looking for places to hide if the real wives came in and searched for them. Ninang Rola and Mommy would block the door, arms on their waists, and tell the real wives that they had no right to barge into our house, that they should all go home and take care of their husbands better so they wouldn't have to look for pleasure elsewhere.

If the mistresses were grass, Pipo was their dragonfly.

After a few weeks, he was buzzing around them, sticking his nose wherever they were. Firsmistress noticed everything about Pipo, complimented him for the little things he did for her. *Buy me Marlboro.* And he did. *Buy me Larawan comics.* They laughed together, as if they both were the same age and understood each other so well. "Ay, so light, so light." Firsmistress pointed to his legs. "Someday you will grow up to be a very handsome man! Women will be falling all over your feet." Pipo immediately ran to the bedroom mirror, turned his head from left to right, right to left, up and down. *Hmmmmm.*

I looked at my own legs. My skin was peeling again like it did every summer, and the new skin was sometimes even darker. When I took a bath that day, I scrubbed myself with a moonrock, the big one with smaller holes.

"Ayyy, look, Pipo is growing hair in his armpits," hollered Seconmistress, teasingly. She helped Pipo grind *tawas*, an alum crystal that Mommy used against odor and sweat. "You soak it in water, a little amount of water, and when it gets thick, you dab it on your armpits."

"Do you do this, too?" asked Pipo.

"We all have to do this. But since boys like you don't shave your armpits, they smell worse." Seconmistress gathered the powder into a little bottle and handed it to him. Pipo took it with both hands and kept it close to his chest, evidence he could show that he was growing up.

I rushed to the bathroom to look at my armpits. No hair. When I took a bath that day, I checked if I had any hair growing on my body. None. None on my armpits, none on my stomach, none, except below my knees, around my calves, but that had been there since I was young. Pipo had hair in his armpits, not one, but a few hairs, some long. He was growing hair and I wasn't. Only my feet had grown, now longer than two tiles on the bathroom floor.

Even the boys in the street were growing hair. Big Boy Jun and his marble-gambling friends were now ending their games by pulling hair from inside their Jockeys, running around with them and having a contest of who had the longest and curliest hair. *From inside their Jockeys?*

I rushed to the bathroom and took off my Jockeys but didn't see hair.

Without knowing it, the mistresses took Pipo away from Daddy Groovie's hands. They also took Pipo's hands away from objects to throw at me. He spent a lot of time in their room even while they were gone. I seldom went there, not that we were not allowed to but it always felt as if it was separate from the rest of our house, with all these strangers moving in and out of it. One morning, the smell of a candle burning pulled me toward their room. I heard a singing voice.

Immaculate Mother, we come at thy call . . . Ave, Ave, Ave Mareeee-uh.

When I walked in, Pipo was sitting at the dresser. The room was full of altars for different saints, and at the center of these altars were mounds of melted wax. St. Jude, the patron saint of lost lovers, was lit by a candle run by electricity.

"Pipo, what's gotten into your head?" Seeing him like this reminded me of the times when we paraded up and down the stairs to re-create the Virgen Maria procession until Ninang Rola told us that soon we would have no place to live because we had burned the house down, adding, "Have you no fear in God that you make fun of him like that?" Since then, Pipo secretly played with Sergio Putita, lighting candles, reliving stories from Ninang Rola's La Litania book, sometimes playing Virgen Maria herself, sometimes Veronica with a handkerchief, Angel Gabriel in the Annunciation, or Virgen Maria before the three kings, and playing all of them, Pipo would always put a blanket over his head.

Pipo turned around. His eyebrows were so thick, one longer than the other, his cheeks the red of floor wax, his eyelids, a coloring book. "Out. Leave. Now!" he grumbled, pointing to the door, his lips, dark, brown, pouty, a pair of dried leaves. A white towel lay flatly on his head. Between his hands, a lit candle. I retreated to our bedroom thinking of the Sunday nights I waited for the procession, only to see him waiting outside at the gate and running to SWAT as soon as he saw him.

He didn't stop there. When it was sunny outside and everybody was too busy to know what he was doing, he would immediately run into the room. Ninang Rola would be in church, Mommy and Maricon at the market, Daddy Groovie with his construction friends. The mistresses would be gone. I would be the only one left, trying not to think that Pipo was next door playing with the mistresses' things again. I had tried to go in there and stop him but he had only ignored me. I sat in the bedroom hoping that one day soon he would get over his silliness.

Pipo had memorized the mistresses' schedules, for they left the same time in the morning and returned the same time at night. But who would have expected the mistresses to come home early one sunny afternoon and catch him? Worse, they caught him in Firsmistress's yellow chiffon, off-shoulder, bareback sundress, modeling and posing. They all laughed. After taking off the dress, Pipo ran to me and didn't say anything. Instead, he walked around to make me know his presence as if to say, "You see, it's okay. They liked me." He returned to the other room. The laughter resumed and echoed in the house.

With their blessing, his visits became more frequent. Even when it rained, his face would have on layers of makeup. He snuck into the room like somebody was watching him, then he tried on a different dress each time, sometimes wearing Seconmistress's bathrobe and a towel around his head while searching through their closets. He put their clothes neatly on the bed so that he knew exactly how to return them. He even played disco music and danced to it while the electric candles twinkled about. He was the master of this room, familiar with its ins and outs. When we didn't have boarders, he stayed in the closets all day, coming out only to eat or go to school. Running away from Daddy Groovie's *yantok* made him discover many secret places in our house, although the *yantok* could always find him.

One late night, I couldn't sleep. I walked downstairs. Mommy's voice suddenly stopped me from going farther down.

"You have to forgive him," she was saying, "he's just a boy. He's too young to know what this means. We know it will go soon. Maybe in a few years. He's at that age when he's adjusting."

I rubbed my eyes. I could hear more if I saw clearly.

"We know he's young. I also had a younger brother. He did the same thing, but he got punished for it so he stopped," responded Firsmistress.

Seconmistress said they had to watch him more. "Many boys don't outgrow these things. They're full of grace until they die."

"Full of grace?"

"You know, like Virgen Maria, never touched anyone . . ."

"Well, Pipo is not circumcised yet. He wouldn't think of those things. That's why he acts this way."

"He's not circumcised?" the mistresses asked at the same time. Firsmistress went on with stories of how boys who were not circumcised grew up acting like girls, wearing girls' clothing.

"Mrs., you must have him circumcised soon. Even Jesu-Cristo was circumcised early in his life. My cousin Efi—Epifanio. Never circumcised, *Dios ko*, he opened the first beauty parlor in our village. Mrs., you don't want that for Pipo. He's too handsome to be like Efi. You see, Efi, he was short, dark, his nose misplaced and big. We didn't think anybody would marry him, so we didn't care. Please, Mrs., just look at Boy Manicure, you don't want Pipo to be like that?"

Boy Manicure. So quickly they learned about him. Everything was about him. My heart began to beat faster, knowing that this would be taken more seriously now that his name had been mentioned.

"How about the other one?" interjected Firsmistress.

"Gringo? What about him? He doesn't—?"

"No. No, Mrs., I just want to know if he's circumcised."

"Oh! you made me nervous. I thought he was doing the same thing. Oh no, Gringo was circumcised at birth." Mommy paused as if taking a deep breath.

I couldn't wait to hear more about myself.

"Yes. He's a nice boy. Too quiet. He needs an older brother to guide him. Pipo should do that but look what he does!"

"Gringo is too young for any of these things." Too

young were the words I hated, especially when they came out of Mommy's mouth.

"And please, Mrs., do something about this. Please, before we run out of makeup."

A stone hit the wall, barely missing my shoulder. "Did you tell him? Did you tell him?" screamed Pipo, whimpering in one corner of our bedroom. "Look what you've done!" He turned his arm around. Bruises. Daddy Groovie's smell was suddenly apparent in the room. "You told him, didn't you? You told him. How could you?" He picked a stone from a heap beside him that he had collected especially to throw at me. "No, you're wrong. I *did not* tell anyone," I screamed at him. Mommy was the only one who knew other than the mistresses, but I didn't tell him that. I ran away from him. One stone hit the small of my back.

Pipo was circumcised the same week. When he came back home from the outpatient clinic, he walked around in a skirt, holding the hem so it wouldn't touch his skin, something he grew to enjoy after just a few days. Sometimes he spread the skirt neatly on his lap and sat like a schoolgirl waiting for the Monday bus. I watched him, thinking of the time we used to spend in the bathroom. We raced to the toilet to see who could pee the fastest. We even drank a lot of water and waited a few minutes until we both couldn't keep our pee anymore. Pipo always lost, while my pee rushed out like turbulent rain. I thought it was because he had too much skin on him, which made him spray pee all over the toilet bowl, the walls, sometimes on me, and if he missed, he would chase me. Even underneath our shorts, we were different.

Pipo stayed home for weeks, wearing a different skirt borrowed from the mistresses and Mommy each day, hiding the yellowing bandage dangling between his thighs. The mistresses began locking their room the second week Pipo came to ask for another skirt. And when he went back again, knocking loudly, the mistresses told Mommy that they decided it was time to pack up and leave.

"Ou-ou." Pipo lay on the sofa one morning for his regular cleaning, lifting the front of his skirt carefully so as not to touch his wound.

I sat right beside him, on the other end, but he immediately tapped the sofa, sending off dust over my face. "Don't sit there. I can't be moved." I jumped up and sat on a chair in front of him.

Mommy came in with a small basin of warm water, which she placed at the foot of Pipo. She raised her head as soon as her reflection appeared on the water. Mommy had proclaimed herself the healer of the house. Because of her, I had never seen a doctor in my life. She simply believed that everything could be taken care of at home. Her *naturaleza* ran through her veins into her healing hands, creating little inventions like the ceremony of circles. I was surprised that Mommy hadn't cut off Pipo's skin herself.

She was a believer in boiling leaves of all kinds, in preserving tree trunks and drying roots. She made tea out of toasted rice grains to clear Pipo's body of germs. Once, when I had a fever, she had wrapped two blankets around me and said, "Once you sweat, your fever will be gone." Daddy Groovie went looking for aspirin in the house. When he finally found one, I was already bathing in my own sweat and Mommy was dabbing me with a wet warm towel and discerningly setting ground Mayana leaves on my forehead like little green hills.

"You can get a woman pregnant now," Daddy Groovie said, walking into the living room. Daddy Groovie of course believed in the magic of aspirin, of the outpatient clinic in the city hospital. He grinned while he rubbed palms against each other, planning the next five years of Pipo's life.

Mommy sighed. While she knelt on the floor, her hands quietly removed the bandage around Pipo's wound. She put little mounds of Mayana leaves on the wound but her face was all knotted up. The wind from the open window began to circle my ears, comforting me at the sight of soft, fleshy skin sticking out of a thick white bandage. It was unbearable for me, although it seemed to be such a delightful experience for everybody, including Pipo. He kept on knocking his knees whenever Mommy put wet leaves on his wound. "Stop," said Mommy abruptly, finally holding his knees. "Don't move or you'll drop all these leaves on the floor!" When she was done, she covered it with Pipo's skirt. "Just sit there and be still."

Everybody was looking forward to Pipo's change, for him to grow up, to enter manhood. My skin tightened at the thought of Pipo leaving me behind. One day, he might turn into those hang-around-do-nothing-boys. And me, what would be my saving ritual? There were no boiling leaves and bandages and weeks of skirts to look forward to.

Daddy Groovie's palms rubbed against each other. *Heh-heh.* I could see in his grin that he was suddenly gaining a son. A Big Boy Jun of his own. A SWAT of his own. A new son, not the one who put makeup on his face or kept nightgowns in a box to sew into a beauty queen gown of sequins and lace. He wanted somebody who would go out with a group of hang-around-do-nothing-boys like Big Boy Jun and his marble-gambling friends—a little Groovie.

I could see Daddy Groovie put his arms around Little Groovie's shoulders, showing him off to his construction friends, saying, "Look how thick my blood is, even this boy has taken after me."

His construction friends would nod their heads with approval, the way they did whenever Daddy Groovie told them a joke before leaving for the pier. They would all speak at the same time, throwing praises for Little Groovie who was enjoying all the attention he was getting.

"You better teach him how to drink beer," one of them would say.

"Yes, beer. A whole case of beer. Soon, he'll have this." Another one started patting his fat stomach. "Just like yours, *páre*."

Daddy Groovie would ignore him and bring the attention back to Little Groovie who was more than happy to know that his own father could taste his hunger for attention. "Look at his arms; someday, they'll be thick. Just like me, *páre*." I could see Daddy Groovie lifting Little Groovie's arms.

Páre was an expression I despised. I had to erase it from my set of words. It had the power only grown-ups had, the face of what men were, and what they should be. The word that I had to use to show everybody that I had grown up, that I was like every young man in our street. When boys said that word, they lifted themselves to the level of grown-up men, demanding respect from everyone whom they made feel lower. Like Pipo and Sergio Putita. And me.

That was exactly what Little Groovie would say, "Yes, *páre*, yes, *páre* ho-ho-ho." He would run into his marble-gambling friends, putting his arms around their shoulders. They would all strut away, these boys. Slowly inching their way into a life of San Miguel beer and Marlboro Country cigarettes.

Pipo knew what was expected of him. In a way, I could tell that as much as he wanted to please everybody, he didn't see himself becoming a Little Groovie or a hang-around-do-nothing-man. By the way he gracefully lifted his skirt, he seemed too far from the effects of circumcision. Maybe that's why when the mistresses walked out of the house with their luggage, telling Pipo, "You better change, you, you, you better change, makeup is not made for boys," he said to them, "Husbands are made for their wives and not for you!"

And as if that wasn't enough, he screamed at them—*QUERIDAS!*

The mistresses stood at the doorstep, motionless, almost dropping their luggage on the floor. They heard the word that nobody had ever dared call them, and from this boy they had once adored. Pipo was never disrespectful of anybody. I knew it was hard for him to say what he said.

"Is that my skirt?" Firsmistress recovered, then pointed angrily at what Pipo was wearing. She was about to grab Pipo when Seconmistress got hold of her wrist and pulled her back. "Let's go. He doesn't know what he's saying. He doesn't know what he's saying."

But Firsmistress stood there staring at Pipo. I waited for her to say something, watching her lips move. She loosened her clutch and placed her hands against her waist.

"*Querida,* Pipo, means *'dear.'* Dear!"

Firsmistress's last words hung in the air.

I stood there inhaling those words and wondering what had become of Pipo. He peered at them directly with those dog eyes of his while they dashed away into a cab.

Querida means "dear," I repeated in my mind. So they were gone, the other women. Their departure was neither celebrated nor mourned. Ninang Rola hardly mentioned their name since. That left me wondering what would become of them, where else they would hide, and for how long.

There were boys on our street who were circumcised the same year or the year before. They were not expected to turn into something they couldn't possibly become, but they did anyway. Big Boy Jun, who was circumcised a month before, was going up the ladder of becoming a hang-around-do-nothing-man. He had stopped playing marbles and took on the habit of smoking secretly. His voice got deeper. Some boys grew taller. Other boys simply stopped playing in the streets and started imitating the young men by whistling at the girls walking by. We were always told that once someone was circumcised, he must expect a sudden burst of growth, as if by removing that piece of skin, the rest of the body would expand.

"You don't have to be like that," Sergio Putita comforted Pipo one Monday morning. "I never did what SWAT did after he was circumcised. I didn't go around looking at girls in the street. I didn't walk around without my shirt."

Pipo had been waiting for his visit for a while, but when he finally came, Sergio Putita hardly bothered to ask how Pipo was. He walked in like a mosquito larva shaking from head to toe. I wanted to tell him that, since Pipo had been circumcised, there wouldn't be any beauty contests anymore.

"Let's go upstairs. Anybody there?" mumbled Sergio Putita.

"No," said Pipo.

I followed while he pulled Pipo to the bedroom carrying a big brown bag I had seen quite a few times.

"Hurry." Sergio Putita waved us up.

Pipo's skirt swayed as he placed his hand over the wound so that the cloth wouldn't rub against it.

"Stand at the door. Make sure that nobody comes up." Sergio Putita pointed his finger. His crew cut looked like it was plucked with a barber's bare hands. He had round blotches all over his head.

I did exactly what he said. I held the threshold of the door, one leg inside the room, the other on the steps of the stairs. Mommy and Ninang Rola were outside on the back patio, hanging wet clothes on the lines while listening to the radio. Daddy Groovie wasn't home.

They sat in front of each other. Sergio Putita took out a luxurious, white, sequined lace veil from the bag and placed it on Pipo's head, and another one on his own.

"What are we doing?" asked Pipo, although they had played the rosary games many times, re-creating certain scenes from the Stations of the Cross, especially on Mondays following the Virgen Maria procession in the street. They had never asked me to play because they knew I would say no to them. I had wanted to play as well, but fear had always overcome me, fear with the eyes of Daddy Groovie looking down with his *yantok* on his hand, and me, sitting on the floor, a veil on my head. I always wondered what he would do if he found me doing this. I simply never had the courage they both had, although in my imagination, I was always with them.

"How do you put this on my head?" asked Pipo. "Like this?"

"No, the little flowers in the front." Sergio Putita adjusted the veil. "That's right."

"Who are you now?" asked Pipo.

"Elisabet. Virgen Maria's cousin, remember her? You know who she is? You know her story? Do you want me to tell you? I know everything about her. Do you want to hear—"

"No."

"Then put them like this, like you're praying." Sergio Putita joined Pipo's hands together.

"And I? Who am I?"

"Mary. Virgen Maria of course. You're always the star." Sergio Putita's words brought a smile to Pipo's face that remained there for a while.

Sergio Putita grew up in the Bible house, which was how we referred to where he lived. He knew every word on every page from years of Bible readings at home. He quickly grabbed the white linen from the bed and wrapped it around Pipo, creating a train on the floor.

"What's that for?" Pipo asked.

"Shhhh. Quiet. That's your dress, *querida mía*." Sergio Putita folded the hem of the blanket around Pipo's neck.

"Where did you get this?" Pipo touched his veil. "Is this—"

"Yes, the Virgen Maria's. Shhhh." He looked around as if there was somebody else there beside me. He chuckled. "The statue is at our house. You know there are two statues, right? I took both the veils. Shhhh. Close your eyes."

It started to rain when Pipo closed his eyes. The room suddenly was dark, as if some huge hands decided to cover the city to punish these two.

"Hail, Mary, full of grace, the Lord be with you." Sergio Putita placed his hands on Pipo's stomach. "Blessed art thou amongst women." If anyone in our street were to take after Boy Manicure, it would be one of them.

The Visitation, I thought. Maybe Pipo didn't know what they were doing. He had stopped praying the rosary a while back and never paid any attention to what we did during the Virgen Maria processions. I imagined a picture from Ninang Rola's La Litania books, and the engraved wall frames of the Stations of the Cross at Iglesia de San Pedro.

The thunder became clear, loud, dividing the sky. From inside all I could see was a long line across and the other houses slowly disappearing behind the glassy hair of rain.

"Blessed is the fruit of thy womb, Jesus," continued Sergio Putita.

Pipo opened his eyes, undisturbed by the thunder. It's a sign. Can't you both see? I wanted to tell them. I was far enough from them to be safe should lightning strike them both.

Pipo of course never learned. He never learned from taking clothes from the mistresses, from being caught with Mommy's nightgown. Daddy Groovie could easily walk into the room and catch them. My being here at the door wouldn't make it any easier for them. Older people took big steps on stairs, faster than they could take off the veils clipped on their heads. I secretly wished Pipo would express himself a little less bluntly, or think of ways to play without having to wear women's clothes, especially now that he was circumcised.

Ave, Ave, Ave, Mareeeee-uh.

Their singing reverberated in the room, their chattering like those of little girls on a school bus on their way to an all-girls school. The rain had become their chorus, the drum of thunder, their heartbeats. And Pipo sat there amid the noise, this newly circumcised boy, mocking the statue of Virgen Maria, but also slowly becoming her—a saint, a pregnant mother of Jesus, a woman.

The door banged downstairs.

"Who's that?" They both turned to me at the same time.

"Run downstairs and find out," Sergio Putita told me nervously, waving his hand.

I didn't run downstairs, nor did I look. I inhaled the scent that came into the house. "It's Daddy Groovie—"

"Why aren't you watching!" Pipo screamed and quickly pulled his veil down, hurting himself.

My mouth hung open. I saw two things happening at the same time: Daddy Groovie, coming up the stairs, and Pipo and Sergio Putita quickly dumping the veils into the big bag and throwing the blanket to the bed.

"Stupid. Stupid." Pipo ran to the window, pretended he was looking out.

I looked at Daddy Groovie again. He was dripping and shaking himself while he walked up. When I turned into the room, a stone hit the wall behind me, barely missing my shoulder.

Sangre

The breath of an approaching rain.

Heavy rain. I wanted to give Mommy an umbrella, so I opened the black one to see if it was broken but she left for the fish market before I could give it to her. Ninang Rola's mouth began to drizzle all over me. "*Malas*. We don't need any more bad luck. Umbrellas are made for outside, not inside." Ninang Rola snatched it out of my hand. "No. No. Not an open umbrella in here. Not that. *Malas 'yan.* Shouldn't you know these things?" She looked upstairs where the ceiling coughed dust through the small cracks with every heavy step Daddy Groovie made.

Lug. Lug. Lug. His footsteps were the most recognizable ones in our house. With our bedroom door closed, I could still hear his voice. "Who told him he could use my Pacorabang? It took two months for this to get here from Dolares. *Puñeta!* Doesn't he know how expensive this is? Spilling it like that? Tsk. Tsk."

I imagined Daddy Groovie taking off his hang-around T-shirt to wipe the dresser with and putting it back on when he was done, spreading the scent all over his body and the house as if to remind everyone of what had just happened. His *yantok* would be on the floor. He never put it away until I saw it, long after he had hit Pipo. The *yantok* spoke to me—the way it was deliberately placed at the foot of the bed told me everything, the nostrils of its tips smelling my presence. Sometimes, the heat of the air inside would murmur in my ears, telling me that Pipo was cornered in the room again, that it was probably an accident, maybe he was just curious and wanted to smell the Pacorabang so he could dab it on his neck, smell exactly like Daddy Groovie.

I was sitting at the bottom of the stairs, in front of the bathroom, waiting for the huge plastic buckets to fill with water so I could take a bath when Pipo flew down the stairs from behind me. He quickly pushed the bathroom door, almost trampling over me. "Yes, Daddy Groovie. Yes, Daddy Groovie," he mumbled to himself. Click, click, he locked the door inside. Water hit the floor. Before I could get up to turn the light on, which he had ignored, before I could stop him from wasting the water I had waited for hours to fill, Pipo suddenly opened the door and found me with his loud voice. "Why are you looking at me like that?"

"That's my water—" Without giving me a chance to finish, he grabbed the small chair under the switch and hurled it at me. It missed and crashed against the wall. The broken legs tumbled down the steps, settling underneath my knees.

Not again, I thought.

Pipo, the one with the talent to kill. Hit me in the head. Slap my face. Pull my hair. Throw things at me. Hot spatula. Banana peels. A fork. The elbow of a pipe. He got me many times and scarred me as well. I carried the scars, unable to explain them to people. He seldom spoke to me unless he needed something or somebody else needed something and he was the middle person. *Mommy wants you, Daddy Groovie is looking for you.* I would drop what I was doing and go, without asking him a series of whys, afraid perhaps that his palms would land on me for no reason at all. His hands had a pair of eyes, roaming our house for anything he could grab, and a nose, sniffing our house to find me. He was in his own world, always by himself, doing his own things. When that world opened to me, it came in the motion of rage.

But the chair took me by surprise. I stood up and started my flight from him. "Stop! Stop!" I screamed. A lightbulb exploded in the corner wall.

Ninang Rola came running to us from the kitchen. "Are you okay?"

"Yes . . . he missed," I mumbled under my breath, sliding my arms between my thighs.

"Pipo, Pipo," she called to him, but he was already running out the door, wiping his face with a towel. The calendar hanging on a nail fell when the door banged.

"You two are always fighting." Ninang Rola checked my

face by holding my chin and pressing her thumb on my cheek.

"I wasn't fighting," I said. I fumbled with my arms, feeling my skin for bruises that weren't there. But he *spilled* my water, I wanted to tell Ninang Rola, as I thought of how much water was left.

"Poor Pipo." She shook her head, moving the thin and long barbecue stick that held her hair bun.

I gave her a questioning look, although I knew she would only say, "Poor Pipo," so I wouldn't feel bad for myself. She had her way of dealing with me when I got hurt, without making me think she favored me over Pipo. Whenever she said, "Poor Pipo," I knew she meant—Poor Gringo, Pipo shouldn't have done this.

She looked at the shards of bulb strewn over the stairs. "More *Malas*." She walked to the kitchen and came back with a broom and dustpan.

Other than opening an umbrella inside the house, *Malas* for Ninang Rola was a list of broken things: glasses, mirrors, cups, plates, ceramic. Anything that accidentally broke was a premonition of something bad. "Spirits always have a way of informing us from the other side what is going to happen next," Ninang Rola would say with rounded eyes. "So always throw them out. Make a sign of the cross." But Mommy would glue them together with colorless nail polish only for them to disappear as soon as Ninang Rola found them. How about broken bones, open wounds? I asked Ninang Rola once. Bad luck, too?

No, she said, you're alive, you heal.

No wonder Pipo and Mommy always healed. Although

Pipo always kept his healing from me and everyone else, never complained about any part of his body hurting, never said a word about what Daddy Groovie did. When nobody could see, he simply took the ointment that Mommy kept on the dresser and applied it on himself before he went to bed. Little white dots on his skin. I wanted to ask him many times how he felt, but he never gave me a chance even when I caught him at the window with that look on his face as if he was about to pull the shutters out of the grooves and smash them on the floor. I stayed away from him; his hands flew too fast across the room.

"Try to understand your brother more, huh?" Ninang Rola interrupted my thoughts, whispering something in Spanish that I didn't understand.

"What does that mean?"

She leaned the chair back against the wall. Her eyebrows twisted up when she picked up the broken leg. She gathered the shards of bulb into the dustpan. I thought she didn't hear me but she turned to me as soon as she stood up the dustpan on the floor. "What?"

"That word you just said?"

"Sangre de familia?"

I wasn't sure whether I heard her right but I nodded anyway.

"Family blood. That's what's in there." A slight breeze moved her to sit beside me. She took my arm and poked the vein on my arm with her fingernails. She pulled up my wrist, closer to my face, and while stretching my skin, said, "See that?"

I could see my pulse. "Yes."

Her face was so close to me that I couldn't avoid looking at it. Her hair was curly, bouncing on her wide forehead whenever she moved. She occasionally pulled her hair and rested it behind her ears only to have it fall back on her face. Her nose was like mine except she had bigger nostrils. She also had big, deep ears with pointed lobes. Signs of a long, long life.

"*Sangre.* Blood," she said to me. In her mouth, words grew. The most difficult ones I had ever heard came out of her mouth. And when I asked her about them, she said they were Spanish, I didn't have to understand them, we didn't speak the language anymore. Gone were those days when we were ordered to speak it, she'd say. But there wasn't a day she didn't drop a word or two in our conversations, most of them curses she couldn't say any other way. *Puñeta,* she would say; nobody really knew what *Puñeta* meant, not that anybody cared. Curses in Spanish always sounded stronger, angrier, and weighed more because nobody knew what they meant. She also claimed that *she* was a Spaniard, although I knew she was too dark to be one. I remembered Miss Spain from TV; her face was too far from Ninang Rola's. Mommy once told me that Ninang Rola was too ugly to be Spanish. "Her nose is too big." I touched my nose when I heard Mommy. *And flat.* My nose was big, too, not as big as Ninang Rola's, but big.

"Sometimes what runs in your blood shows in your family. From fathers to sons, from sons to grandsons," she continued.

"What do you mean?"

"Certain things will never change. Something inside you

that you inherit. Like blood. *Mala sangre.* Bad blood will always be bad blood."

Mala sangre, I thought. "Pipo has bad blood?" I asked.

She didn't expect me to repeat what she said, though I was only thinking of pig-blood stew and how we put big peppers in the steamy pot and stained our clothes afterward.

"No. That's not what I meant. Forget it. You just make sure you don't hit anyone in your life, that's what I'm trying to say."

Meaning not to take after Daddy Groovie, or Pipo even. Their hands, so light, so easily lifted by the wind. Everywhere, their hands could be found, hovering in the heat, landing with the rain. Winged.

I nodded my head when I noticed Ninang Rola staring at me with her hypnotic eyes. "Even when you're very, very angry, keep your hands to yourself, don't even think about lifting them up, you'd never know where they'd go." She folded my hands on my lap and pinched my ears. She knotted her nose, exposing the hair inside. "No good to hit someone." Beads of sweat formed around her forehead, staying there, without the need to slide.

"My Pacorabang!" Daddy Groovie hollered upstairs.

We both lifted our gazes to the ceiling. Ninang Rola wrinkled her face.

"They're father and son all right." She pointed her finger up in front of my face. Women were supposed to grow their nails but her fingernails were cut to her skin. "When your brother hits you again, tell me."

She left me with that. *Tell me.* I never told her anything.

Sometimes, I thought that what happened was the natural progression of things. Handed down from one to the other, from older to the younger, like she said. So if it was meant to happen, what would be the point of telling her? Maybe it was in me, too; maybe some time soon I would be hitting someone. I cringed at the thought of doing it. I couldn't even step on a roach. I couldn't bear the sight of welts and bruises. I couldn't imagine myself being the cause of them. I stared at my palms, followed the lines with my finger. I knew Ninang Rola had a way of knowing; she knew exactly when Pipo was going to come after me, although she could never tell when Daddy Groovie went after Pipo. Nobody ever did. I always waited outside until it was all finished, when the noises had finally left through the windows and all that was there were sweat and the strange smell of Daddy Groovie's subsiding anger. I also waited for someone to rescue Pipo, waited for the sound of Mommy's footsteps to come upstairs and grab the *yantok* out of Daddy Groovie's hands, breaking it with hers. Then she could scream at him, too, tell him to never ever do that again. Daddy Groovie would just stand there, holding his Pacorabang, accidentally spilling it on himself. But Mommy always ignored what went on, as if she couldn't hear the noise. For as long as I could remember, she always stood where she was—frozen, like meat in a plastic bag left to defrost on the kitchen counter.

Always tell Ninang Rola.

Because Ninang Rola is always there.

Everywhere. I felt the dog bite scar on my hand, the little depression that was darker than the rest of my skin. I was too young then to remember what happened, but Ninang Rola was there. She told me the story so many times that even if I hardly remembered anything, I had re-created exactly what had happened, imagining Sgt. Dimaculangan's dog Superdog as the one who bit me. The real dog the neighbors killed immediately after; they hit his head with wood and nail, called him crazy. I wasn't the only one bitten, though judging from the scars mine was the worst. "Poor Gringo, so delicate," Ninang Rola would say after a long pause at the end of her story, and always with a sign of the cross and a kiss on her thumb. "You bled too much. You bled like a fifteen-year-old girl." Even then I knew what she meant. Mommy was not a girl anymore but she bled the same way. That was why she sewed *pasador* to stuff her panties with, the same thing she put in my Jockeys when I used to wet in my sleep.

Sangre. The marks on Mommy's back I had seen one morning, the ones she had kept so well hidden until they healed. I often wondered if Ninang Rola knew of those, too. I had woken up many times, tempted to step down from the bunk to watch Mommy and Daddy Groovie again, in their cockfight that nobody seemed to know but me. Or maybe Ninang Rola. She seemed to know everything.

"Like a fifteen-year-old girl," she would say to herself whenever she saw the mound on my hand.

My scar. That dog. Pipo was very much like that dog, I thought, always ready to jump. It was something Daddy Groovie had planted in him with his *yantok* while he hit him, screamed, called him names. It was in his *sangre* to hit me, to put what Daddy Groovie gave him inside my veins. Mommy. Pipo. She had given him something she never knew. Hitting. Bleeding. Hitting. Healing. All these years. Another ceremony of circles. I had longed to become a part of this. Always wondered when Daddy Groovie would pull me into the bedroom, hit me instead of them.

"A year apart," sighed Ninang Rola when Mommy arrived. "Pipo was followed too soon." She shook her head and walked to the kitchen with plastic bags of fish, her pants so big at the bottom they dusted the floor.

I looked at Mommy. She, too, shook her head after handing one of the plastic bags to Ninang Rola. They both disappeared into the kitchen, mumbling to each other, while I stood there still waiting for Mommy to say something about what happened. A few words would be fine. She only had to acknowledge something had happened and didn't have to know Pipo almost hit me again.

A year apart, I thought.

I was born too soon. The fights were bound to happen. Written on our palms, half on Pipo's, half on mine. Oozing in our *sangres*. I looked at my palm, imagined my brother's. I imagined the veins on his hands, too.

But we were never far enough apart that the sight of me quickly attracted objects coming out of his hands.

A year apart. One older. One younger. Both, swollen.

But no, it wasn't always like that. Wasn't he my brother once? Didn't he used to teach me things?

Wasn't he the one who introduced me to the bathroom?

"I'm a rabbit," Pipo screamed. He was only nine, but already with long legs. Even then, his face didn't need the reflection of the bulb to show how light he was. Soft, almost invisible veins could be seen on his cheeks, so light green you wouldn't think they held blood. The bathroom door opened. Pipo had a towel around his chest. His head full of lather shaped into two horns. When one of his rabbit ears began to sink in, he closed the door.

I was sitting on the stairs again, twisting my legs, holding my pee. "Hurry," I begged.

The door opened again. "Nefertiti." There he was with a crown-shaped lather on his head. I didn't know how he did it, thickened Prell shampoo like that. All I knew was, if Daddy Groovie saw him, he would certainly get hit, not only for wasting water but for wasting Prell, another Stateside product floating in the house, one of the very few not locked in his cabinet.

"Who's Fer-ti-ti?" I stammered. *Titi,* of course, meant "penis."

"She's the E-Jeeptian Queen." He closed the door.

Jeepney Queen? I thought.

Mommy had just stopped bathing me then, which was really a daily ceremony of pouring water on my head with a big plastic scoop she cut from a Mazola Cooking Oil container, after scrubbing my whole body with soap and moonrock. I remembered Mommy saying to me, "Your veins are thick enough to pour water over your head yourself." There was a pipe on the wall that was supposed to be a shower but never worked. *Scoop, pour, scrub, scoop, pour, scrub, scoop.* Pipo, on the other hand, had been bathing himself since he was six. Mommy had always treated him as if he were too old. Our age difference measured by the length of his legs and the big veins on his arms.

Pipo raised his arms and screamed, "Miss World." The lather wasn't quite round on his head; it quickly melted down his face.

I laughed. Didn't stop laughing. He opened and closed the door probably ten more times, coming up with the silliest characters he could think of. I laughed too much, my shorts were wet when I finally got up to go to the bathroom.

That was the first time I was going to be alone in there. Pipo's laughter accompanied me inside the bathroom. This room of high ceiling, cracked white tiles on the floor and on the lower parts of the wall, sometimes diamond-shaped, sometimes square, plastic pails of water against the wall, a bulb hanging from the ceiling that seemed to come down to me whenever I looked up, and a spider web where the ceiling met the wall.

"The spider is your guardian angel. It will watch you." He warned me about the dark drain, a passage to purgatory, told me I should always make a sign of the cross before I did anything, and said the word *purgatory* many times as if he knew what he was saying. I never saw him pray in his life. "If you look at the drain and it starts sucking you in, call on the spider and it will come and help you," he advised while he sat outside, dripping and on guard with a towel neatly wrapped around his head like a turban, another towel around his chest, his shoulders exposed, beaded with water. He placed one hand neatly on his crossed legs, the other hand dried his wet face with a bamboo leaf fan. He held his back straight to balance the weight of the towel on his head. A few times, he knocked on the door to reassure me that he was still outside.

I came out of the bathroom laughing for no reason. Pipo looked at me and started laughing himself. The bathroom was one place in our house he knew much about. He had even told younger kids in our street about it, creating stories around the insects that lived there, which I had looked for but never found.

"You're dripping wet." He pointed to my bare feet.

He went upstairs. I followed him. He had his own way of walking up and down the stairs. The slightly heavy way his feet landed on the tread, so that even with eyes closed, I knew it was him. In our house, I knew who was coming by simply listening to the footsteps, by the weight on the floor, by the time it took for the other foot to land. His long legs gave Pipo the speed of a cat, although he always made thumping noises.

Even then, he already showed signs of what had always been in his *sangre*. Like when we went upstairs, I would always have to climb behind him. Behind, where I could watch the way the towel was wrapped around his head, different from the way that Mommy wrapped hers, without the careful planning. But that was Pipo, the way I had always known him. He had started doing things on his own early in his life. I always thought he was born knowing how to do all these things. I couldn't remember Mommy bathing him and he never really bothered to ask her even if he saw her taking me to the bathroom every day before I learned to do it myself. He never asked for much of anything. He just waited for something he never got.

"Where did you find this?" Ninang Rola exclaimed as she turned the fish over in her hand. "Mama de Jesus! How much?"

"Too much!" Mommy pulled the other fish out of the plastic bag. "The price of fish is so exorbitant!"

"I guess we'll have to eat this for a week."

Mommy took the fish from her, sprinkled it with salt crystals.

"Fish is cheaper than meat. More nutritious, too," Ninang Rola commented, washing the plastic bags then hanging them behind the door so we could use them later. The door to the back patio had several nails on it, each one with a special purpose. The one next to the doorknob immediately above the cloth floormat was especially for dripping shopping bags.

"But still not cheap enough." Mommy took a big knife and started to grate the scales of the fish. She sliced open the stomach, splattering blood all over herself and the tiled counter. She pulled the innards out and whisked them into the open plastic bag. She searched for something in the bag. "Eggs. I can't throw this." So she put it back in the fish. She never turned the faucet on when she worked on fish. She always saved a bucket of water in which she would throw the fish, after slicing it into small steaks.

"Slowly," warned Ninang Rola after watching fish scales get strewn all over the kitchen. "I saved some water on the patio if you want to use it. They're cutting off water at four today. You know that?"

"I heard. Sometimes I wonder how we can live in a country of a thousand islands and not have enough water."

"We can't drink that water. We're not fish," Ninang Rola answered, laughing at her joke. Mommy shrugged her shoulders.

They were both in front of the counter, which reached a little bit over their waists. They were each as tall as the other. Mommy had changed into her everyday sundress. Ninang Rola was wearing hers, too, the same faded orange one she had worn for almost a whole week. She had a green bath towel around her waist to wipe her hands on when she cooked and cleaned. In front of them was a big window with sliding shutters, a smaller version of the one upstairs. There was no sunlight coming through the window; the kitchen was usually brightly lit on late afternoons.

I could feel the thickness of the wind. The clouds must be moving very fast above us, circling the city and looking for a place to pour. It had been dark the past few days. A slight thunder here and there but no rain. I knew we were only counting hours now. I had never seen the skies so heavy, as if the clouds were going to drop all together. My thoughts slipped out of my mouth. I lifted my hands and pointed outside, mumbling, "Rain."

I knew they heard me, though they didn't pay attention

to what I said. What took their attention was Daddy Groovie descending the stairs. And the smell of Pacorabang that approached us before he could. While walking toward us, he sniffed his armpits, twice, one for each arm—something he always did before he left the house, his nostrils getting larger, little hairs sticking out. I did that once but couldn't smell anything.

"Hang-around," he said, almost a shout so we could all hear. *Hang-around,* he said for anyone who would listen to him, the word he used to tell everybody where he was going, what he was doing, as if we couldn't tell by the way he was dressed: his T-shirt tucked into his dark blue Levi's, which were tight around his thighs and so huge at the bottom you couldn't see his shoes. *Hang-around.* It also meant he would be coming home late, when everybody, already in bed, would be awakened by the smell of San Miguel beer.

I had never been to the pier where he did his hang-around. It always seemed so far away. It would take two jeepneys to get there. I couldn't imagine taking one jeepney, much less two. Too much smoke to absorb. The dizzying smell of the city that everybody here never failed to mention after a long trip outside. I always thought of the pier as a place to stay away from, where only thick-skinned men like Daddy Groovie could get to. Nobody would touch them there. I had been told many times about places where people had to always keep their eyes and ears open because other people might hurt them. That was exactly how I imagined the pier to be—dark, muddy, full of left-over cement blocks and huge pieces of wood, burning tires, and shadows drifting past smoke.

When Daddy Groovie walked away, his scent stayed with us, the same scent that I thought of whenever I imagined the States. The scent of all of Auntie Dolares's letters.

In front of the house, his construction friends were waiting. From where I was, almost in the back of our house, I could hear their voices getting louder upon seeing Daddy Groovie. I stuck my head out the kitchen to watch Daddy Groovie leave but only caught his hand closing the door.

Before Mommy could say anything, Ninang Rola began her usual litany of Spanish curses, words whose meaning we never knew: *"Puñeta! Qué se Joda! Dios de Alma! Paralítico!* Hang-around *na naman. Puñeta talaga 'yan!"*

"Rola?"

"Why wasn't he born a fish? Make life a lot easier, huh? Chop him up into pieces then eat him afterwards. *Dios de Alma!* He would be one piece of hard *tubol. Qué se Joda!* Would he smell, huh? *Santíssimo!* Hang-around. States. Hang-around. States. That's all that comes out of his mouth. He should go to Central to fetch some water. What's this life, huh? *Puñeta!*"

Mommy pulled the gills off of the fish and shook them off into a little plastic bag. The fish's mouth was open, facing me, as if wanting to say something, too. "*Paciencia,* Rola, please remember what you used to tell me? *Paciencia.*" She raised her eyebrows, lifted her hand, almost touched Ninang Rola with her bloody fingers. Whenever Ninang Rola's blood went up to her head, Mommy would take the calm side.

Ninang Rola jolted away from her at the sight of fish blood. "That would look nice on his face, huh?"

They always took turns trying to calm each other down.

"Paciencia." Mommy took a big knife from a drawer and carefully chopped the fins off of the fish. I had often seen patience in her eyes. Her face was always waiting, for what I never knew. Her daze told me that something was going to happen soon. After she had washed the white clothes and left them to dry on the corrugated aluminum, she would sit there as if they would dry faster if she guarded them. Many times, she would just stop sewing and stare ahead, watching pictures that only she could see appear on the wall.

I leaned my shoulders against the Frigidaire and felt the vibration of the motor. I lifted one leg and rested my foot on my knee, something I picked up from watching birds in our street.

The smell of fish mixed with Pacorabang.

I listened to the clic-cloc of Mommy's knife on the cutting board. Ninang Rola took a clove of garlic out of a jar and pounded it with the bottom of a soy sauce bottle. Then she walked around, rubbing the mashed garlic in her hand.

"What are you doing?" Mommy asked.

"Getting rid of the stupid Pacorabang." Ninang Rola sniffed, walked around, raising both of her arms. Her shaved armpits had a little growth of hairs.

"I don't know what it is about him. So Pipo played with his Pacorabang. Doesn't mean he can swing his hands and just hit the boy like that. Then Pipo goes around throwing stuff at Gringo."

I waited for Mommy to respond, taking a step back and

holding my breath. Maybe if I wasn't there, she would begin to talk.

The scent of garlic had taken over the kitchen.

"But it's too much. For little things, he hits the boy. Too much. Sometimes punishment can be left to the Lord." I knew what Ninang Rola wanted to say—Why aren't you doing anything about it?—but Mommy didn't hear her. She knew like I did that Ninang Rola only talked, slipping a piece of her mind after something had happened. She never stood up to Daddy Groovie herself, although I thought she could have, because she was the oldest person in our house. I could never understand the way they passed responsibility to one another, as if one was supposed to handle it alone. It would have been better if Ninang Rola did it herself; after all, she never stopped talking about it.

Mommy hurled the sliced fish into the glass bowl of water and watched it sink, ending their conversation with a deep breath and silence.

I had learned to speak without saying a word, too. Just like them. Whenever they stopped talking and only the sounds their hands made could be heard, I could hear so many things being said. And I learned to read their hands. The way they moved. And their eyes, the way they looked at things that nobody else could see.

Ninang Rola put the garlic on a saucer. She put the fish guts and gills in an old plastic bowl that I would later put on the sidewalk curb for the stray cats to eat.

"I will not be here forever, you know, Estrella?" Ninang Rola mumbled. "I am much older than you. Before you know it, I will not be in this world anymore. Sometimes I wish you would take matters in your hands, especially when it comes to your boys. I always wonder . . . I always wonder what would have happened if I didn't live with you. Would things be any different, huh?"

Mommy would have probably done more, I thought. Daddy Groovie would not have gotten away with what he did. On the other hand, she probably would not have done anything either. She might have just taken Pipo and me away and left. Somehow I wished that would have been the case. It might have been a lot easier for everybody here. But I also knew Daddy Groovie would fight to have us back; he would never lose sight of any one of us. I thought about many possibilities but the truth was, without Ninang Rola, anything could happen.

My thoughts were interrupted by a sudden downpour outside. "Mommy, it's raining," I shouted. There were drops of rain rushing down.

"The buckets. The buckets." Ninang Rola tapped my shoulders. "Go, get the buckets."

I hesitated at first, my eyes on Mommy. She was chopping on the cutting board even though there was nothing there to chop. The fish had slipped off to the counter; she didn't notice even though she was staring at it the whole time. But she continued chopping, adding more knife marks on the already rough board. The drumming sound echoed the drops of rain. I looked at her face—knotted brows, sunken cheeks, the constant swallowing of air—and tried to listen to thick thoughts running through her head.

"Gringo, go. Get the buckets," Ninang Rola insisted.

I went to the bathroom and noticed how most of our buckets were half empty. It usually took a whole night to fill these buckets with water. I wrapped my arms around one big empty plastic bucket and walked back to the kitchen. "Here," I said to Ninang Rola when I ran into her.

She grabbed the bucket and yanked it onto the back patio. "Get more. Quick!"

I ran to the bathroom as fast as I could and emptied a bucket into another. Ninang Rola and I ran in and out of the kitchen to the sound of Mommy chopping, each trip taking more buckets with us. In no time, there were buckets and drums all over the patio floor, filling up with rain. Then, Ninang Rola started to look for more containers like the huge Del Monte pineapple cans she collected underneath the counter. She pulled the curtains apart, saying, "They must be here somewhere."

"Ouch!" Mommy screamed.

"What happened?" Ninang Rola looked up.

Mommy cut her thumb with the knife, but she didn't put it in her mouth the way she always sucked my finger when I cut myself. Her blood mixed with the fish's. She stood there and watched her finger drip.

"*Dios mío!* Gringo, go get Band-Aid. *Agua Oxinada.* Quick. Band—" But before Ninang Rola could finish her sentence, Mommy walked out to the back patio.

Ninang Rola stood up and leaned against the window, watching her, hands on the grill. *Band-Aid,* she whispered as if the word didn't mean anything at all. Her eyes were steady, as if by not blinking she could stop the gush of rain from soaking Mommy. The rain splattered Ninang Rola's face but even that didn't pull her away.

I took a step back to avoid getting wet. The rain had begun to flood the floor, soaking the handmade cloths we had spread all over the kitchen. I didn't say anything, nor did I go down to pick up the floormats. I continued watching both of them.

The sound of the front door banged open behind us, then again, louder, when the rain pulled it closed. Very rapid steps followed. Slightly loud thumping of wet slippers. Another recognizable footstep. The wind pushed Pipo all the way to where we were. He was still holding the towel he had left with, which was as soaked as he was. He was going to run upstairs to change perhaps when he suddenly turned around, stopped, and stood nearby, staring, breathing very hard. His skin was visible on his T-shirt thinned by rain. He wasn't looking at me.

My eyes followed Pipo's stare, outside, to where Mommy was standing, covered with rain. She was still for a while, then she slowly lifted her hands and opened her palms as if trying to catch the drops. I couldn't see her bloody finger anymore, I was looking at her head, the way she moved it back so that her face was directly facing the sky. The drops drummed on her face. Her hair looked like one thick line down her head. The heavy rain weighted down her clothes but she ignored it. There was so much of it, I could hardly see the ground. The sewer hole in the corner was vomiting rain. The white clothes on the corrugated aluminum were also drenched, which meant they had to be washed again.

Nobody had thought about bringing them inside. They were so wet they floated on the aluminum as if little bodies were being blown up inside.

Pipo looked as if he wanted to run to her, tell her the containers were filling up with rain. I wanted to carry them back inside, maybe take Mommy along with me. Pipo would hold her one arm, and I, the other. But I couldn't even move. Pipo and Ninang Rola were both staring at Mommy, at the rain.

I had never let myself get soaked in the rain. Afraid that I might get *pulmonia* and shiver to an early death. But I had always wondered how it felt when one's whole body disappeared into the rain's arms until you couldn't hear anything else but its voice trickling in your ears, or couldn't see anything because the drops were so thick, so strong, they forced your eyes to shut. Or so magical, perhaps, they could even heal, and wash the dirty blood beading around a wound.

Godmother of Words

Certain things are better kept than said, Gringo.

But certain things you have to find out now. I won't be with you always. This is my last trip in life. Something I have always known, especially in my old age, time has a way of showing up again with a similar face, similar gestures, a never-ending cycle of circles. It was different then, our time. All of you might have changed now, all you young people, but you will always carry something of your parents in your veins. I am not talking about the way you look, no, not that, not even the way you act, but of the way you are. Some things we carry in ourselves no matter how much everything changes around us. People like your parents who were born after the war, yes, they are unique, unlike people like me who came before. Each decade brings so many strange new attitudes. My time, Santíssimo *Rosario, those were the real times, when we believed in ourselves, when we had respect.* Moralidad. *Forties, fifties, sixties—I lived through it all, each decade a different song. The words change but the tunes, Gringo, the tunes are always the same. You understand? Come, sit by me, right here,* hijo, *where my shadow can hide you. Let me tell you a story, but first say that you will keep this, all of this, to yourself.*

Your parents, Gringo, they were not supposed to marry each other. They met at Miss Tanso. I remember when . . . Oh, they were young. . . . Oh, your mother, beautiful, beautiful. Always looking good because in the sixties, people had too much hair, and wore those strange-looking clothes. Tight miniskirts. Liberated daw. Como Puta *the women then. It was a sign of new times. They listened to strange songs, rock-roll-roll? Whatever. No more Sinatra. Oh, Sinatra, Como-Perry, Matis, how so many years have gone by. When I told your mother to join Miss Tanso, she laughed at me. She said, "Why in the world would I want to join that?" Told her we could use some* puhunan *for our buy-and-sell business. The prize money wasn't bad. I wasn't thinking of the money, of course, although I bothered her for weeks until she said yes. People like us never join beauty contests, you know? Some people think we smell. Or have some kind of malaria or TB. But that's not true.*

Your mother was the most beautiful woman in our block, you see. Hermossíssima. *So* meztiza. *Look at your mother, can't you tell we're related, Gringo? I helped her sew her own gown for the preliminaries. We bought flowers to put around her head like a crown. She smelled of Sampaguitas and Gumamelas. Hmmmmm, the scent of those days comes back to me. Oh. In her white lace gown, and a crown of white flowers on her very big hair bun, she looked like a screen goddess, like*

Dorisday. Dorisday! You don't know her, Gringo, you're much too young. Your mother looked like her when she descended down the steps to the center stage. I fell off my seat looking at her. Who would have known she worked at a market to sell clothes, huh? When she made it to the finals, I made her a new white gown because she still wouldn't buy anything for herself. But I thought since she was already there, I'd do the work. I dressed her up, put makeup on her, light one because she already has a beautiful face.

Then she made it to the top twenty. Oh, Gringo, I screamed and screamed so loud I fell off my seat again. The people behind me pulled me up, saying, calm down, calmante, calmante. *I told them, be quiet.* Magtigil nga sila! Santíssimo! *That's the dress I sewed that they were all looking at, you see? Some of the women were even daughters of prominent people. One is an actress so famous now. People took Miss Tanso seriously, you know? And one of them was my Estrella. I always knew she would make it. I told her to sing that Dorisday song—Qué Serasera—you know that song? Qué serasera, whateber wilbi, wilbi. Gringo, Gringo. The stage was decorated with balloons of different colors like the ones sold near Iglesia de San Pedro, remember? Yes, birthday balloons, that's it. Fiesta banners crisscrossed above us like stars. Estrella was right in the middle. As she walked to the center of the stage, my heart started to beat fast. She stopped. I thought my heart was going to fall down my chest. She turned, smiled, turned again. I could feel everybody holding their breath. I looked up to catch a breath of air. All I saw was a heaven of lights, blinking Technicolor lights all over.*

Certain things never cross our minds, like how we first met someone we've always known. I'm not sure when I started to wonder why Ninang Rola lived with us. All I knew was that when I was born, she was already there. And because the word *godmother* had always been attached to her name, I never questioned who she was. Sometimes I also wondered why Daddy Groovie and Mommy stayed together; I never asked. But like everything else, it was something I was bound to find out. *Certain things are supposed to happen.* That was Ninang Rola's answer to everything, what-God-willing-always-happens. I was thinking of that when I looked at Boy Manicure one day and smiled at him. He waved at me and smiled back. I didn't move away, but in the corner of my eye, I looked around me to make sure that nobody saw. I found myself walking toward his beauty parlor, watching him change Delilah de Samsona's hair. She had on a brown wig this time, a white dress with little round sequins hanging on the hem and flowers on the shoulders. I could smell her, imagine her walking around inside the display window, singing. The sun was out. Delilah de Samsona was wearing something that made people look at her, her mannequin face so smooth, it made me always wonder who she was modeled from, if there ever existed a real face that looked exactly like her because, if she were real, she would be the most beautiful one here. A beauty queen. A *meztiza.* Like Mommy. Our own Miss Tanso. With Boy Manicure's expert hands making her beautiful every day, no doubt she would have eyes following her wherever she went. I watched Boy Manicure change her dress. She even wore a bra, brown one like Mommy's. I laughed when Boy Manicure took it off. He had a way of touching the mannequin, touching her skin as if it was soft and it pulsed, handling her as if she would break the moment she moved from where she was. He was dressing her the way a woman would dress herself, with all the care so that young men would look at them, would notice them. But somehow, in my eyes, Delilah de Samsona and Boy Manicure were becoming one. I slowly walked away from him when I saw Big Boy Jun coming toward me with a handful of names to call me. I could already tell even from afar what he was about to do. Seeing me in front of Boy Manicure's would not help, for sure. My insides started to jump up and down. Boy Manicure didn't notice I was going away. Under my heavy breath, I was thinking about how much he probably wanted to be Delilah de Samsona himself—by putting layers of makeup on his face, like a beauty queen, so that when people looked at him, they would want to get to know him, talk to him, not run away. Laughing. And would definitely not call him names. Names that were better kept than said.

"*Who is she?" That was the look on his face.*

He was the only one left sitting in the audience. He looked Stateside in his nice suit. I knew, I used to sell Americana fabrics, too, you know. That was your father. I invited him to come. There he waited looking so posterioso, *waiting to be introduced to the new Miss Tanso. The new Miss Tanso, Gringo! Imagine that! Hayyy . . . and your father, he looked like Elvis or he thought he did. In those days, after the liberation from the States, everybody wanted to look like Elvis. I knew of him. I had sold him clothes before. When everybody left, your father stayed. He wanted to speak with her. I told him about your mother a few weeks before. I told him that my cousin will be the next Miss Tanso. You know what he said: "Your cousin, Miss Tanso?" as if by looking at my face he could tell how your mother looked. I told him how beautiful your mother was, how I didn't want her to become an old maid like me, how they would look so good together. Then I told him that he was the best Elvis look-alike I had ever seen. He bought twenty raffle tickets. Your father wore his best suit from the States. He told us later on how he had lots of them, all Stateside suits, which he wore at different occasions. In those times, suits were tight, very tight on the body. He wore the best one, he said. He watched your mommy as she walked past him, his face so red, his eyes fixated on her. I was taking Kodak then. I got everybody to pose. I remember the pictures, those beautiful black-and-white ones with Estrella holding her sash and your father flashing his teeth. I don't know what happened to them. I took pictures of everything, even the boys who were running to the stage to steal the balloons on the bamboo stands to sell them again. I screamed at those culprits!*

Ahh! Gringo, it was different then. Your father was much younger. He was still in parochial college, not working in construction. His face was still clean, free of wrinkles and mud from work in the sun. Guapito. *When he came up to Estrella to say hello-*kumusta-ka, *she only stared into his eye then walked away. I caught her shoulder and said to her, "Wait,* *this is Germano. . . .” Estrella turned around, her crown tipped over and she caught it with her hand.* “Jesucristo—” *Germano whispered in awe and took her hand. He said that he would have bought a hundred more raffle tickets had he met her before. I started laughing. Hah! You see that? And he didn't believe me at first. He couldn't get his eyes off of your mother, looking so young in his Stateside suit. Me and my mouth. I told him where we worked. Germano found out where we lived. He did almost anything to win your mother's hands. He courted her for months, sometimes skipping parochial college to visit her at the market. He brought calachuchi flowers every time he came. Calachuchi? HAH! Those flowers are for dead people.* Qué se Joda! *I took them anyway and sold them.*

I told Estrella that the college boy who thought he was Elvis liked her a lot, but she wouldn't pay attention to me. I asked Estrella many times if she liked him, too. She only looked at me. Your father's family is well-to-do, you know that? Buenaventuras have some money. They descended from Hacenderos. Land-owning, Gringo, land-owning from the province. They have a name where they are from, up in the north. You know how important status is to us, especially to people like us. Anything to get us out of this. But you know what your mother said, “Buenaventura or not, it doesn't matter to me. Do I look like the type who goes after men with money?” That's my Estrella. She's not one whose eyes glow when someone with a nice Mustang drives by. Something about that woman. Even now she's still like that. So much she keeps to herself without telling anyone, too. So I told her that it's going to be the seventies soon, women will be more independent, especially her, the six-

ties woman. They will have more choices. The war has been over a long time. Time to be practical. They can use their heads a little bit. Your father might be good for her. Estrella looked at me and laughed. "Did you see the way those men looked at me, at Miss Tanso? They looked like they would buy me. Sixties women? There is no such thing as sixties, seventies. The men today, if they don't love, they'd buy you. And Germano. He looks like he always gets what he wants." I thought, "What's wrong with that?" Ahhh, Gringo, I would be lucky if a shoe shine man noticed me.

Who could escape the thin, all-seeing eyes of Big Boy Jun? He made it a point to notice everybody who got near him. He was always in everybody's way. He had grown, too. Wider. Wide enough to cover a great part of our narrow street when he stood in the middle. His body cast a shadow that covered the entire block. His head was bigger than ever, too. Balder. His stomach had a life of its own by the way it bounced over his belt. His belly had an eye at the center with plenty of hair coming out of it. And although his marble-gambling friends had split up into different groups, he was far from being on his own. He had made friends with others who smoked and watched girls walk down the street. Sang songs nobody could understand. Or whistled, even if no sound came out of his mouth, which looked like a twisted earthworm whenever he pointed his lips. Nothing escaped his eyes. He called the cats that walked hungrily around the streets. *O, ano, pusa, o ano?* As if they could respond back to him. Then he would kick them in the stomach and watch them twist in pain. Whenever I walked outside and caught a glimpse of him somewhere, I would look at my watch, or try to fix or wind it or check a bag I was carrying, or maybe count change if I went on an errand. If I were inside our house, I would not leave at all until I was sure he wasn't there anymore. But even then, Big Boy Jun would find me and make sure I noticed he was there. He would whistle, or whisper something to the person next to him so that they giggled like little boys. Big Boy Jun. Or just Jun, the way he would say his name now. But nobody ever said just Jun. Jun Páre, his friends would say. All these Juniors were slowly growing into the monsters that they were expected to become. They frightened me. I wasn't one of them, would never be. Every time they saw me, they knew that. They hung out in our street, day and night, as if the street would go away if they didn't stand guard. Sometimes they played this game by throwing a ball against a flat wall with a racket carved from Mazola Cooking Oil plastic containers. Jai Alai, the game of the season. The sun was out, their shirts sweaty with little muddy circles that came from being hit by Jai Alai balls many times. One, two, you could count them. The more, the better. That was their way of showing who they were. Another stage into becoming a hang-around-do-nothing-*sanggano. O Gringo, Jai Alai, O?* Big Boy Jun asked me one day. I thought about the parable of the rocks. Of how much I wanted to make a racket of my own and put rocks in it and throw it at them, one by one, especially at Big Boy Jun, the creator of everything that had nothing to do with what I was going to become. "N-n-o," I stuttered. No.

Stonewomen, that's what we called them in my time.

They never got married, never had a need for men, for the love of men. Yes, that's what she was, a woman of stone. Told her that if I were as beautiful as her, I would marry a lawyer, someone who can buy a big house here. Somebody titulado. *Estrella only stared into my eyes. I said, "You are like a younger sister to me. I will give you opportunities I didn't have." She only smiled at me, that smile of hers that came so seldom that I wanted to wring her neck sometimes. The next day, I told your father that he would have to work twice as hard. Harder. "You know the women of today," I said, "not like us women of the war, women of too many atrocities. We were a lot easier to get. We'd marry anyone, as long as he had his limbs intact." That's true, Gringo. Things I learned in my lifetime. Sometimes you have to use your head, not your heart. Too much trouble in the heart. Had I used my head, I would be married with grandchildren by now. Your father started laughing at me. That* idioto. *That was when he planned it all. I should have known what he was thinking. Gringo, I should have known better.*

The old Dorisday movie was playing in Deluxe Theatre, so your father asked your mother to see it one early evening. He was looking very slick with his well-pomaded hair, with his long sideburns that were down here to his jaws. He thought she wouldn't say no to that. After all, she loved Qué-sera-sera. Outside, he parked this newly polished Mustang. The car was like his shoes. Even his belt had a silver horse like the one on the hood of his car. I found out later the car wasn't his. Only God knows where he got it from. But then, I laughed. Elvis, lover boy, I called him. He was once again wearing his

Stateside suit. He looked at Estrella who was wearing a white dress. She always looked beautiful in white. "Must cost a lot of money, these suits you have," I said to him. He told me his sister Dolores lived in the States. The suits were sent by her. She also sent the shoes with metal on the tip. Dolores, huh? I was thinking how sometimes parents name their children without knowing what certain words meant. Dolores meant pain, much pain, in fact. Haven't I told you this before, Gringo? Never name your children Spanish names you don't know.

Anyway, I nodded when Estrella looked at me for approval. "Okay, take me home early. Okay?" she said to him. I repeated what she said, so he knew, and I added, "Take care of her, make sure you return her alive." I even joked about it that your mother gave me an angry look. I knew somehow that she was excited about the Dorisday movie. I had seen it many times but I still got excited. Estrella sang the song but never saw the movie. She was too young in the fifties to even get to the theaters. Don't you know that song, too? Everybody does, it had a special place in our hearts, specially in the older judges' of Miss Tanso. When she sang, the judges almost cried, then the applause that never stopped. Estrella moved closer to me before she left with Germano and whispered, "After this movie, Germano will leave me alone." Somehow, I didn't want that to happen. They looked so good together. And I was right, that was the night that would connect us forever, that would create this house.

Sometimes when I look at you Gringo, I think maybe it's meant to be. Maybe God wouldn't punish me for allowing my little Estrella to go off with a man she wasn't sure about. Your mother said yes to everything: to the movies, to the long drive by the bay, to the cocktail drinks at the Hollywood nightclub, to the dance. It was weeks later when she told me all these details. I waited for them, too. I waited. And I would have waited forever because I wanted to know. At Hollywood Club, he asked her to dance the twist. Estrella shook her head, grabbing the glass of beer half full of ice, finding a reason not to be taken to the dim dance floor and be watched by strange drunkards. That's my Estrella. I thought that was good, not dancing with him like that but Germano insisted, "C'mon, just like in the Elvis movies." He stood up and began to shake his body in front of her. She covered her mouth in embarrassment, looked away and threw little giggles of laughter to the mirror beside her. When she looked back at him she was thinking that maybe this wouldn't be the last night she would see him again. "He's quite funny when he's been drinking," she kept on saying to herself. She was beginning to like him. He pulled her to the dance floor. She wasn't sure whether she was shying away from him or from dancing. Germano held her around the waist, one arm extended, doing the twist. She never knew how to dance. Sing, yes. Dance, no. Qué Verguenza! *But how can anyone do both? But your father—he's been drinking from the day he was born. Estrella only learned it later in life. I was the one who taught your mother how to drink. She had to have drinks with people in important places after winning Miss Tanso. She said beer tasted bitter, that bottle that women of our time never touched. But men love their San Miguel, you can tell by the way they touch their bottles, because they take the shape of a woman's body. I wished I never taught Estrella how to drink. That night, she used what she learned from me. One beer. Two. The third one she said stop. She knew her lips didn't touch the glass. She was sure of that. I asked her if she got drunk. She said no. She wasn't even dizzy. Even months later when she asked herself again, she knew she didn't drink the third glass of beer. She remembered because that was the glass that didn't have ice in it. And she never had beer without ice. I taught her that, too.*

She was sure she insisted that he take her home that night. Your father said it was too early; he probably didn't know what he was saying because he was too drunk. She stood up and said, time to go. He convinced her into finishing her second glass. After that, she told me she hardly remembered leaving the nightclub, or going into your father's borrowed Mustang to be taken home. I believed everything she said. I can never forgive myself for what had happened to her. Putang-ina niya! Putang-ina yang tatay mo! Ahasss! Microbio! *Forgive me for saying these things,* hijo. *But how could he do that? And my Estrella—I took your mother into my arms when she told me all this. I wouldn't let her go. Never again, I promised myself. Oh, Gringo, never forget any of this. I have kept this to myself for a very long time. I want you to do the same until the day you are ready to tell.*

When your mother woke up the following day, everything looked different around her. Then she noticed she was in somebody else's bed, that she wasn't home. I usually woke her up in the morning to go to the market. It was Sunday then. I would have woken her to go to church. I had no idea where she was that night. I was up all night wondering what had happened. Every time there was a car pulling by I would run to the door. But it wasn't them. It wasn't like your mother to stay out late. I was thinking of accidents, maybe Germano couldn't drive the Mustang he borrowed. I was thinking of all these horrible things that sometimes you can't read from your palms. Accidents are not written on Estrella's. Disaster is. That line on her palm that twists the wrong way.

She told me that when she woke up and her eyes began to clear, she pulled her body off the bed and stared at everything around her. All at once. Everything darkened around her. Dios ko. Dios ko . . . *She hardly noticed that Germano was sitting on a chair, in front of the bed watching her the whole time.* Putang-ina niya. *Your mother didn't cry, didn't scream, even when she felt herself naked under the sheets. My God, my heart shrinks when I think of this. Hold my hand, Gringo. I never quite understood how anybody could do that. How could he just sit there and watch her? Your mother told me she couldn't scream although she wanted to. She took deep breaths, her lungs almost running out of air. Oh, how could he take advantage of her like that? Estrella had never been touched by anyone before. Your father started calling her name. "Take me home," was all she told him. Your father begged her to stay, cried in front of her, told her how much he loved her. How could anyone believe him then? I wanted to kill your father, Gringo. I wanted to kill him. But then, I thought there was something else . . . something good might come of it.*

Sergio Putita told me SWAT was gone. Gone where? I asked. He only looked at me. Gone. Gone with a girl was what I learned later on. He eloped. It was raining so nobody knew. Why would he do that? I asked Sergio Putita.

He didn't answer me. He only unwrapped cellophane off of tamarind sweets. Then he put it in his mouth, darkening his teeth. I asked him many questions, all starting with a why: Why didn't he tell anyone? Why didn't their parents try to stop them? Why would he want to take off with her? He doesn't know, was the answer I read from looking at Sergio Putita's mouth. I shook his shoulders to get a word out of him but he wouldn't tell me anything. "What's gotten to you?" he finally asked, spitting a tamarind seed into his palm. Why do you care anyway? He raised his voice, pointing his lips at me so that I quickly slapped his mouth and ran. I only heard him coughing, but that didn't make me turn around. I wondered if he coughed out all the tamarind sweets. I stayed in the bedroom for hours, sitting in the corner, staring at my hand, folding my fingers again and again, wondering what the elopers just did. When I got up, I stood at the window to see another cart of pig slop being pushed by a boy I had not seen before. The boy's arms were too thin, they would break from picking up the frozen chickens buried in the pig slop. He never took off his shirt, and I didn't want him to. I simply wanted him to go away, maybe sink in his pig slop. I thought about the girl. I wondered who she was, where she came from, whether she also spent time watching SWAT when he delivered pig slop, whether she watched him walk outside during the nights of procession. Had she ever been to the procession? Did she like the way he smelled? Did he court her, send her flowers—calachuci, sampaguita—so she would give him a kiss, so he could hold her hand? Did they go to a motel? Did he take her there and do things to her? What were they doing together? I stood at the window every morning for days, not knowing what I was waiting for. I would hide whenever I saw Sergio Putita walk by. Behind the curtain, where he would think I was Pipo. He had not talked to me since I slapped his mouth. He told everybody I made him bleed. I didn't see any blood on my hand. After he passed, I would move back to the window, just in time to see Boy Spit walk by, with other newspaper boys, all of them chanting names of their newspapers. I would watch his steps carefully and study the way he pushed his cart on the rough street. He looked up and saw me. I wasn't afraid he might see me. It didn't matter. So I stood at the window in full view. Look at me, I said to myself. His spitting was something I wanted to see. His voice, I wanted to hear, because I knew it was getting deeper, the words coming from somewhere down inside. I waited until I was overcome by fear that he might be like all these other boys, that someday he would probably elope, too.

Love is strange, Gringo. It makes people do things that they don't usually want to do. I had only felt it once and never again. In our time, we always believed we would only love one person all our lives. Maybe that's still true for your generation. Maybe that was what your father was thinking when he took your mother to the motel, without her knowing it. Maybe he loved her too much, I don't know. That morning at the motel, your father told her that he would marry her, that he would be responsible for what happened. But your mother only wanted to go home. She said she almost fainted when she saw stains of blood all over the white sheets. All dried up. She couldn't bear looking at the people behind the register at the motel. She couldn't look at anybody on the street. I knew that. Because she wouldn't look at me straight in the eyes for a long time, as if by looking at me, she would make me disappear.

This is what I always tell you about shame, Gringo. Shame. Verguenza. *It is within us, in our blood, it stays in there for as long as we are here. That's why it took a long time for your mother to tell me what happened. She didn't know that was the night that would bring both of them together, like a rock in a ring, never to be separated again. Your father lived up to his word. He did not disappear. It was your mother who did. She went away when she found out she was three months pregnant. We had argued about this. She didn't want the child. But God forbid she should get rid of it. I convinced her to go away if it was the shame that was bothering her. I felt for her. Even though it was already the sixties, it was still a different time. Liberated is what we're all supposed to be in the sixties. Liberated? Hah! Like many things in this country, that is another Stateside word nobody understood! Inside us, we are all afraid, afraid of so many things.*

Estrella had gone north, close to the sea, to the water. South was where she should have gone, where her family was. But it was hot down there. Heat is not good for giving birth. She didn't tell your grandparents about what happened to her. She just took the train to the north. It wasn't until much much later that your grandparents found out. Before she left, she could still hide her stomach. Only I knew what had happened to her. While she was gone, I was thinking of how we could explain the child to our relatives. I wanted to keep the baby.

Estrella wanted to give him away. She never fully believed he was hers.

Your father knew why she left. He probably read my mind. People don't just leave for no reason, you see. Once you've moved to this city, there is no going back to where you came from, north or south. He came to my house one night, very drunk, the first time I ever saw your father like that. He dropped on the floor. He begged and begged for me to tell him where your mother was. But I couldn't do it. I couldn't do it, Gringo. I was very angry with him. I could have killed him at that time. Then he started to cry. I had never seen a man cry in my whole life. But those were real tears. I could tell his tears from his sweat. I told him. I said, over and over again, that if I told him where she was, he would bring her back and marry her. A child needed a father. There was no way I would have given your brother away. That was a sin against society and God. We as people are not raised to do such horrendous things. Pananagutan, *that was the word I told your father. He would be responsible for all the lives he touched. He would be responsible for mending the broken parts. And whatever Estrella felt for him at the time, he would have to accept that, too. So I sent him off to the north.*

When they came back, it was their wedding. Nobody showed up from your father's side of the family. The wedding that your mother kept from her family. That was the time when your father's parents stopped sending him to the parochial college. I never knew how poor we were until then, and these things you really don't realize until someone, somewhere reminds you of them. Germano was my constant reminder. His family said—he's one of them now. One of us.

Poor. They don't know how we live, how much dignity we have. That's why you had only seen faces of your grandparents in pictures, Gringo. They are alive. Except for Dolores, they all turned their backs on him. Dolores is a different lot, a modern woman. That's the real liberated woman there. Maybe because she's in the States, she thinks different. But since then Germano was on his own and his life wasn't the same anymore. Both of them, and Pipo. And I was there, too, and am still here, although I may not be here for long. I couldn't leave them then. I was responsible for them. They had nobody else, nobody watching them, Gringo. At their wedding, I played everyone's role: maid of honor, witness, bridesmaid, and ring bearer. I was to carry their crosses since. Your mother, she was like Virgen Maria. God forgive me for saying this. She was like her, her body ballooning with a son she never asked to have.

I had always felt that the Jesus with the glowing heart on our bedroom wall knew everything. But since he never spoke to anyone and I could never read his blue eyes the way Ninang Rola did so she knew whether it would be a good day or not, I had no way of knowing what would happen next. I was out one day because Mommy asked me to buy a spool of thread. The sun had pulled everybody out of their houses. There would be a brownout soon, the radio announced. Even the newspapers had it printed all over the pages: BROWNOUT AT 3 P.M., CONSERVE ENERGY, the song of the summer. Outside, people stood, fanned themselves, gossiped. I was walking back home from Tarina All-Around store. Ahead of me, Sergio Putita and Pipo, drowning in the heat of laughter. Their giggles made me walk more slowly so that nobody would think I was with them. So that there was enough distance should they decide to stop and giggle more. Who could have seen what was coming? There they were—Big Boy Jun and his friends, walking toward them. I wanted to stop and turn. Moving back would make it seem like I was running away. Maybe dropping the spool of thread until it rolled back to where I came from? But the eyes came sooner than I thought, followed by the mouths. The voices—AYYYYYY! I waited for the name-calling. My knees, I could feel my knees hitting each other as I walked. Sergio Putita and Pipo only continued walking, as if everything would be all right. "Hi! Hi!" Big Boy Jun started teasing. They should have run. But slowly they walked. Or more slowly. "Hi! Hi! Jai Alai! Ayyyyy! Ayyyy!" The teasing went on, louder even. "Stop it!" Sergio Putita screamed, raising his arms quickly above his head. The birds flew above him. I froze where I was. Jesus, I whispered. But even Jesus couldn't help them then. "What do you mean stop, who are you talking to, huh?" Big Boy Jun approached them. His strut confirmed what was going through his bald head. "Who-do-you-think-you-are, HUH?" Watching him beside Sergio Putita made you know how big he was. Faces looked out the windows. "JAI ALAI," Big Boy Jun yelled. The clouds came down in shape of Jai Alai balls, round, bouncing, and white. Sergio Putita and Pipo were spinning where they were, arms over their heads to protect their faces. The other Jai Alai boys were also throwing their balls all over. Sergio Putita caught one of the balls, threw it up into the air, so high that when it came down it got stuck in the aluminum gutter. He started laughing. There was nothing to laugh about. Even Pipo knew that—he was still staring at the roof where the ball was caught. Big Boy Jun swung his racket-wrapped arm and quickly sling-shot Sergio Putita with it. The moment stopped. We all watched the ball speed past his face, missing Sergio Putita, Pipo. Faces turned around. Boy Manicure came out of his beauty parlor. He screamed at Big Boy Jun, told him to stop pestering Sergio Putita and Pipo, pointing his finger at the sky. "*Ano ba?* Leave those two alone! Go home! Go home!" But it went so fast that when I heard a noise again, it was Boy Manicure falling on the sidewalk, his hands on his face. Laughter, lots of it. Stone throwing. Ball throwing. Sergio Putita and Pipo spinning out of the group, so quickly they left me not knowing what to do. The voice of Boy Manicure took over the street. "Leave them alone, you fat, ugly bastard!" Words shot back at him: *bakla, binabae. Malandi. Puta. Lalakwe. Pakalalake ka, o ano? You better be a man, or else? What? You wanna fight? What? Whatchalookinat? Huh? Baklang 'to. Mahiya ka sa sarili mo. Fucking bastard.* I felt a hand around my wrist, pulling me. I went back to the opposite side of the street. "Faster," Boy Spit said. "This way."

"Pipo," I said to him. "Where is Pipo?"

It rained so hard when your brother was born. It was as if the world was angry. We already lived here. See that wallpaper up there in the kitchen? That was the very first wallpaper we used to cover this house. This house had old, peeling paint on the walls so we decided to wallpaper it. I told your mother never to cover that part up there so we would always be reminded how we began. It was purple. It's been turning gray through the years. When your brother was born, this whole house was wallpapered with purple flowers with bits of yellow background. Your father wasn't home then. Stuck somewhere he used to work. It was beginning to flood outside. The heaviest rain I had ever seen in a long, long time.

Your mother wasn't supposed to give birth yet. I wasn't expecting her to. I didn't even know she was going through labor. I was too busy trying to get rid of the flood on the floor with a dustpan, and running around shutting the windows with a flashlight in my hand. I thought I heard screams but I wasn't sure. It could have been the scream of the rain. The rain screams like a woman, you know, but not like a woman giving birth. When I heard it again, I stood there, in that kitchen, looking up. The scream wasn't coming from upstairs but down where I was. I ran around the house. The lights went out as soon as thunder hit the electric lines. That's when I heard your mother in the bathroom. She called my name over and over. I didn't know what to do. I wasn't thinking that she was giving birth right there, in the bathroom, during a brownout.

Pipo came to the world that way. I thought he was dead. I didn't know what to do. I pointed the flashlight at them. I can't tell you what I saw. It wasn't life I saw, the way life is brought to the world. It was death. Two dead people. But as if God-willing, Pipo cried as soon as his buttocks hit the tiled floor. Your mother had collapsed. There was blood all over. And water. Water all over. I did what I could do. I ran back to the kitchen and boiled water. I also boiled knives and scissors so I could cut his cord. Look at your brother's navel. It sticks out. That's because I didn't know where to cut. I just cut and knotted it. I kept the cord after all these years. Put it in a plastic bag. It's all dried up now. Someday I will give it to your brother. Remind him what brought him to this world. Your brother, he could survive anything. I knew even then. When I looked at his body, it was full of veins. Felipe was what we called him. Pipo after Felipe. That's the name of your mother's father. And many fathers before him. Tell me, isn't that a beautiful name?

A COMPANY OF RATS

The sun poured and poured on the ground.

Even with my new thick rubber slippers, I could feel its heat. The windows were wide open but no breeze was coming in. The streets were so still that the roar of electric fans could be heard from other houses. This was the time when most of our neighbors left for their provinces to get as close to the water as possible. If we did, we would take the long, narrow north road to the place where Daddy Groovie was from. But we stayed here, in the sun, where water was scarce because we never had money to go anywhere. I knew I lived in a country of countless islands, but I was born in the heart of smog so I hardly saw the sea.

"Rats." Pipo came running to us, screaming. "There are rats under the sink. Rats as big as cats. Their tails this wide." He described them with his hands. "This thick." He made little circles with his fingers.

We were all in the living room. Beside us

were glasses of water. Mommy was at her Singer Machine, stopping every minute to stare at the wall. Ninang Rola had a basket of rice grains on her lap, separating the white grains from the unpeeled ones.

"How can rats be as big as cats?" I asked, although I had seen them in the back patio many times. I always knew they lived around us. I had seen them running past me, their long tails sticking out of their hiding places. "So you haven't seen rats before?" I wanted to ask Pipo but I kept it to myself. We both knew that at night, the house became a playground of rats, lizards, and roaches. They crawled on the ceiling, the walls, into the deepest parts of the house, leaving traces in the morning: droppings, chewed wall-paper and clothes, roach sacs, zigzag tailprints on the wall. They flew all over the empty dark spaces of the room, sometimes landing on our skin while we slept, leaving their marks, red as an itch. A good part of the morning was always spent cleaning up after them, and putting ointment on rashes that grew on our skin overnight.

"Of course, they can be as big as cats. In the rice fields, they're as big as you!" exclaimed Ninang Rola, winking at me. She grabbed a handful of rice grains and threw them into her mouth. A few slipped and landed on her lap, which she quickly picked up and put back in the basket. I looked away before our eyes met again. The closer she was to me, the more I remembered what she had told me about how Pipo was born. I had been wondering since then where she hid Pipo's cord. How does it look now? Dry? Wrinkly? Like *longganisa* after we had removed the stuffing?

Pipo sat down, panting. His brown cut-off shorts were down below his knees, and so big another pair of legs would fit in just as comfortably. "Come and see this. They were huge. They were all staring back at me. How they got under the sink I don't know but we must kill them."

"The drain. That's how they got there," replied Mommy, sounding as if she had just woken up, her face glued to the needle, where the light shone directly from outside. She moved her head about so as not to block the sun. "But you can't kill them. Not even touch them a little bit. These big rats, they're very smart. If you kill one, better kill them all. Otherwise, even if only one of them survives, it will go after you, ruin your clothes, eat your food. You're better off if you leave them alone."

The Singer Machine's motor vibrated with her voice. I could tell its age, like heartbeats slowing down through the years.

"Are we just going to leave them there?" I asked. Killing rats was how Daddy Groovie spent his time with his construction friends at the pier on Sundays while everybody else dressed to go to church. Maybe these rats were the survivors, hiding under the sink, planning ways to get us. Daddy Groovie once said after killing a rat he had found on the back patio, "These damn rats live off poor people's blood and sweat. Got to get rid of them." He cornered it with his arms spread so wide, anyone would be fearful. His eyes grew so big, so veined, one look at them you'd close yours. He wrapped the rat in a plastic bag after hammering it with big fat sticks, big nails sticking out of the tip, only for the rats to multiply a week later. That was where Pipo got his idea later on, even if he himself knew that rats were one of those things nobody could get rid of, not even Daddy Groovie, or his construction friends.

"Why don't you leave them alone, both of you?" asked Mommy. She would never say that to Daddy Groovie. Nobody could tell him to stop his favorite pastime with his friends once they had all lost their jobs. I never really saw them doing that but I knew they had spent more time together the longer they went without jobs. The last time he lost his job, he was hardly home. The window no longer attracted him. It could have been because Ninang Rola wouldn't leave him alone once she caught him sitting at the window for hours. She would follow him around until he left, then she would ask him whether he was going to go chasing after rats again. Daddy Groovie would annoy her even more, by saying, yes, yes, and by rubbing his palms together. "Looking for his own kind," Ninang Rola said when he was gone. "Rodents never had to work."

"We can kill them all," Pipo said.

"Why do you want to kill them for? Why are you so afraid of rats? They don't do anything to you. You must be afraid of people. They rob, they kill, they do all bad things. Rats live off your garbage. Under the sink, too, where you can't see them. When the rats go to live under your bed and start squealing like pigs then you should be concerned. But they're under the sink. You won't know they're there unless you stick your head under it." Ninang Rola stood up.

As if he just heard a brilliant idea, Pipo stood up and walked to the kitchen. The big white pockets hung lower than the hem of his shorts. They were full of whatever he had collected a few hours before: bottlecaps, little shiny stones, coins. They made sounds as he walked away. I followed him, staring at the bulge lap-lapping on his thighs.

"Where? Where?" I asked, also looking under the sink, moving the kitchen counter curtains apart, greasing my fingers. Under the sink was a huge storage space filled with used soft drink bottles full of roach eggs and dirt, rusty appliance parts, and a lot of other junk. The floor was wet, greasy, and smelly. Sometimes the pipes dripped with water and dirt that collected on the bottom of the sink.

"Where are they?" I saw this hole of darkness. I could hear a flow of water. I was excited partly because I had never had the courage to peek in under the sink. "I don't see anything."

"You all are so silly," said Ninang Rola behind us. "During the war, we ate rats. We had to. We had no choice. Rats or death. Field rats actually taste like bullfrogs." She placed the basket of rice grains on the counter and filled a rice pot with water.

Rats. Frogs. I stared at a pot of boiling pig feet. Ninang Rola started cleaning the counter while Pipo stuck his head deeper under the sink again.

"Wasting your time on stupid rats. You should be praying for your father so he would pass the embassy interview today," continued Ninang Rola, pinching Pipo's behind. She took a handful of round black peppers and pounded them with the stone block she used to sharpen knives.

"Out of the kitchen, you two," demanded Ninang Rola, sprinkling the boiling pot with ground peppers. The scent escaped. No more than two people could move around our kitchen so we hardly stayed there. It was where Ninang Rola could be found if she was not anywhere else in the house. Kitchen to Ninang Rola was what the little Singer Machine corner in the dining room was to Mommy. Even in the other houses in our street, kitchens were usually small. They weren't small to begin with. It's just that we had this thing for big cabinets that were placed against the wall, tightening every room in our house, much like in other houses. Cabinets: the bigger and older the wood, the better. Again, something about luck.

"Ou." Pipo's head, which was still under the sink, hit the counter. He wrinkled his face, rubbing his head with his fingers. "Am I bleeding?"

"Inside your brain," Ninang Rola said. "You little rat."

Mommy spent hours at her Singer Machine, taking turns between sewing and staring at the wall in front of her. Sometimes, she spent more time staring at the wall so that even if a lizard were to cross her sight she wouldn't notice. I had never seen her sew as much as she did today. Sitting there, her whole body curved to a letter *C*. She, the Singer Machine, and Sonja Carolina Santa Cruz's head became one. Whatever she was sewing didn't make any sense either. It was a cross between a pillowcase and an underwear bag.

Perhaps a jacket, the one that Daddy Groovie went looking for before he left for the day for an interview at the States embassy. The blue, striped, tailor-made one he was supposed to wear for his graduation that never happened. Even when he grew a stomach, he still wore it on special occasions, oftentimes popping the buttons out. He chased after them while they tumbled and wheeled about on the floor, then once found, he slipped them into his pocket to be completely forgotten. That was the same suit sent from the States by Auntie Dolares. Anything sent from the States, however worn out it was, he kept and wore. "Why don't we just buy a new one?" Mommy used to ask him whenever he wore his suit. "This is Stateside. Who can replace this?" he answered. Most of them had missing buttons; he never made an effort to sew matching buttons into it. That early dawn, as soon as Daddy Groovie woke up, long before the six o'clock roosters crowed, he rummaged through everyone's clothes to find his suit. He woke us up with his loudness and heavy footsteps in the bedroom. Pipo and I immediately found ourselves running around the room to catch the rain of clothes, both of us half asleep.

What Daddy Groovie didn't know was that a few weeks before, Mommy had sold the suit along with other old clothing. She did this occasionally when she needed money. In fact, we had already eaten the food bought with the money she got from selling the suits. I could remember the sudden change of fish: from milkfish to those more expensive, big, steaklike ones with strange names. Daddy Groovie himself wondered where it was bought from, finally answering his own question by saying it must have been from the north, where he's from, fish from the north were always bigger and tastier, much like the people who took them out of the sea. *Big, tasty, that's me.* He ended up wearing an old suit that also hardly fit him. I could tell that wouldn't be the last time we would hear about it, by the way he angrily emptied the remaining Pacorabang Cologne he had kept in his locked cabinet since Pipo spilled it. He mumbled about his suit while his head became a sculpture of pomade, some parts thicker than the rest. He swaggered in the street, holding his documents and a sealed envelope of X rays under his arm. Cursing in whispers, he left, wiggling a tail of keys on his back pocket. Instead of wishing him good luck, Mommy said instead, "We'll find your suit somehow," as if as soon as he walked out the door, it would all be forgotten. We all followed him with our eyes until the smog took him into its arms. I quickly looked at Pipo and was glad that he didn't say anything about the suits either. I was afraid that he might open his mouth, say something uncalled for. But he woke up with his mouth sealed with dried morning spit.

Pipo had finally calmed down and sat in front of our General Electric fan, wiping little drops of sweat on his face. I imagined him a little boy again, putting crumpled paper through the steel frame, watching the paper go round and round inside until it got caught in the metal blades and shot at him like an arrow. He was sweating more than ever, which, according to Ninang Rola, was a sign that he was growing up. He took out what was inside his pockets and arranged them neatly on the floor beside him. They turned out to be marbles, empty bottles of nail polish, little squares of ceramic chalk. He started arranging them into a heap, then drew circles around them on the floor.

I sat close to the kitchen so I could see the rats firsthand should they decide to come out. Ninang Rola ran to the stove at the sight of the pot boiling. She took the lid off and dropped it on the counter, shaking her fingers as if they were burned. Steam rose to the ceiling, clouding the kitchen with the smell of boiling pigs' feet and yams.

It was late in the afternoon when Daddy Groovie came home. The sun was beginning to go down. The streets were still quiet. He staggered into the house. The rats started to come out from under the sink. I wanted to tell everybody but Daddy Groovie's presence muffled me. I stared at the rats, my mouth gaping. Everybody could have seen them as well but had no time to notice. They all looked at Daddy Groovie, motionless, as if they all stopped breathing.

"Where—is my suit?" he screamed. "My blue suit, where is it?" He held the arm of the sofa for balance. Mommy stood up from the Singer Machine and didn't move from where she was. She put her hands together.

Pipo ran upstairs, shaking. I, too, ran, but only to the bottom of the stairs, grabbing the rails, ready to go up.

"Where—is—my—SUIT?" He struggled to put words together.

He was fuming, hotter than the sun. I could see all the signs of heat on his face. His hair was disheveled and dry, ridges all over his once pomaded hair. The sleeves of his old jacket were wrapped around his waist. His shirt was unbuttoned to his navel, wet.

I could smell bottles and bottles of San Miguel beer approaching the room.

He was going to explode, I could sense it. Even the rats knew an explosion was about to come; they all ran out of their hiding place onto the back patio. In the corner of my eyes, I saw them fleeing, one by one, their long muddy tails leaving tracks on the floor.

I had never seen Daddy Groovie like this. Even when he was drunk, he would usually just collapse on the sofa or on the bed. This time, he had energy. His body was a pot of boiling water about to kick the lid off any minute and burn anybody in its way.

And Ninang Rola was in his way.

"What happened, Groovie? The embassy?" She went straight to him, tried to hold his arms so he wouldn't fall.

"Get out," he yelled at her. *"Malas!"*

Ninang Rola stood in front of him, appalled by what she heard. *Malas?* she repeated but she didn't move. Only her lips moved. And her eyes, staring at Daddy Groovie while he tried to balance himself by holding the back of the chair beside him.

"What's wrong? What happened?" Ninang Rola appeared to have collected herself quickly.

"Didn't you hear?"

"Hear what, Groovie? What happened?"

"You didn't hear what I just said—"

"You're drunk, you don't know what you're saying."

"I kn-know what I'm saying. YOU! You're the *malas*! *Malas!*"

"You don't call me *malas*, Groovie," Ninang Rola's voice

was low at first, as if by doing so she could calm him down. "What are you trying to tell me, Germano? What *malas* are you talking about?"

"Out of my way, you—"

"*Tranquilo,* Germano." The sudden switch of names meant that Ninang Rola was paying closer attention, that she was beginning to believe he knew what he was saying.

"Ma-las. Maaaa-las!"

"You're the *malas*. Why are you calling me that, huh? Are you out of your mind, Germano?" Ninang Rola raised her voice as well. I had never heard her yell, at least not the way she did now, as if Daddy Groovie was not close enough to hear her.

For a brief moment, Daddy Groovie leaned against the wall completely soaked in sweat, looking so resigned in the way his eyes and lips drooped. He shook his head repeatedly, gathering thoughts in his head, mumbling something we couldn't hear.

"Germano, what is it?" It was much like Ninang Rola to push herself into matters she shouldn't be a part of anymore. I didn't know why she couldn't tell it was time to just leave him alone, to get out of his drunken space.

"Did you take my suit, Rola?" Daddy Groovie moved closer, cornering her against the wall, trapping her between his arms, ignoring what she asked.

"What suit? What suit are you babbling about?" Ninang Rola turned around to find Mommy. We didn't tell her what happened in the morning before Daddy Groovie left. By the expression on Mommy's face, I could tell somehow Ninang Rola didn't know what had happened to his suit. Mommy's eyes spoke for her—don't push it anymore, Rola.

"My suit! My blue *Americana*. My suit. Did you take it?" Daddy Groovie pressed his hand on her arm.

"Son of a whore!" Ninang Rola cursed at him. She tried to move his arms away from her. "Son of Satan."

She was losing her religion.

I could feel my pulse when I heard her. I didn't notice how much I was sweating until I put my hand on my cheeks and it slid down.

Then the many years collided.

Without her prayers, Ninang Rola was subdued. She was pushed against the wall even more, listening to all the words Daddy Groovie was screaming at her face while pulling the knotted sleeves of his suit to tighten it around his waist. "You're one unfortunate woman. You old, born-again witch."

Ninang Rola just as quickly threw the same words at his face, her hands raised over her own, palms facing him. "Don't touch me. You're the fart. You're the son of a dog. Nothing more than that." Her face was all teeth and spit. "Estrella . . ."

Mommy moved a step up from where she was. I remembered what Ninang Rola had told me about her. Estrella was her name when Daddy Groovie first met her. I had never paid attention to how her name was said until then. There was a sense of desperation, the way Ninang Rola had pronounced each syllable. *ES-TRE-LLA* . . .

"You stole my suit, didn't you?" Daddy Groovie accused

Ninang Rola. He grabbed the back of a chair, pushing it down the floor. The chair fell beside them.

Mommy finally went to them. Each step was calculated, hesitant. She tried to pull Daddy Groovie away from Ninang Rola, by first holding his right forearm, then the left.

Daddy Groovie's jacket slipped off his waist. It twisted on the floor, kissing dust and the red Johnson's Floor Wax. Mommy's feet got caught in it but she only ignored it. "Germano. Stop this! Rola knows nothing about your suit. Stop this!"

"What do you mean she knows nothing? What . . . what do you mean?" Daddy Groovie turned around, releasing Mommy's hands on his back. His arms took Mommy, shook her, and pushed her away.

"Estrella." Ninang Rola tried to catch her with her voice. I saw Mommy land on her knees, slide against the fallen chair with the jacket.

Ninang Rola spat at Daddy Groovie's face. "How could you do this to her? Enough of your hurting your family, Germano. Enough! Enough of you! I've had it. You can't do this!" She drummed Daddy Groovie's face with closed fists. Ninang Rola was strong, had always been strong. She could carry two buckets full of water from one corner of the house to the other without stopping to rest.

"You mind your own business, you bitch." Daddy Groovie grasped her hands with one hand and pointed his thick finger at her face. "G-G-GET OUT. I don't want to see your ugly face."

"This ugly face has been taking care of your family since

you came into our lives." The picture on the wall next to them tilted on the nail and fell.

Mommy got up from the floor and went to them again. "Stop. Stop this now. Rola, he's drunk, he doesn't know what he's saying." In her right hand, Daddy Groovie's jacket.

"I know what I'm saying. Get the hell out before I kill you!" He screamed again, and finally, as if it was what he had been waiting for for so long, slammed Ninang Rola's face with his closed fist.

Spit flew out of Ninang Rola's mouth. Her whole body shook. She shielded herself with crossed arms and for a minute choked on her words. Daddy Groovie appeared not to regret what he did by watching every move she made while saying, huh? huh?

"G-g-get off." Ninang Rola pushed Daddy Groovie with all her strength. "Maria Consuelo. Mareeeee-a Consuelo." She shouted in panic. "Pack your clothes. Quick. We're getting out of this hell. I've been here long enough, too long." She looked straight into Daddy Groovie's eyes. "How dare you think I would steal your suit. Nobody would want your suit. I can make better suits than you can ever have in your life! *Tonto!* How dare you, after everything I have done for you and your family. *Santíssimo.* Have fear in God, Germano, have fear in God, you good for nothing *Lasengerro.*" She spat at him again. She grabbed his jacket out of Mommy's hand. "What do you call this? This is not good enough for you, huh?" She threw the jacket at his face.

Daddy Groovie caught his jacket and wiped the spit off of his face.

"Go, go upstairs." Mommy saw me. I ran. Pipo, who was also watching from the top of the stairs, went into the room. I stopped at the landing where he used to be.

"Your time will come, Germano. You haven't paid for your life," Ninang Rola screamed. She ran to the stairs, past me, and stopped. "You see this child, Germano, you see this?" She pointed at me. "*This* is the one that you are going to pay to. Don't you ever forget that!"

"Get out before I kill you." Daddy Groovie's fists were so tight they seemed they were going to rip his fingers apart.

Ninang Rola went to the other room and came out with her luggage. I could hear wheels rolling on the floor, luggage being zipped open. "Maria Consuelo, plastic bags. Get plastic bags. Now!" Maricon ran around carrying empty plastic shopping bags. She looked at me. Her lips were trembling. She kept on putting her hands over her mouth. Her hands were shaking, too.

Only Daddy Groovie stood there, a beer bottle overflowing with foam, watching everything around him.

"Rola, you don't have to do this." Mommy tried to keep her from stuffing the plastic bags with clothes.

"Don't, Estrella, don't stop me." Ninang Rola lowered her voice

"Rola, please, we need you here," Mommy begged. "You're just upset. It will go if you give it some time. He's just drunk. You know how he is. Don't leave, please. You're just angry."

"I am," said Ninang Rola. "But I've been upset for a looong time."

Ninang Rola took Mommy into her arms, very tightly, telling her, "You'll be all right."

"Don't go," Mommy said into her ears. "Rola, please—"

But Ninang Rola threw the luggage on the dining table and started throwing her clothes into it. Mommy stood there, watching her push her clothes and belongings into one big luggage. She zipped it closed and threw it to the floor. She opened another luggage. "I knew this time would come, Estrella, I knew."

"It doesn't have to be now." Mommy pulled the clothes out of the luggage. "Stop this nonsense."

"Don't, Estrella, don't." Ninang Rola snatched the clothes back from Mommy's hands and piled them up quickly in the luggage. "Maria Consuelo, take this." She handed Maricon the smaller one. "Go out. Call a taxi." She turned to Mommy again. "Even you, Estrella, *you* knew this time would come. We can't be together all our lives."

Ninang Rola raised her head to look at me. I pushed my head between two rails, holding them tightly with both hands, looking down at her. I wasn't sure what I was thinking then. She took a deep, deep sigh, her eyes not wanting to let go of mine. Her lips, wide open, without anything left to say. A part of me didn't want to know any more of what she had to say. She had told me so much. That part of me wanted her to leave. The other was begging her to stay. What would happen to Mommy when she was gone?

The answer might be in the way all three of them stood there in the living room. This moment when Daddy Groovie had finally joined them in their language of eyes and hands. Quick and quiet gazes lingered in the room. The expressions on their faces explained their emotions. Daddy Groovie's anger was shaped by the tightness of his body and the sweat continually bursting out of his pores. Mommy's confusion was in her pleading eyes. And Ninang Rola's resignation was turning with her head as she moved it back and forth, between Mommy and Daddy Groovie, between their past and their present.

Daddy Groovie was first to leave. He approached the stairs, dragging his jacket on the floor, hitting chairs, tables, and everything in his way. A succession of banging noises made me stampede into the bedroom. I could hear Ninang Rola and Maricon leave. Their luggage rolled on the floor. The taxi stopped outside. I heard the driver's voice asking where they where going and Mommy answering him with, "Nowhere, they're not going anywhere." I heard her calling Ninang Rola's name over and over again until the doors of the taxi slammed. I could see Mommy in front of the door, its shadow climbing to darken her face. Now it was just the four of us, the way it was supposed to be from the beginning. I wanted to run to the window to watch but I couldn't move my legs anymore. Somewhere deep in me was a person who was glad that Ninang Rola was gone. Somebody saying, she started all this. If not for her, they would never have met.

Daddy Groovie came in and opened all the cabinets that divided the room. He went from one cabinet to another, pulling, pushing, swinging them all open. He took all the shirts and clothes off of their hangers and began to throw them all over the room again. His hands just threw anything they could touch. Hangers crashed against the walls, others broke underfoot. Pipo and I watched the clothes fall, one after another until the wooden floor disappeared. But we didn't move. We waited for Daddy Groovie to tell us what to do, but he didn't say anything. He kept on saying, where, where, where, ripping some of the clothes while he pulled them out of the racks.

"Where!" Daddy Groovie's voice was fuller than ever, the loudness that wouldn't give up, a firecracker popping every minute.

Mommy walked in the room, her anger gathered in every part of her body, especially her face. The four of us were all in this room once again. "What is wrong with you?" Mommy looked at Daddy Groovie. I thought about the time when she had woken up naked in the motel. I imagined her voice then. I felt that suddenly that voice was back. "What-is-wrong-with-you?" She said every word slowly, as if by saying it faster Daddy Groovie wouldn't understand.

"They told me I couldn't get my visa."

"What are you talking about, Germano?" asked Mommy. She sat herself at the foot of the bed, covering her mouth with her shaky fingers, wrapping her body with her left arm.

"Can't you see? It was my suit, my lucky suit. Without it, I couldn't pass that interview."

"You didn't pass the interview?"

"They told me I was sick. Something in my X rays. I have to see another doctor. I have to come back. I am sick, you see, I am sick."

Sick of what? I thought. Does this mean he's not leaving for the States?

"Sick of what?" Mommy asked.

"I DON'T KNOW," he raised his voice again. Sweating like that, he did *look* sick. Of what? I could only think of San Miguel beer.

"Lower your voice. I *can* hear you."

He dropped to the floor, shaking on his knees. He closed his eyes. Tears mixed with his sweaty face. He clutched his face and screamed words I had never heard before. Down there, he looked like a flowerpot made of mud. On his forehead were roots, green roots of veins, exposed and pulsing, each about to burst.

I looked toward Pipo. He held himself. His eyes were big, staring at Daddy Groovie. He was sitting on the bed, partly hidden by the shadow of the cabinet beside him. He was chewing the hem of his T-shirt. One eye of Speedy Gonzales on his T-shirt was looking at me. Mommy had given that to him for Christmas, although I was the one who had asked for it.

"What am I going to do? That was my only chance." Daddy Groovie put his hands on his head, pulling his hair back, pomade oozed between his fingers. "I never asked for anything else. All my life—all my life, I-I never wanted anything more."

Mommy sat there. I didn't expect her to go to Daddy Groovie and she didn't. At the edge of the bed, her face was not the same face whenever she did her ceremony of circles. The pattern of her sundress matched the bedsheets. Red, red fire of flowers.

Stonewoman. I thought of what Ninang Rola had told me about her. Her face was suddenly as hard as stone.

"*Puñeta!* A stone. A stone in my kidneys. How did I get a stone in my kidneys? Why—why did it appear now?"

I didn't know what he was talking about. I didn't know where the kidneys were. He pointed to his stomach. I thought it could be somewhere in there. But what were stones? How could anyone have stones in their kidneys?

"How could you hit Rola like that?" She wasn't listening to him anymore. "How could you just scream at her like that? What is wrong with you? Are you so fucked up already, huh? What the hell is wrong?" Mommy buried her fingernails into the sheets, clawlike.

Suddenly, Daddy Groovie rose from the floor. One side of his shirt was still tucked in, the other hung like a huge green leaf on his waist. He walked to the window and pulled the shutters closed. The bright eye of the window silhouetted his figure. I could see the sweat in the middle of his shirt. His arms were very tense. The bracelet of his watch snapped open. The watch dropped on the floor. He only stood there. *Clic-cloc.*

We were shrinking in his eyes.

"WHERE-IS-MY-SUIT?"

His voice banged against the walls, hitting the ceiling, the floors, circling the cabinets in the room, and finally pulling us toward him.

I held my breath when his voice hit my face. I looked away from him only to see his reflection in the mirror on the wall.

"Don't do that, Germano. Don't." She clutched her hands guarding herself from him.

Pipo was crying in the corner. "Daddy please, please, not anymore." He pulled his T-shirt higher, covering his face with it.

It was the moment I had waited for all my life. Each minute I saw was every minute of the many years I was kept from this. Finally, I watched Daddy Groovie go to Mommy, watched him pull her hair. She yelled at him, pounded him with her fists, kicked him everywhere her legs would go, slapping him with her clawed fingers. But he was too strong. He ripped her sundress, hit her hard enough with his swaying fist that she tumbled on the floor, like fish on a cutting board.

Pipo cried louder and louder with each word. "Stop. Stop. Stop. Daddy, please stop. . . ."

"Mommy . . ." I whispered. I saw my hands move up to my face. My knees folded even more, closer to the rest of my body. I pushed myself against the wall behind me, trying not to look or close my eyes.

Mommy crawled on the floor, lost in the layers of clothes. Her body limped but her voice was loud and strong. *STOP.* She took the ripped string on her sundress and held it up to her breast. She struggled to get up, her other leg appeared as if it was being left behind. She caught the edge of the bed and lifted herself up. Sweat slid down her face, even her hair was wet. Rings formed around her mirror-like eyes.

Daddy Groovie slowly walked toward the cabinet, reached

behind, and took the *yantok*. He swung off the web that had formed around it.

Pipo began screaming Mommy's name, his eyes and mouth were filling up with tears.

"Damn you, Germano! I said stop this now! Don't touch him anymore." Mommy was finally on her feet.

It was the first time I noticed that my whole body, even my insides, were shaking very fast.

"You're bad luck, ever since you were born. You can't even be a real boy, you're bad luck." Daddy Groovie's *yantok* swung in the room, catching Pipo who was attempting to run away from him, pulling the sheets toward him.

"Why are you always doing this to me?" Pipo screamed. I could see on his face he was ready to strike back any moment. "It's not fair, you never hit Gringo, you never hit Gringo."

"Leave him alone, Germano. Leave him. Don't touch him anymore." Mommy grabbed Daddy Groovie from behind, her arm around his neck, lifting up his chin. I could see the dark holes of his sweaty nose.

Daddy shook her off but she continued tightening her arms around his neck. It was as if time slowed down. I watched his elbow lift up again, high up, above his head, and slowly, very slowly come down, right against Mommy's chest, hitting her so hard that she squirmed and spat, her tongue sticking out of her mouth, drooling. She dropped on her elbows and knees, hands around her neck. She couldn't breathe. Thick veins lined her neck and forehead. She coughed out words that I couldn't make out. When she finally caught her breath, she howled, a dog howl, so loud her voice pushed me against the wall even more.

"Mommy—" Pipo and I yelled at the same time.

Daddy Groovie pulled Pipo back closer to him. By his hair. Which he grabbed as if it were a piece of dirty clothing. He didn't think it was connected to somebody's skin, somebody's head. He didn't hear him screaming, didn't see the tears bursting out of his eyes. Pipo didn't let go of his grasp of the blanket, pulling it until the bed was naked.

I buried my head between my knees when I saw his *yantok* hit Pipo. Pipo crawled away on his back, then covered himself with that blanket, as if that would shield him from the stick that Daddy Groovie pounded on him repeatedly. "You never hit Gringo. You never hit him," he persisted.

When I heard Pipo mention my name again I knew I was now a part of them. Daddy Groovie must have heard his pleas, for suddenly he turned around and swallowed me with his angry red eyes. I saw him coming toward me. I sat there, staring at the *yantok* swinging beside him, its shadow was already wrapping me around.

Mommy managed to get up from the floor and leap at him, wrapping her arms around his waist, hanging her hand on his belt. "Not Gringo. He's too young. NOT HIM. Germano, NO!"

No. No, I thought, I'm too young. *I'm too y-young.*

Pipo jumped off the bed hands first and very quickly crawled on the floor, coming toward me. As soon as Daddy Groovie swung the *yantok* to hit me, Pipo pushed me away, getting himself hit instead.

"Not him," he yelled, and curled against the wall beside me. He looked at me with his tearful eyes, his fingers shaking in front of my face. "Run, Gringo. Run."

I would always remember his face: those watery eyes, those cheeks once so beautiful and light but now darkened by sweat, dirt, and tears, his lips cracked with blood. The face of an older brother, the one who used to hit me.

"Pipo—" I said, though no word came out of my mouth. I tried to hold him but he pushed me away.

Our fingers touched.

"Go—"

The thought of doors appeared in my mind interrupted by the sight of Daddy Groovie's *yantok* swinging above me. I jumped to grasp the doorknob and pushed it open. I dashed down the stairs in four big leaps. *GO!* The door swung and banged behind me loudly.

"MALAS. MALAS. MALAAAAAS." I could hear Daddy Groovie's screams over and over again as the door bounced open.

"No, they're not. They're not," I mumbled.

"STOP HURTING HIM," Mommy screamed.

The mirror fell on the floor.

The sound of shattering glass.

I hated the thought of what it could do to the skin upon the slightest touch. I started to shake at the image forming in my mind. Although I wanted to go back upstairs, my feet took me outside our house where the streets were still empty. With the shutters closed, I could hardly hear noises.

I thought I was running very fast, my insides running

ahead of me, my shadow left behind and unable to catch up, but when I looked at my feet, they were walking slowly, my knees knocking against each other. I wanted to go back. I wanted Daddy Groovie to hit me. I wanted to scream at his face.

Spit at him, with everything I had kept inside my mouth.

BUTTERFLY EYES

His last words to me—*Run, Gringo. Run*—whistled in my ears.

Pipo lay on his bed, limbs all over as if they were born separate from each other. His back was turned so I couldn't see his face. But I could hear him picking the wall with his fingers, removing layers of paper that covered it, revealing the years we had spent plastering the whole house with big square technicolor wallpapers. Soon he had those years all over him, a shower of little tamarind leaves, each torn piece a different color, a different time. Every hour, his fingers drummed and picked the wall, his fingernails became the teeth of hungry night rats.

He had not said anything to anybody.

The General Electric fan roared in his place, its metal screen covered with thick dust, and spitting out more dust all over our room, especially in the sun rays that entered through our window. Streaks shone directly to where Pipo was, hitting one leg of the bunk, splitting our bedroom in the middle with light.

His ribs moved quietly. Ninang Rola had told me once that nobody died lying on their side, always facedown or on their back, so that their spirits could see where they were going or where they had come from. Pipo was on his side, his thumb, halfway into his mouth, facing neither heaven nor earth, eyes closed, his cheeks moving in and out, making sucking noises. His shirt was pulled up so that his bruised back was exposed, so fresh that it hurt to look at it. His blanket was pushed down to his feet. The mattress was so bare I could see its stained striped lining. Hanging above him was my own blanket, left undone like the one on the big bed in the middle of our room. I could see from the spring underneath my bed that the weight of my body was in the middle, the middle part being more depressed than the rest.

But Pipo's bed had no middles, no sides.

The familiar smell of bruises.

He didn't move as I edged to him. I touched the dark blue metal of the bunk, which creaked as soon as I sat down. He didn't even hear my loud breathing, didn't hear my insides tumbling like a rubber band ball as soon as I smelled him so close to me. I remembered the times I waited outside this room and watched him flee; the scent of the room always swallowed me in.

I waited until the day after to see him. I didn't want him to remember that I wasn't hurt by Daddy Groovie, didn't want to remind him of his bruises, the shape of Daddy

Groovie's palms. I wanted to tell him that he could keep inside what hurt most, deep inside, in Ninang Rola's words—when you buried something so deep, you would not know it was even there. There would be no need to suck his thumb, pick the wallpaper, because doing those wouldn't bring him back to the past, or remove Daddy Groovie from him.

I moved my hand closer, slightly brushed his skin. His hair, disheveled and thin. Looking at his scalp made me see Daddy Groovie's hands again, dragging him all over the room. I heard heavy footsteps and I quickly pulled my hand away and ran to the window. The bed squeaked. I sat behind the curtains, peered out the window. The sun cascaded down my face.

The door swung. I sensed Daddy Groovie's scent inside the room. I didn't turn my head. I could only hear him walk over to Pipo.

"Tsk, tsk. Get up, don't you want to eat?" he asked in a low voice after standing there for a while. He probably shook Pipo's shoulders as he did to wake us up every morning. He didn't know Pipo had already eaten, in the middle of the night when nobody could see him get up from his bed. Pipo didn't answer.

"Pipo . . ."

Daddy Groovie never talked about what happened. He didn't ask why I was walking up and down the stairs with a dustpan full of shards of glass early that morning. He didn't know I was cleaning up after him. He didn't know how much I wanted to remove the traces of everything he had done to this family. Every time I picked up a piece of broken glass I saw a part of his face in it. Every time I emptied the dustpan and heard the clang of the broken mirror I thought about what he had done. Mommy didn't bother to remove the shards of glass that could have hurt them more if they accidentally stepped on them. Daddy Groovie just stepped over them. He spent much time standing in front of that mirror to spray himself with his Pacorabang. As I slowly put them in the dustpan, I was also removing parts of Daddy Groovie from my mind, throwing them out, wishing his memory could stay in the garbage can.

He probably would never know that the mirror was not on the wall anymore. Only Jesus with the glowing heart, still staring into space, was left, something Daddy Groovie would never dare touch. He hadn't said anything about the thick paddings of bandages around Mommy's arms, or asked why she wouldn't turn around from her Singer unless nobody was looking, or why she wouldn't answer when I repeatedly reminded her that the rice was already simmering and flowing over the sides of the pot. He had not mentioned that Ninang Rola and Maricon were gone. He probably never heard her haunting voice the way I did whenever I turned to certain corners of our house where Ninang Rola used to be. What he would say was a new word—*stone*—and whenever he said it he pointed to his stomach and frowned. *Puñeta. Stones. Anak ng Bato.* But nobody listened. He spoke with the walls, the sink, and the rats underneath—none of them listened.

I wouldn't look at him. I pressed my elbows on the windowsill, stared at the dead cat lying in the street and the big-winged, bad luck flies hovering in waves. I fingered the crevices on the wood with a matchstick, and pushed the dust out. I couldn't smell the dead cat, my nose full of the scent of the bedroom and everything in it. But I could hear the flies buzz like mosquitoes over my ears on brownout nights. I wished they would all come in and take all the bad luck out to the street. The cat looked stiff on dark asphalt, its hair so hard it would break like its tail, folded and smashed. Dead black cats were double bad luck. Besides, flies, in their moment of hunger, were difficult to shoo away. That's why nobody had bothered to throw it. But nobody was around, really. In the heat of the summer, everybody ran way, even the birds. Without people throwing old bread into the streets, there wouldn't be any food for the birds.

It felt as if we were the only ones there.

Without thinking, as if needing to witness something, I turned back to the room. Daddy Groovie was still standing there, back bent, hand scratching his head. He walked backward to the bed and sat on the edge. He grabbed his shoes, took the socks that he kept rolled up in them. He slipped his hand into each shoe to check if there was anything there: roach sacs, pebbles, sometimes roaches themselves found their way into his shoes. He turned them over. When nothing fell out, he put them on. He reached out for his hang-around T-shirt, which was on the floor, and after wiping the dust off it, put it on.

He crossed the sun streak in the room. I noticed his color, the color of this room, of this street—they were all the same. This was where he belonged, here, not anywhere else. He should grow old leaping over puddles of mud and dead bodies of little animals left in the streets to rot.

He and his construction friends.

An occasional breeze came into the room, lifting the curtains up. Pipo pulled down his shirt to cover his back and, just as quickly, his fingers rushed back to the wall and started picking the wallpaper again, feeling perhaps that Daddy Groovie was on his way out the door.

The curtain softly landed on my face and pulled itself away. I watched Daddy Groovie through the little holes. His veined hand caught the threshold and stayed there awhile. I looked out the window again, fearful that he might come back. I knew he was going to Mommy next. His footsteps were slow as if he were counting them while he descended. The cabinets were still open, clothes piled on top of each other. They would normally be folded, a task Ninang Rola used to perform after ironing and starching them in the corner of the room near the sockets on Sunday afternoons. The broken hangers were in a paper bag, waiting for someone to match and glue the pieces back together. On the floor, the mouth of the General Electric fan roared endlessly, its cord circling around it, spotted with dust.

Behind me, the wind lifted the curtains up again, hovering above, a wave of soft fingers.

The hallway that led down the stairs was always warmer than the rest of the house. It was always darker, too; the bulb that hung down from the ceiling was never lit. The plywood walls were fastened by nails of different sizes, some of which were bent. The lower part of the hallway was covered with wallpaper, but not the same one that covered the rest of the house. This was always the last one we touched because it was always too dark, the ceiling too high. Two picture frames of trees seemed to be permanently fastened on the wall, aged by the many years they had been there. I sat on the top steps, clutching the rails.

From there, I could see where Daddy Groovie was going.

Mommy had always been different to him. What he couldn't say to Pipo, he could say to her. He would tell her he didn't know what happened, that he was drunk, too drunk and angry. That he cared for her very much. From the very beginning. Same thing all these years. But it had never been this bad.

Nobody had ever been kicked out of our house.

But Mommy sat at her Singer Machine, listening to the zigzagging of the needle, ignoring him. He put his hands on her shoulder. Mommy shrugged at his touch.

"Estrella," he called her quietly. "Estrella." He moved his lips next to her ear. He never called her Mommy. He seldom addressed her by any name. Sweetheart, Honey, the words of afternoon black-and-white movies, Dear. His mentioning her real name could mean something important, something worth holding one's breath for.

Mommy's fingers shifted, pushing the piece of cloth to the needle. She had not talked to anyone. Not to me. Not to Daddy Groovie. Not even to Pipo who probably needed her the most.

Daddy Groovie walked to the kitchen and opened the Frigidaire. He came back holding a towelful of ice cubes. He wore loose shorts down to his knees, without a belt as usual, so that his hip bone hung over.

"Estrella, I know you're listening to me. Here, let me put this ice on your face. Turn around. Look at me."

She didn't budge. The side of her face was a face of little stones. Bruises were something she used to be able to hide from us by wearing long sleeves or long sundresses. She never had them on her face.

She could hear him. I knew she was only waiting for the ice to melt in Daddy Groovie's hands. *Cold things burn,* was what they used to tell us whenever we played with ice. And Mommy could burn him as well, by sitting there, by not responding to anything he was saying.

"Estrella," he said her name again, this time like music, slowly moving his hand closer to her face. The wet towel dripped on her shoulders and the Singer Machine.

I didn't mean to do it, was what I expected him to say. What I didn't expect was him breathing so much air into his body and keeping it inside his chest, as if he was about to sob again.

"I didn't mean it. Believe me. I know what you're thinking. But I didn't mean to do this.

"Forgive . . . me." Each word was as heavy as what I was feeling inside, yet as light as the wings that took the words out of his mouth without him thinking twice.

Mommy stopped sewing. There was a long, long pause. Daddy Groovie stood there, inhaling over and over again, perhaps trying to breathe his words back in. It was the loudest noise of all, what I heard in my head: the repetition of screams, sounds of faces being slapped, spat at. "Don't lay your hand on her anymore," I wanted to tell Daddy Groovie after seeing him tighten his grasp of the towel, making it drip on the floor some more. But he only raised his other hand and curled his fingers over his face, as if about to scratch it.

The ice cubes dropped on the floor, one by one, crashing. Daddy Groovie started to kick them angrily, holding his head, pulling his hair back tightly, moving his eyebrows high up on his forehead. From above, I could see the whites of his eyes surrounding the two black ones that sat at the bottom of his lids, only seeing Mommy, and nothing else. He clutched his hand again, tightly, and raised it up over his head. I held my breath. His fist started to shake up in the air. *Ahhh.* His growl made me bite my jaw and tightened my skin even more, but it didn't move Mommy. I don't know what I wanted her to do. Her weapon had always been her silence. She knew that the stitching sound of the Singer could irritate Daddy Groovie the most, could send him away in no time.

Daddy Groovie did walk away from her, slowly, backward, then turned around, toward the door, leaving shoe marks on the wet floor. *Ahhh.* He unfolded his fist.

I crawled my way down the stairs, a little child afraid of making the slightest noise, my eyes gazing at Mommy, first the top of her head, the sides of her face, then her full body, still sitting there.

"Mommy, Ma . . ." I said, when I reached the bottom of the stairs. She didn't respond. She started to pedal the Singer Machine faster. I stepped on the ice, crushing it like little balls of dry mud or hardened Johnson's Floor Wax.

"Stonewoman," I whispered. But in my head, I screamed—*stonewoman! stonewoman!*—repeatedly, swallowing each word after saying it. She only continued to pedal the Singer Machine.

Her face was a mound of blue and black. I could hardly see her eye. She had cuts on her shoulders. Her lips were swollen, the upper part fatter than the other. She didn't look like she once had a face at all. Closer, her face didn't look like stones. It was softer, so delicate that even a blow of breath could hurt it.

I wanted to ask her, Why? Why she had allowed this to happen? Did she fight him? Did she protect Pipo from him? Did she shield him? What had happened after I left the bedroom? Who shattered the mirror on the wall? I wanted to ask her many things but I knew that her ears probably had lumps in them, too, and she wouldn't hear anything I was saying.

And it was hot inside, and outside. There was no rain to bathe in so that she could heal faster. All she had on her face and on her back was sweat, waiting to drip and slide and be absorbed by the bandage around her arms.

I felt angry watching her not say anything, letting the Singer Machine speak for her. The Singer Machine was much like her, smooth and shiny when she sewed there happily, but rough and sounding angry at other times. It was the only thing in the house that she never allowed us to touch. I wanted to hold her in those moments, maybe that way she could stop hurting, so she would know that I had every intention of taking after her, that I would never hit anyone in my life, that Daddy Groovie's blood did not run in my veins. But she let out a long sigh held deep within for some time. She rocked the pedal. The Singer Machine buzzed in the thick heat around us, the only sound I could hear other than my loud thoughts.

I didn't touch her, didn't say anything; instead, I walked away.

Stonewoman. The breeze came in and interrupted, a voice that sounded like my own.

I looked at the corner of the room where Ninang Rola used to always sit. For a moment I thought, What would she have done had she known that everyone in this house had learned not to speak? What would she say if she saw Pipo picking the paper off the wall for days? *Everything heals with time.* Or does it? I heard her voice as I walked out. Could Mommy heal herself without Ninang Rola? Why did she leave so abruptly? How could she leave us when she herself put us together?

What would Mommy do without her?

Was there more to know about everything around me?

When I walked out the door, Daddy Groovie was already halfway down the street. The sun was too bright, our shadows too dark. The cars parked in the street were mirrors deflecting the heavy rays. Daddy Groovie was at least ten houses ahead of me. He didn't turn around, even when I banged the steel gate shut so he could hear it. He didn't ask me to go back home, as if he didn't know I was following him. He continued walking, arms swinging to keep his armpits cool. His huge, round calves wobbled, tensed when his shoes touched the ground. He walked past the store where he used to get crates of San Miguel, not looking there once even when someone yelled his name.

Lasenggero. I wanted to scream at him, curse at him, call him names. *Basagulero. Tonto.*

He never turned. I didn't know why I wanted him to. He walked beyond the houses whose residents hung clothes to dry at the windows. His shadow behind him was darker than the asphalt street and very long—it almost reached my feet. The houses on both sides were two high walls of wood that shed shadows in the morning. The sun lit the whole street in the afternoons to the point that even the depths of the little marble holes on the ground could be seen.

When he walked past the dead cat, some of the big-winged, bad luck flies followed him as well. He didn't shoo them away. He wasn't slightly bothered by the irritating touch of flies on his skin or the sharp buzzing sound they made over his head.

I leapt over the dead cat but the flies only lingered over their meal.

I stood there, not knowing where to go. There was nothing at home but two people staring at walls.

"Butterfly eyes," said a voice around me.

I turned around and saw my own reflection on Boy Manicure's glass window. At first, the light hurt my eyes. I looked again. CUT: 5 PESOS, a board said. Lining the window ledge were flower boxes. Inside was Delilah de Samsona, wearing a gown with a rainbow of gems all over her, a gown like a wedding dress except it was black. Her hands were above her head, which was capped with a pearly hat. Her face looked toward the jeepney street, toward me, looking into my eyes. It was those comforting eyes that drew me closer to the window.

Boy Manicure stood behind her. Parting the curtain, he waved at me. I didn't ignore him, didn't look away. I watched his face closely, switching between him and the mannequin. Both of them were looking at me. Never in my life had I thought I would look at him like this: so curiously staring at someone as if I had not seen him before. But nobody was around. Nobody would know that I was there, walking closer and closer to his beauty parlor.

"Butterfly eyes," he called again, a different tune this time. The quiet of the street echoed the music of his voice. He stood between the curtains that always matched Delilah de Samsona's clothes. His voice, something about it pulled me in. It was telling me not to be afraid, inviting me to walk up the steps, toward the door, and forget the times I used to run away from him. I imagined what could be inside: a manicuring table by the window, this strange-looking red box with long metal legs. This was where I had seen equally strange faces of old women while they were getting their nails done and watching us play. There would be frames on the walls with paintings that looked so thick you could actually touch the huts and trees. A huge hair dryer hung on the wall, looking like our aluminum white urinal except this one was upside down. The floor would be polished clean.

There would be quiet in his house, not the same quiet that we had in ours because everyone had stopped talking but some kind of quiet, a quiet the children were not afraid of.

There would be frames and calendars with different shapes of moons and stars; his walls would be bare and painted dark blue, not hung with wallpaper like most houses were. There would be mirrored shelves, behind which nail polish of many colors, but mostly shades of red, would sit.

Butterfly eyes . . .

I imagined touching the aquarium that I could see from outside. It was lit, with little black fish and leaves moving slowly in the corner like fingers. There were bubbles coming out of little straws. I saw myself sitting on the sofa, feeling a sting when my skin touched its plastic cover. It would be a nice sofa, unlike ours with its thin slashes of holes and foam coming out like guts.

People came to this beauty parlor from faraway places. Most of our neighbors had never set foot in this place. Women here, especially the older Mrs., wouldn't spend money to have their fingernails painted. For what? They wouldn't even bother to grow them. Their hands were made to remove fish guts, gills and scales, to chop pork thighs, to sink in Tide lather.

Boy Manicure continued to wave at me. *Come. Halika.*

"May I see your bruises." He opened the door and stuck himself out. Through the door, I could clearly see the little fish in the aquarium, the bubbles. The plant rippled inside. My knees knocked. I bowed my head and caught his toes sticking out of the wide bottoms of his pants. His toes spread apart when he realized I was observing them. *Your bruises?*

I had no bruises but I turned my arms around. I didn't ask him how he knew. In our street, cries and yells traveled like the aroma of food cooking and became subjects of conversations at dinner.

"I heard screams from your house," he continued softly. "It's so quiet these days, you can hear everything. There's no one around." He started asking me questions but I failed to answer any of them. *Was it Daddy Groovie? Aling Estrella? Where is your brother? Did your father hit your brother again?*

My eyes rounded as I stared at him. As if he had moved closer, I could suddenly tell that his face was bare, without the colors that made him so fearful. He had little deep pits on his cheeks. His lips were much like mine, thick and sticking out. His ears were unusually small. Abnormal, children always called him. Up close, there was nothing different about him.

"Don't worry, beautiful eyes. Tell your brother to come here. It's going to be okay. Pipo would be fine here."

"Pipo?" the first word that came out of my mouth was my brother's name. I hadn't said it in days. I hadn't called him. It sounded different when I said his name to someone else. Fear slid out of my tongue and I swallowed it back inside. "Pipo?"

"Yes, Pipo. And you, beautiful eyes."

Boy Manicure told me my eyes were big, my lashes long, beautiful. *Like butterflies.* I heard what he said. Beautiful never had anything to do with me, especially my eyes. He said other things. His voice was unusually deep, very eager to please. Comforting. *Fly, fly the butterfly.* He started singing something we used to sing as little children. He made gestures with his hands, joining his thumbs together, flapping the rest of his fingers over his chest like wings. They created a shadow on the door.

Fly, fly the butterfly . . .

From the end of the street, I could see Daddy Groovie disappear into the jeepney street, his face becoming like those boarding the jeepneys in the traffic of smog.

I looked at him again, Boy Manicure. He continued to talk but I wasn't hearing what he was saying anymore. I imagined myself being left in the house, still watching Pipo on his bunk, still counting big and small swollen mounds on Mommy's face. Still waiting for Daddy Groovie to touch me, hit me instead of them, because I knew that if he did hit me, he would have tired of doing it, and he probably would have spared them or, at least, hurt them less.

Suddenly I remembered the drum of water I used to dream of as a child. As I slowly sunk in, Boy Manicure's voice got bigger and bigger, as if laughing. I would wake up in the morning bathing in sweat and pee and run to the window. I wondered if he had drums in his patio like we did, if his kitchen smelt of spilled fish sauce. Was it small and dark, walled by cabinets? A window overlooking the cemented counter? Was his faucet new, a shiny silver, like at Sergio Putita's? Were there plastic bowls on the ground outside in the patio, colorful ones, lined up on the sides as if they were placed there as decorations, some empty, some filled with fish bones, whole ones and leftover, for the stray cats on the aluminum roofs? Were the drums lined up against the tall walls just like ours, greened with mildew? Did his patio crisscross with clotheslines, with white T-shirts swinging on one side, some dripping heavily on the wall, the dry ones flapping in the wind, with the sound of birds flying?

"Won't you come in? Huh?" His face had that strange smile I used to always see on him. There were no teeth on his smile. Only dark lips and gums. That kind of smile little children had whenever they did something or were about to do something that needed approval. But somehow, I wasn't afraid of him.

At first I thought it was a cat meowing from above that brought me back. When I looked at Boy Manicure again, he was motioning me to come inside. *Come in,* opening the door slightly.

I felt his hand grabbing my wrist, slightly tugging.

Diario. Diariooooooo.

Boy Spit's voice could scare off anything alive in our street. I didn't notice that he was already halfway up the street toward me. He had a way of breaking the quiet, of sending cats to scurry away when he rolled his cart on the street. He looked at me as if trying to say something. The warm grasp around my wrist disappeared as I continued to look at Boy Spit. When he got closer, I looked back toward the door again, and it was closed. The curtains behind the mannequin were drawn together, the aquarium light behind it disappeared. *Meoooooow,* I heard a cry from inside Boy Manicure's house. Boy Spit walked by and looked at me and shook his head, eyebrows knotted. He looked at the swinging sign above the door then back at me. It must be the summer, I thought, the quiet roar of the summer heat that made people not say any word, that made their eyes speak. Boy Spit wiped his hands on his pocket and grabbed the handle of his cart and pulled away. And there she was again. Delilah de Samsona. A mannequin in black. Her eyes followed me as I walked home, but eyes without expression, without any sense of emotion like most people I have known.

The smell of skin healing.

Mommy seemed to have sent off this scent while she extended time: everything she did took longer, the times she spent at her Singer went beyond what she used to do, she even washed and ironed the clothes longer, pressing on the shirts more firmly as if the wrinkles weren't already gone. She did what she had to do for us, the usual, and perhaps more, now that she had taken over Ninang Rola's everyday chores. Except she did them quietly, without a hint of reaction on her face. As she gathered the clothes, separated the white from the color, and soaked all of them in water, the mounds on her face subsided, the cuts on her shoulders healed. Slowly, the bandages were taken off. I wasn't sure if she felt pain because I never saw her cry since she had them. I saw her dressing up in the bedroom and she didn't ask me to leave, as if telling me that it was okay for me to see everything that Daddy Groovie left on her body. Mommy did everything slowly. From the time she woke up in the morning, she would be in the kitchen cooking, measuring water in the rice with her fingers, scrubbing pots later until all the stains and grease were gone, only to use them and darken them again. She never rested. She just kept on moving. Her hands were either soaked in Tide lather or inside a fish's stomach pulling guts out.

The moments she spent doing our laundry were perhaps the times she craved for most. She was constantly washing clothes. She sat on a stool in the back patio by herself. The sounds of the morning accompanied her: the chatter of people from nowhere, the meowing of cats, the occasional chirping of birds, the flapping of clothesline. I wondered if she even noticed these sounds, or if the thoughts in her head didn't allow her to listen to anything at all. I was much like her, always thinking, except what I thought about always showed on my face: knotted eyebrows, twisted lips, open mouth. She had nothing on her face; one could never tell what she was thinking at all. While Ninang Rola expressed herself with every possible movement in her body, Mommy seemed like she was just there and her body was disconnected from all her thoughts.

When I looked at Pipo, I wondered if like me he wanted to say something, too. I waited for them to cross each other's path—Pipo and Mommy—watched them go from the front of the house to the back patio, one scratching his bruises, the other bandaging her arm, because once they crossed maybe they would realize how much they had in common. Pipo was healing, too. One day, he just stood up from the bed and stopped sucking his thumb and picking the wallpaper. He walked back and forth in the bedroom, sat by the window, went to the bathroom, stayed there for hours, this bathroom where he was born maybe gave birth to another Pipo. Because as soon as he came out and paced around the house, he became somebody else. Perhaps because he couldn't see bruises on his back, he healed faster. In a few days, they were gone. He went about doing his own things, quietly though, just like Mommy, without any need to say anything to anybody at all. But once they ran into each other, Mommy only told him to pick up the dry clothes from the line and put them in a pail. No mention of what had happened, or of how each one was feeling.

Certain things are better kept than said, said a voice that was once Ninang Rola's but now theirs. So quickly they had learned to keep inside what hurt most. It was something I had wanted to tell Pipo: keep it inside, nobody would find it. Someday you would tell, just like Ninang Rola had, the day you felt the need to tell someone, you would. *The time has come,* was Ninang Rola's response to me when I asked her why she told me Mommy's story. *Certain things you have to find out now.*

Now for us was all these people in our house not saying anything much to each other. What I found out was no matter how small this house was, the farther the distance grew between everybody in it. At times, Pipo would sit at the window, the way Daddy Groovie used to, and watch the empty street outside. Even when I called his name, he would only look at me then turn his head back to what he was doing. He left a big hole on the wall after hours and hours of picking the wallpaper every day. Did he know I picked up all those pieces of paper he left in the corner of the wall under his bed?

Healing took many days. I used to think that perhaps in the process, one would lose his ability to speak. I was afraid that because Ninang Rola wasn't here anymore that that would be true. The difference she made was no matter how hurt Mommy got, Ninang Rola would always be there to talk to. Maybe there were times that Pipo spoke with her that I didn't know about. Now their only connection was gone. It was those times I had wanted Mommy to start talking to Pipo. I felt separated from both of them. I felt there was nothing I could say. And Daddy Groovie continued to spend time talking to himself about his stones or his visa to the States. He was the only noise left in the house, although nobody paid any attention to him. Pipo had been so quiet, sometimes I would catch him walking by himself in the street or sitting on the sidewalk curb throwing dry summer leaves at the few birds that came by. Watching him from upstairs, sometimes I wished he would grow wings so he could fly away with the birds. Sometimes I wished I would, too.

I would hold his hand, take him away.

I saw Boy Spit outside from our window. I was the only one there. Pipo must be taking his long walks again. Mommy was outside on the back patio. Boy Spit was about to yell when he caught me looking at him. He was always the only one in the street. I didn't know why he continued to walk our streets when nobody had ever stopped him to sell used bottles or old newspapers. I noticed that his cart was always empty. One day, he would lose his voice because of all the yelling he did. Besides, it was getting dark. Even if there were people there, nobody would sell anything around that time. Bad luck.

I went outside and followed him. The lamp posts were beginning to light up the way it did before dark. The sun was coming down; the shadows of the power lines still crisscrossed the street, slowly disappearing.

Boy Spit stopped right across from Boy Manicure's house and sat on the sidewalk curb. His cart was right next to him. I stopped to look at Delilah de Samsona. On the window, I could tell that Boy Spit was watching me. He didn't move. He rested his chin on his knees and started digging the buried soft drink caps on the pavement with his fingers. How could he scream *Diario* at the top of his voice and not be able to say a word to me. Delilah de Samsona was probably watching him, too. She had watched every child in this street, much the same way that Boy Manicure had. If she could speak, she would call my name, ask me what was bothering me. I would perhaps tell her there was no one left to talk to in the world. Maybe she would sit me on her lap the way mothers did with their sons. Boy Spit could move closer and take turns with me. He always looked like he needed to talk to someone, too.

I was conscious of Boy Spit's presence. I would shy away from his reflection on the glass, afraid that he might catch me looking at him again. I never thought that he could not see me on the glass, that he could only see my back.

It was in that moment that I noticed the curtain moved behind Delilah de Samsona. I saw a hand grabbing its side, tugging and then letting go. It wasn't Boy Manicure's, too small to be his.

Meoooowwwww. A sound from inside the house.

The door moved. The door opened. First, I saw the same hand holding the threshold. Then I saw it wipe his T-shirt. When I saw both hands, I noticed they were shaking. When they went up to wipe his face, I saw Pipo.

It went very fast. It seemed as if he jumped out of the door, and three steps down to the street. I froze where I was, not knowing what to do next. He wasn't running, Pipo. For a minute, he only stood in front of Boy Manicure's house, behind me. With the door open, I could see what was inside. The summer wind pushed open the door a little bit more and I caught Boy Manicure standing there, naked, wiping his dripping body with a towel.

Meoooooowwww. Cats were rubbing their bodies against his legs.

He stood by his aquarium, and started to feed his fish. At a quick glance, I realized his maleness, like Daddy Groovie's, but Boy Manicure's was much leaner. Without his makeup and the colorful clothes he displayed without shame was a whole new body. A masculine one. With veins all over. He frightened me.

Fly, fly the butterfly. It was hearing that song that made me turn around to find Pipo. *Fly, fly the butterfly.* Boy Manicure sang gleefully.

Butterfly eyes. The wind pulled his door shut.

Everything went slowly this time. I descended one step. Pipo turned toward our house and took one step forward. He was soaking wet, and walked as if afloat in water. The wind roared wildly around us. Pipo shivered in the early chill of the night. His skin was moist; he was trembling down to his knees. My hair stood on its end. I followed him. *Pipo,* I called softly. The asphalt street suddenly seemed like a street full of upside-down bottle caps, very rough on the soles of my feet even with my rubber slippers on.

I didn't look back at the beauty parlor once. Delilah de Samsona must have turned her face around to continue watching us walk home.

Pipo, I said again.

His behind was bleeding, blood slowly dripping down his thighs.

I slowly moved behind him, to cover him. Although the street was empty, I didn't want anyone to see the blood on his shorts.

The world slowed down even more. My chest was beating very fast. Pipo was shivering even more. It was then that I realized that Boy Spit was still there. I couldn't recall what he was trying to do the whole time, but somehow I took a newspaper from him, and opened it, put it around Pipo's behind.

Pipo grabbed the edges of the paper with both hands. I held the middle of it. "This way," I told him. "Like this." I continued to walk behind him, making sure that he didn't drop it while he wrapped it around his back. He walked painfully as if his legs were torn apart.

Boy Spit looked at me as if trying to tell me more with his eyes. I was afraid of eyes. Anyone's. And he stood there but I didn't know what I was supposed to say. I thought his eyes were not the only ones watching us, that there were others, behind closed shutters, behind clothes hanging at windows, behind termite holes, even if our street was empty.

I didn't know why I left Boy Spit without saying anything. I didn't know whether he was still behind us as soon as I closed the door of our house.

The smell of silence.

It was that smell that made me want to scream Mommy's name over and over again, to know if she would come to Pipo's aid. It was also that smell that prevented me from uttering a word, realizing that she probably wouldn't pay attention.

In the dark, Pipo continued walking inside the house. I wasn't sure whether he knew I was there the whole time. Still clutching the newspaper behind him, he entered the bathroom. One page fell down to the floor, landed flat, weighed down by the blotch of blood. I picked it up and carried it.

I stood outside the bathroom. I knocked slowly to see if Pipo was all right. He didn't answer. I remembered the time I used to wait outside while he took forever to bathe. The times I peed in my shorts because he wouldn't come out no matter what. As much as I had banged on the door, he wouldn't unlock it. Worse, he came out laughing at me. This was also the same place where he had thrown stuff at me. Everything seemed to always revolve around this part of the house between Pipo and me. Something about knowing we were within the same space, and yet separated by this bathroom door, this wooden door that had aged in years.

When I touched the door, it creaked. It wasn't locked from inside. I slowly pushed it open. I stuck my head in. Pipo was squatting on the newspaper, smearing blood all over it, shitting whatever Boy Manicure left inside his body. I imagined what Daddy Groovie did to Mommy at night. Those long nights of whispers and cries. I didn't say anything to Pipo. He didn't look at me once. His eyes were hollow, his face, blank and pale. My body was hollow. He grabbed the edge of the plastic drum to support himself and got up. He poured water on his legs.

The door opened wide. Pipo moved around me without looking at anything. I felt his hand on my arm. He didn't grab me the way he used to when I stood in his way. He felt as soft as the look in his eyes. Slowly, he climbed the stairs, holding a towel he found in the bathroom. The light of the bathroom led him up.

I locked myself in the bathroom. I poured water on the stains of blood on the floor. Slowly, it flowed into the drain. I began to hear a squeaking sound coming out of the drain. I felt numb to everything around me. I only continued pouring water on the floor. I found a rag in the corner and started to scrub the floor with it. I watched the drain closely, watched the head of a rat come out of it, its nostrils sniffing the blood that was oozing in. It didn't mind my presence. I completely soaked the newspaper in water and squeezed the blood out of it. The whole body of the rat came out of the drain. Its noise became very apparent. I waited for the rat to come to me. But it stayed around the drain, its whole body bigger than both of my feet combined, its tail waggling as if it had a life of its own. Another rat came out. Then another.

I looked up to see the hanging bulb. It was watching me, knowing what had happened. The spider web was frozen as always casting a shadow on the wall and all over, holding me. There were pails and pails of water that Mommy had patiently filled, considering the way water dripped out of the faucet in the summer. The drain was there, where it had always been, this time swallowing blood, allowing three big rats to eat it.

I didn't want a spot of blood to remain on the floor, not in the little cracks on the broken tiles, not in the corner of the wall where dirt sat for days, not around the bottom of the pails. As I imagined Pipo upstairs change into new clothes, I scrubbed the floor more and more. I felt Pipo's touch on my arm. I heard him say, "Run, Gringo. Run." I remembered the empty look on his face before he went upstairs. I smelled the air around him when he was picking the wallpaper off the wall. I saw the mark of Daddy Groovie's hands on his back. For a while, I squatted there the way he did, holding the ball of newspaper in my hand, squeezing it harder and harder until it turned into pulp. I sat there quietly; hours might have passed, the wet floor might have dried underfoot and the rats have gone, but I squatted there, staring at the hanging bulb perhaps, thinking of Pipo, of Mommy, whispering to myself over and over.

Certain things are better kept than said.

STATES OF BEING

A year is not a very long time.

If you could count moons and stars and suddenly your ten years of waiting would be over, I could also count mounds of red and black ants on the asphalt street and, one day, a year would be over. One year. I want to go where you are, anywhere but here.

I'm afraid of this place, of what it's done, of what it's going to do to me.

So I squat here all the time, across our house, on the fence that was never finished, holding the steel that sticks out of the concrete blocks, watching the window. I have seen you many times, the way I'm looking at you now. In my mind, you are always there, watching us play in the street, keeping Big Boy Jun away from Pipo and me, throwing peanut shells at the other marble-gambling boys for teasing us, cutting newspaper clippings about the States. The same things, again and again.

You may not know this, but you are always here.

I think about the States a lot more, wonder what is there. I know where you are but I'm not sure what it's really like. I think in circles—rain, flood, heat, sun, then back to rain again, but where you are it's not like that. It's cold there, isn't it? Like sticking my hand in the Frigidaire? And not too much sun. There is snow, isn't there? Before the snow, I think of the States as a coloring book house, wider than our street, sometimes green, sometimes white, sometimes you can lie on there and sometimes my feet could sink into the snow. Not like the houses here, with peeling paint that nobody thinks about repainting. These brown boxes all attached, each day one looking older than the other, like the faces of the people who lived in them. You don't live in one like that. Yours must be newly painted, the whole house, not just the doors. A Christmas card house with rows of green trees outside sparkling with lights, snow half-melting on the twigs. I think about how you and Auntie Dolares walk together in the streets of Woodside, Nuyork. D'merica, sorry, that's the way you write it now. Sometimes you walk with my cousins, too. You laugh. You forget all about the window. You forget all about the street that overlooked it. You forget about our bedroom, the noise, your *yantok*, how often it kissed Pipo's skin, the night you hit Mommy and broke the mirror on the wall, the only one we ever had. You forget about many things. I know. I can see you now. You laugh with Auntie Dolares, with her children. You practice your English with them. She tells you how you should learn to pronounce her name right, with an *O* not an *A*. Do-LO-res, she will tell you, just like what Ninang Rola said, but you are so used to saying her name your way, you don't hear her. I'm so used to saying her name that way, too. You tell them about us. But you don't tell them what you did to us. Never once do you mention how you came home drunk from the embassy, thinking you failed your interview and beat up everybody and got rid of Ninang Rola and Maricon. You only speak of the paper boat times, the hours before the hitting. The ones after. You tell them how Pipo took after you, just like you. How you brought us up so well. They will see us soon.

*

An aerogram at the doorstep.

Handwritten in a backdrop of blue. Blue, the color of the States. Mommy looked at it then ripped the edge with her fingers, so slowly I could almost hear. Before unfolding, she released a very deep sigh, then handed it over to me. *Read this.* Inside, lightly penciled lines. Daddy Groovie's handwriting, practiced to perfection, over and over, on scratch paper. Then transcribed. I could tell by the way letters curved and angled, time must have slowed down when he wrote this. I couldn't see him doing that, taking his time.

It's been so many years since I saw Dolares last. She has changed a lot. Her kids are all so big now. This picture was taken recently. See how her kids are now, your cousins? See how healthy they are? Very busy here. More jobs than I thought. Many jobs here for those who aren't very picky, unlike there, not much to choose from to begin with. I have two, day and night, at a hospital and, in the evenings, at a restaurant nearby, washing plates. Dolares recommended me there. She told me, right now, take anything you can get, you need the experience. She knew the owner. She knows a lot of people, people like us.

His voice. My auntie's voice. Dolares, his only sister, whom I had never seen except in pictures. On the back of one, he wrote her name, the same way he had been saying for years. Dolares. She was Daddy Groovie with a huge wig and nice Stateside clothes. She always wore that big-teeth smile of people who were well fed, so much like her two older brothers who came to our house when Daddy Groovie left and covered their noses while they walked on our street. Dolares. The one who petitioned for us when I was two.

So many places here to go. So many things to buy. So much food here. Bacon, do you know what that is? I eat bacon in the morning. There is no Spam here. Dolares is a good cook.

Dolares this. Dolares that. Dolares. She spoke to me in pictures and Christmas cards she sent to us regularly. She called me "little one," and never seemed to remember my name. Once, she wrote it: Gregorito. So glad I was that I showed it to all my friends. English-speaking Titay almost ripped the Christmas card because she hated to see anybody with anything from the States. Auntie Dolares. The goddess of Daddy Groovie's future—he'd probably build an altar for her.

I *finally got a schedule for a medical checkup at a local doctor. So you, you always take care. Eat well.*

He used to always complain about us getting sick, comparing us to my cousins, Auntie Dolares's children, making statements such as, there, they don't get sick—he took the picture out of his thick wallet, this wallet dangling with several keys—you see, healthy, healthy children. I saw the picture once. Once and never again. He always kept it in there, this brown, cow-skin wallet that, like this house, had a window on it except he wasn't the one at the window, it wasn't me, Mommy, or Pipo, but Auntie Dolares and her two children, outside their house in Woodside, in the snow. They wore thick clothing, around their heads and neck, all over themselves, as thick as the whiteness around them. I could tell by their dark faces that I was related to them, except they never looked hungry. Whenever I thought of them, I smelled the difference of another country, a story of coloring book houses I saw on TV at English-speaking Titay's house, its theme song repeatedly playing in my mind, and in my mouth, a taste of melting ice.

Eat well, he always wrote.

Hunger, the taste of it I could never forget. It melted in my tongue when my stomach began to ask for something I could never get. Then I became conscious of little things, leftover bread that the ants rushed to in a blink, or roaches. I gaped at children eating ice cream, watched it melt on the cone, watched them lick their fingers, and when they finished eating, watched them go back to buy another one. I reached down into my pocket and kept my hand there, wishing my coins would multiply. The corn vendor would roll by with his cart. Our neighbors ran to him, one peso for a corn, so hot and steamy they burned their hands and their tongues as they licked the rounded surface before they bit into it and drooled. From our window, I watched all kinds of food being sold. In the morning, the *Taho* man with his carts of soybean drink, in the afternoon till the evening, the parade of fishball carts, cotton candy, rice cakes, coconut that got chopped in front of you and many others as if they knew how hungry our street was, as if they didn't know that there were ones like me who only sat there and watched the whole time. So one day, I began to dry stale rice in the sun, mold it into balls to make crunchy rice cakes afterward. And fish, the taste of fish, dried and salted from the *tinapa* women—it became even more flavored because I'd want it to stay longer in my mouth, after dipping in vinegar.

Eat well, he said. But I wondered what he was eating now that made it easy for him to say that. When his letters arrived, I skimmed through them until I found the part where he listed what he ate that day, my new vocabulary of food, most of them I never heard of before: pizza bigger than your two hands, extra cheese; steak, medium-rare; fish fillet, a fish without bone he called it, without the head, how could that possibly be? He was saving money, he added, saving to rent a house for us.

A houseful of food.

Because here, things were getting worse. Or maybe it had always been this bad and I just never noticed until now. I could tell by the way our neighbors looked. Everybody seemed to be complaining more, finding it more difficult to cope. Prices were going up too fast. Bread was shrinking in size.

That was when the States filled people's faces, blinked in everybody's eyes. And when they got tired of brownouts, the heat, the mosquitoes, the States appeared in every word they spoke:

So much food in California.

Ako? may sister *ako,* CPA *sa* Nuyork. She will send me a Balikbayan box, full of fruitcake! Fruitcake, imagine, we don't have that here!

My son—*abogado* in Ha-why.

Look at my shoes. PX Goods. Stateside *'yan.*

Kumusta to your father, huh? Tell him not to forget us here, huh? Say hello for me, huh? But tell me, where's Woodside, D'merica?

When is he going to send me my Samsonite? He promised me, you know? When is he going to send me Yardley and Ivory? Also, I want some Stateside Colgate, what do you call it there, Crest? They're not too expensive in the States I hear?

Every day, everywhere, a reminder of where he was.

*

States was the body of an imagined brother.

Born in Daddy Groovie's mouth, he grew up in the mouths of our house. He was the youngest one, the boyish one with an enormous power over Pipo and me, occupying the empty space in Daddy Groovie's insides, one made especially for him. States would sit beside me, hands between his thighs, sitting like Big Boy Jun, smelling like Boy Spit, not looking like me, not looking like anyone else, like himself, a look all of his own, the face of the future that might not be there. He would stare at me, his eyes, blue like English-speaking Titay's dolls, his skin as light as the stomach of a dead toad in a flood and lighter than Pipo's. He would speak English so well. "This Gregorio, so gooood in English," Miss Huffy used to say about me, but now she would say States was ten or twenty times better, after all he's States, the only one that made Daddy Groovie's small eyes grow big as a coin, so big you'd think he just had San Miguel beer again.

"What do you want?" He appeared, sitting beside Jesus with a glowing heart, looking much like him, a child's face of him. "Why are you looking at me like that?"

I wouldn't think of him being there, if there was somebody here to talk to, if those newspaper clippings could talk back. There were questions I wanted to ask and he was the only one who could answer.

"What is it really like there, where you come from?" I asked.

"Where I come from?" He folded his arms, pushed his head back to stare at the ceiling. Pointed his lips.

"Where Daddy Groovie is now?"

"Woodside?" he asked, not looking at me.

"D'merica."

Then he fell in silence as if he was climbing the ceiling with his eyes, searching for the answer there, something he did very well. He pulled his little body back up. "Why do you want to know?"

"I don't know. Curious. I just wonder . . . is there a place for someone . . . like me there?"

"What do you mean someone like you?"

Like me. I didn't answer, didn't know what I meant. Perhaps I wanted to know if I could be as happy as Daddy Groovie, or happier. What was I like? Someone who thought much, said less, someone whose expertise was to keep everything inside, someone whose role in life was to hold the secrets of everyone around him.

*

The day you left, I waited for the rain, but it didn't rain.

Your construction friends were there. I could smell them, their breath, your breath, their hang-around T-shirts so stiff with dry sweat. All so alike. They're just like you. Sometimes I wondered why you left them. They even tucked in their shirts the same way, without belts, so that their shirts kept on popping out. Their arms were as big as both of my thighs combined. Their bellies stuck out, hanging over their shorts. Burnt skin. I couldn't tell them apart, especially Mang Bok and Mang Bic: from their sticky hair to their slippers, from hand-sewn shirts to their broken zippers, everything identical. I always remembered you when I saw them in the street. When I walked there and saw one of their backs to me, I imagined you being with them. The only difference was you never smoked in your life. They all did. That's how you got your hang-around T-shirts, gratis from their having bought boxes and boxes of cigarettes.

"Time to go," you hollered so loud, everybody moved their chairs. You hugged and kissed everybody. Your hang-around friends circled you, recounting memories in your last minutes together. "Don't forget us. Don't forget us. Huh, Groovie?" In his very heavy breath, Pipo also said your name, "Daddy Groovie?"

"Groovie . . . Groovie," your friends kept on saying. They said it so well. From their mouths, it became a full word. *Groovie.*

They were the ones who gave you your name.

Their faces were red, saddened. The same look after finishing a whole crate of San Miguel. Even now, when I saw them, they looked like that.

They didn't drive to the airport with us. Everybody left, their stomachs full. They all watched the jeepney leave. From inside, I imagined them waving at me. Me, the one who was about to leave.

At the airport, the coming and going of people was inviting. Amid airport boys pulling and pushing carts full of huge boxes, it was easy to tell who was coming from the States. It was as if a cloud was floating them into the airport by the way they dressed and acted, cutting through the dust with their Stateside luggage with wheels, holding battery-operated minifans and little boxes of tissue paper. And I could tell the ones who were leaving by looking at the boxes wrapped with hemp and the anxiousness of their faces as they stared at the closed gates.

You didn't have that on your face. The excitement you had before you left our house had then disappeared. Pipo kept on walking close to you. In the middle of the crowd, where other people were also saying goodbye, you went after Mommy who skirted away from you. She asked you to stop, slapping your hands whenever they touched a part of her body, telling you to go. Her hair was in a bun with a black *peineta*. *Tama na.* She had on an orange blouse with colorful fruits on them. *Sige na.* I had never seen that before. She never wore that again.

From behind, Pipo grabbed you tight. His hair was pomaded with the same sticky thing you put in yours. Before we left our house, he sat looking in a hand mirror for hours, combing his hair over and over until it was so flat, it looked like a car tire. He was wearing your T-shirt, one of those you decided to leave. He even picked one that would fit him right, though none of them really did. The whole time at the airport, he was staring at you, his palms on his hair, flattening it even more. He almost pulled out your shirt that was neatly tucked into your gabardines when he held you. "Please . . . not yet . . ." he begged.

Perhaps he wanted to tell you something. Perhaps had you sat down and listened for once, he would have told you what Boy Manicure did to him. I would have told you that I was there, outside; I saw him bleeding. I cleaned up after him, the way I cleaned up after you. I had been watching Pipo a lot. I was afraid of what he would do next. He was never himself, but this time, I wasn't sure at all of who he was. He was changing, and very quickly. Now he was wearing your T-shirt and I didn't understand. Why would he want to be you, of all people? Why you? Why would he want to do his hair the way you did yours?

"Please, Daddy . . ." Pipo pleaded again.

You had the word *what?* written all over your face when you turned around and looked at him. He bowed his head, stared at his own reflection on your too-polished black shoes, mumbled again—not yet. I thought you were going to hit him by the way you looked but you simply let him go, ruffled his hair. Then you shook your head.

Pipo stood there, watching you go to Mommy instead, twisting the hem of his T-shirt into knots.

"How do I look?" you asked Mommy. "Like these navy pants? This shirt looks okay *ba*?" The bottom of your pants swung quickly, left, right, left. I thought your tight pants would burst around your thighs. This was what you called your *despedida* attire: navy was your color, your *despedida* color, navy would bring you luck. You bought them yourself, which you rarely did, at a department store, you boasted. "O-kay?"

Mommy nodded her head, pulling up her bag. "You look fine."

You hesitated to leave. Standing there, you looked at all of us for a long time. It was different, the way your eyes saw us. Something I had never seen before. That was the face I saw at the window, when I thought that you were there. The fallen look of your eyes. Your last days here, you had the same look when you pursued Mommy wherever she went, holding her with your eyes. While Mommy's bruises healed, you sat there and watched, always asking her how she was, breathing words of comfort. You froze water in little plastic bags. "Put them on your face." You handed them to her. She took them only to leave them outside to melt in the sun. Then she pounded Mayana leaves to soak in water and wore them on her wounds. The night before you left, I saw you standing at the window. I had never seen you there at night. You enveloped her with your gaze, the same you had at the airport.

There was nobody else in this world for you but Mommy.

Your feet paced with your hands, back and forth. You couldn't seem to lift yourself. There was much heaviness inside you. You couldn't say anything anymore. You took me into your arms, kissed me on the forehead. Then you took Pipo, held him tightly. And when it was Mommy's turn, your eyes pooled with tears though you didn't say anything to her. Go, she said under her breath. Please go now. So you finally turned; it didn't last long for you to look back again.

I knew you were only looking at Mommy.

She wasn't even looking back at you. She was watching people walk through the gates, outside, through the glass windows, where airplanes were moving around. They were huge. I had never seen anything like them before. One of them was yours. One of them was another one of your favorite words, *PanAm*.

"Daddy Groovie. Daddy . . ." Pipo waved and tiptoed so he could catch the last glimpses of you. "Is that his plane, is that it?"

Mommy pulled Pipo away more but he shrugged her off.

"Wait," he said, then with a whisper, "Daddy Groovie." He spent those last minutes following your passage through the gate, his hands half-raised, prepared for the moment you would turn around again. You didn't and when you finally disappeared, Pipo stood there, trancelike, ignoring Mommy's succession of calls. Then he pulled up his arm and smelled the sleeve of your hang-around T-shirt. He kept on doing that until we left the airport.

Mommy's jaws were again locked on the bus during our trip back. Like Pipo, she just stared into the space outside. I watched the commotion of people. The parade of colorful umbrellas in the heat. The Stateside movies painted on big plywood boards hanging all over the buildings. Those Holy Week movies.

It was almost Semana Santa when you left. The roads and streets were filling up with all the signs. Giant Technicolor picture of Moses, with rays emanating from his head, holding two slabs of stones that mechanically opened and closed causing more traffic jams. There were children in front of rows of moviehouses selling a variety of comics, peanuts, cigarettes, rosaries, and Litania books. There were many different faces of Jesus painted on big plywood boards with the brilliant light coming out of his face amid suffering. His face was beautiful, they twinkled while thorns poked through his skin. The fake blood. So fake it smelled of manicure paint. And his eyes, so blue, watching us all, the quiet blue of the sea that watched Daddy Groovie's PanAm plane slowly hover to the States.

Mommy would never go there. There is no rain there.

The sound of water filled the house for weeks. She had been washing the walls of the house since you left. She began in our bedroom. She had me carrying buckets around and throwing the dirty water in the back patio. Each time I brought in a clean bucket of rainwater and soap, I saw her rip another one of your hang-around T-shirts. She tore them with her teeth, her fist so tight, I thought she was going to break her arms. Water dripped down the wallpaper in front of her. I listened to the sound she made squeezing your clothes that she used as damp cloths. She folded and lay one against the wall, then scrubbed it so hard she could break a hole through the wall. She climbed tables, cabinets. I found her sprawled on the window grill, reaching into corners of the ceiling. She pulled the bedsheets off the big bed. The cardboards placed inside to cover coils fell off. She picked them up and tore them one by one. Without the boards, I could clearly see the pee stains I left as a child, still big, round, and browned. She covered them with big cloths, the ones she had been sewing weeks before you left, piled them one on top of the other. Then she sewed the sides into the mattress. When she finished, she covered it with a thick embroidered blanket, turning it into a different kind of bed altogether.

As soon as the walls dried, she washed them again. She spent days, patiently moving from the bedroom to the living room then to the rest of the house. I thought she was going to finish the buckets of rainwater we had saved in the back patio. She kept on asking me to bring more in.

Your clothes had appeared in many parts of our house. Sometimes in the kitchen sink, wet and dirty with fish bones all over, sometimes in the corner of the bathroom to clean the toilet bowl with. Mommy used them to clean the table, the floor, even the windows. There were shredded pieces she would make floormats with that lay in a small bag close to her Singer Machine. She had given some to me and I was soon waxing the floor with them. When she saw Pipo walk in, she quickly threw one at him and asked him to clean the stairs. You should have seen the look in Pipo's face when the torn T-shirts fell in his hands, as if he was the one who was ripped into parts.

For days, we cleaned. The three of us. I thought it would never end. The whole house had the scent of soap and rain.

"Let the air come. Let this new air come into this house, once and for all. I have waited for this for so long," Mommy said while she opened the windows, and she kept them open night and day. "Ahh. The smell of this country."

The odor of the jeepney streets? I wondered what she was referring to. The smell of the afternoon sewer, of dead animals? Of children who had not bathed for days? Of newspaper boys who had been working a whole day without food? I could stop breathing for a whole year, I thought. But not Mommy, she wasn't thinking of a year the way I did all the time. She had never mentioned the

States once, you know that? And that frightened me. I didn't think she wanted to leave, as much as I wanted to, especially now.

Mommy had slowly removed your things, packed them away in boxes of powdered milk that she asked me to get from Tarina All-Around store. She placed all of them underneath the kitchen counter, along with dirty soft drink bottles and rats.

"Collector of garbage," she mumbled, pulling out all the things you had collected in boxes and cracker cans. She knelt on the floor, sifting through open cabinets. Medicine bottles. Old newspapers and magazines. Empty bottles of cologne. At least five of them were Pacorabang, empty to the bottom so that they didn't smell of anything at all. Then there were your construction tools that she stared at for a long time before putting them in shoe boxes. Some of them were almost unused, like the nails of different sizes, thick and thin ones, in small Gerber jars.

"Garbage," she said again, while she grabbed piles of newspapers and yanked them into the room. I didn't think of garbage when I saw the pile sliding across the floor. I thought of you sitting at the window, peanuts in your hands, some of their skin stuck around your lips that you didn't even notice. You were flipping through these newspapers.

And I am sitting here again, outside, on the fence, ignoring faces of people walking by, thinking that if there was any way I could take after you, it would be in this desire to look through these pages, to see for myself what had interested you so much to gather all of them together and not throw them away. I will immediately take all the newspapers and keep them under the bunk bed. Open them one by one, page by page, read them while making sure not to tear the brittle and yellowing pages. Look for everything written about the States. About Nuyork. And no, there will be no peanut shells on the windowsill when I sit there in your place. Just ants. Marching slowly while I count them. One for each day.

*

Whenever I closed my eyes before I fell into deep sleep at night, whenever the coils in the mattress began to poke the small of my back and I slowly began to forget the lingering smell of fried salted fish in the air, I would tell myself that someday, somehow, I would also leave.

D*ear everybody . . . how is the family? Hope everything is well. Very soon you can join me here. . . . Are you working on all the documents? . . . It's winter now. The snow is falling outside and it's very chilly here. Christmas is here again. It's different here, Christmas. Children don't knock on doors to sing carols. Hardly any midnight masses. People don't take it seriously as much. But the snow, the snow, you can't imagine how beautiful it is. It seems that time is flying fast. We are okay. Dolares's kids are already off from school and shopping for gifts. I hope you will have a wonderful Christmas and New Year. I heard about the big typhoon. Hope everything is all right . . . Here, we have no floods, just snow. It's wonderful. . . . Thank God I left. Merry X'mas . . . All the love in the world, ho-ho-ho, Daddy.*

A Stateside Christmas card wrinkled in my thought. Mommy left a Christmas card on the table. Pipo saw it first. I waited for him to leave then I took it, kept it, put it under my pillow, memorized what was inside. I have never forgotten it since. In my deep thoughts, it formed like a crumpled ball of paper, slowly unwrinkling.

T*hank God I left.*

CURFEW

Daddy Groovie's T-shirts hung on Pipo like a burlap sack, empty of rice.

His favorite one—gray with a peeling Stateside flag and thread curling out of the seams. He wore that every day. Every time he put it on, he brought it close to his face, inhaling perhaps Daddy Groovie's scent. While he sat in front of the dresser, he would look at himself in the mirror and comb his hair endlessly until it was flat. When he walked away, he carried himself with some kind of heaviness, his shoulders hunched. Bowed his head wherever he went. Covered his face with his hair. Long, for his age.

Sometimes, when I sat on the unfinished concrete-block fence, looking for Daddy Groovie at the window, I would see Pipo instead. His eyes were always looking in. When he looked at me, he always turned his head.

He was completely different now. Sometimes

I wanted to read his mind, hear what he was thinking. I wondered if somehow he remembered the night he walked home bleeding. I wondered if he knew all this time that I existed. Because whenever our eyes crossed, it seemed as if he didn't know that I knew something bad had happened to him. I never caught him crying when he was by himself as other children did when thoughts occurred to them from deep memory. He hardly said anything at all. Like Mommy, his sentences were short, abrupt. Almost wordless, nothing to say, or maybe with much to say except they were trapped in his throat, lumped in the middle.

He had stopped playing outside, stopped seeing Sergio Putita. He had stopped throwing things at me. He was always at home now, always chewing on raw mango slices dipped in fish sauce and vinegar. He had grown tall, his legs were longer and thinner. They curled around the tall chair.

He was always waiting, always, for something I did not know.

And he spent his days in the room next to us. The door closed. There was absolutely no noise. You'd wonder if he were sleeping the whole time he was in there. Mommy had not made an attempt to rent out the room again. So Pipo took over the room. If Ninang Rola came back, she would stay there and not on the folding cot downstairs now harboring webs under the stairs. When I went inside his room one day, it didn't seem to be a place I had been in before. Some sights were familiar: the uneven edges of wallpapers, the old Iglesia de San Pedro New Year calendars, the thread and needle box, the green metal bunk beds, and Daddy Groovie's cabinets that Pipo had moved into the room. But everything else was different, especially the strange smell of a boy when his armpits began to sweat, and his hair grew thicker.

Even I, perhaps, changed, because I was thinking then, No, I don't have to talk to him. He didn't have to look at me for more than three seconds. I, being the one who always followed him around, now thinking like this? We didn't have to acknowledge anymore that we were around each other. No more holding my breath because he might say something or do something, forcing me to answer him back.

There was this dream: I was pulling Pipo out of a drum. I couldn't see his face. His hands flapped on the surface of the water. He was inside, deeper than I thought. He was breathing in water. My hands were slowly going in, searching for his arms. Our arms knotted around each other. As soon as his face touched the air above the surface, he sank back in. And Boy Manicure suddenly appeared from behind him, naked. He grabbed Pipo from behind, locking his hands over Pipo's chest. Pipo screamed but I didn't hear a word he said. Water splashed all over me. Blood floated on the water. Pipo completely sank in, his hands last. This time, to the very bottom.

The noises next door at night.

I had ignored them many times. I always thought that

Pipo was still on the bunk above me, that Daddy Groovie was making all the noise. But it was some kind of noise I had never heard on curfew nights. Not voices. Not cockfight movements. I didn't dream of Mommy when I heard it. I thought of how dark it might have been outside the room. And outside the house, darker. I pulled the blanket over my head. Somebody was walking. But not really going anywhere in particular. I shut my eyes, kept my body still. Listened to footsteps. Then just as quickly, everything would be hushed as if the noise knew that I was wide awake, that I could hear even my own nervous breathing.

Boy Spit had never stopped at our house. We had not bought a newspaper since Daddy Groovie left. I knew who bought newspapers in our street. I knew when they bought them, too. The *New Society*, that's what our neighbors wouldn't stop talking about. *Green Revolution,* I never knew what it meant. Boy Spit would go to those houses every day. I would wait for him to do that, sometimes playing deaf to Mommy's calls so that I could watch him from our window. Each time, I pressed my finger against my palm. I'd say to myself, go, follow him again, talk to him. I wanted to sit in his cart while he pushed me away from here. Away, and so far, I wouldn't know where I would end up. Perhaps in the slums, where newspaper boys lived. Even if it's very dirty there, there would be people to talk to. Boy Spit could sit with me and listen. I could tell him many things, many, many things. But thinking all this, I only sat at the window, legs frozen, the curtains blowing dust to my face. Shame, a word I learned when I was young, was so close to me, like the little hairs growing above my knees.

A thin curtain over the moon.

Sitting on the edge of the bunk, I stared at its brightness. The moon moved slowly. I continued staring, my eyes getting stingy because I wouldn't blink. A night cat danced around the roof and covered it, its long tail dividing the roundness in half. Before I knew it, the moon was hiding behind the roof of the house across the street.

Slowly walking away from my bed, I waited for the noise next door. It had stopped. I left our door ajar so I could hear more. Somehow I knew Pipo was wide awake, too. I could hear Mommy's deep breathing, which showed how much sleep she had gained since Daddy Groovie left. She wouldn't even know that everybody else was up in the house.

Carefully I sat by the door. The moon was gone. The room had gotten dimmer. A sound of a door opening. Feet were being lifted slowly so as not to make any sound. I had seen him do this before, Pipo. I could tell by merely listening how quietly he went down the stairs. In the darkness, nobody could hear him.

His shadow at night.

A dancer on the street. The big cart was its partner. The night light, its music. I could almost step on his shadow but when I did, it quickly moved away. Boy Spit pushed the cart handle down. The newspaper bundles inside slid down toward him. I saw they were recent newspapers. *New*

Society, printed all over it. Everybody was making songs out of the new slogan of the year. Martial Law's loud mouth, the way Daddy Groovie would put it. Bottles quickly followed, rolling over each other. They made clanging sounds without breaking. SWAT could have done it better. More control with his bigger arms. The cart expert. Although SWAT had splattered pig slop over the street, leaving mounds of smell that lasted all day. With Boy Spit, nothing to worry about smell.

My toes slipped over my slippers as I made a quick stop.

His shadow stopped moving. The three wheels of the cart weren't making noise against rough asphalt. I wasn't looking at him. But he knew I was there. He could have turned his face but I wouldn't know, because most of the time I kept my head bowed. I wondered why he wasn't saying anything.

Are you following me? If he asked, I would say, Yes, yes, but I can't if you just stand there, so go.

The wheels rolled. Crag-crag. The bottles shook inside. Newspapers snapped out of the strings and bounced. A melody of some kind. His shadow danced again. I continued to follow. This time I slowly lifted my face. I had wanted to talk to him for so long. I could see we were reaching the end of the street. I could see his back. His hands clutched the handle of the cart. Tight.

I raised my head quickly.

Boy Spit turned around. I bowed my head again. He didn't ask me any questions. Before I knew it, I was just standing there. My legs were hard as sticks. He had disappeared in front of me.

I was left standing on my own shadow, the rhythm of the six o'clock street honking around me.

After dinner, I handed Pipo an aerogram from Daddy Groovie. "You know what to do with this," I said.

"I've been looking for this." He grabbed it out of my hand, couldn't get his face off of it, sniffing it even, and by doing so, ungluing the flaps.

The aerogram unfolded in his hands, like a peeled banana, then was swallowed with his eyes. He didn't even bother to clear the supper table. Lucky he was because Mommy wasn't there to tell him that. He began reading the letter in his mind while he walked upstairs. His steps slowed down. Daddy Groovie's voice, I heard in my head, always starting with *Dear everybody . . .*

Pipo was in his room again. The fluorescent lamp was busted, so he had put a lamp on a small table. The put-together table we had both climbed as children and crashed on the floor with. He must have been sitting there. The moon was never on that side of the house. It was always darker there, even as early as seven at night. And noisier. Because cats loved the dark. They could see in the dark. And fireflies, they're lit at night. But that wouldn't bother him. He had his letter. He would sleep with it.

He would feast on Daddy Groovie's words in his dreams.

I stared at his plate. He must have lifted it close to his face and licked it. I always left something on my plate: a bone, rice grains, at least five; white eyes of fish. He always ate the whole head of fish. Only cats left their bowls clean.

If I saw him again, I would follow him. I would not bow my head. I would talk to him. I would know who he really was, his real name. I promised myself that. I memorized my promise, the same way I recited "Our Father" without knowing what came out of my mouth.

I would follow him.

Waking up, his face appeared with my foul breath. The first thing I saw: his stare. I looked at the scar above his eyebrows, only to realize I was dreaming again, and I couldn't remember any more of it. And every day, the image of him giving me a newspaper became clearer. I began to see how he looked like then, those sorry eyes of his, as if blood was all over my face, clotting.

So one day, I waited. I waited until night.

When I saw him, I ran downstairs. I followed. Boy Spit, Boy Spit, his name a steady heartbeat.

Piko. Children skipped blocks drawn on the street. Some waited for their turn outside the chalked borders. *Sipa.* Boys were kicking rubber bands they tied together, counting while they bent their knees to catch the falling rubber bands. One of those last minutes before the night took over the street, when the feel of that last strong kick of the rubber band ball and the biggest and most heroic skip of blocks became so important because it made them all sleep better.

I felt the same way; I thought it was my last chance, too. So when I caught his shadow, I immediately ran after him, brushing past the children scattered in the narrow street.

Why he never said anything to me, I didn't know. But as if I would never see him again, I stopped as soon as I caught up with him, observing, waiting. Hadn't you pulled me out of the Jai Alai boys once? Hadn't you given me a newspaper when Pipo left Boy Manicure's house? That was you, wasn't it? But now you don't say anything?

Pssst. The children-call. I looked back. Pssst. A succession of whistles. The moment to stop and go inside the house. Dinner. TV. Homework. Faces at the windows. Hands waving children to go back inside. The hours before curfew. A sudden panic in the faces of the children playing outside. Everybody wanting to win their games. *Sige, sige.* Hurry. Kick the ball so high it'll get caught in the aluminum gutters. Step one, step two, oops, out, out *ka na*. Pssst. Mommy wasn't calling me. She didn't know I wasn't home anymore. Her face flashed in front of me. I took a step back. The rest of my body resisted. In my mind, I could see Mommy walking into our bedroom, finding out I wasn't there. I took another step back. No you mustn't go, I said to myself.

All I wanted was for him to turn around.

His cart rolled on the street.

He could have read my mind because he turned. Waved. The come here wave. What was I to do? I stood where I was. I was supposed to be following him. Boy Spit, I whispered to myself. He waved again. He did that like he was fanning the wind into his face.

So he walked and I finally followed.

We were at once in the corner of the street, facing jeepneys. At night, the lights of the jeepneys were big, tired, red eyes. You could hardly see the even more tired faces of the drivers behind them. Their voices, you could hear.

There was always the commotion of voices. Light whirled above and below. Footsteps of passengers flew with the speeding jeepneys. Some people were endlessly waiting for their turns to get into the crowded vehicles, turning their heads patiently, slapping their hands for the occasional attack of mosquitoes, pushing people who were cutting their way in.

The smell of gasoline was more pronounced. The smog I couldn't see but I knew it was there.

Lamps were lit in every corner of the street. Fireflies circled the leaning electric poles. A whole gang of children selling eggs marched side by side, steadily, baskets on one hand, strings of bottled vinegar dip on the other, chasing after hungry drivers. My throat tightened at the thought of the preserved eggs that men melted into their tongues in the dark.

Why was Boy Spit still out?

Baluuuuuut. A chorus of children's voices.

"Take this side," he said. He was nervous, I could tell. He knew I was waiting for him to say something. Boys our age were usually not like this. Hearts usually didn't beat fast when we talked to each other.

"H-huh?" Hands usually didn't shake.

Get over here. Come. Touch. Push.

The touch was different. I was expecting roughness, splinter, raw wood. But the handle was clean, smooth, a newly polished dining table. Skin without bruises.

Push. Push. Down.

I pushed the handle of the cart. It was heavy, at least heavier than I thought. The cart was full. He must have been rolling this through the streets all day. Too full in fact, the newspapers didn't slide down to our side. The bottles didn't make clanging noises.

Our elbows touched. I quickly moved my arm away. He looked at me, surprised. I slapped my arm. "Mosquito."

He laughed. It was a young laugh. He was just my age, maybe a few years older. *Mosquitoes,* he repeated. He covered his mouth with three fingers. Mosquitoes, he yelled, then laughed again.

That was the laughter that grew up in the streets. That never went to school. Newspaper boys were schooled in the streets. *Educated about a life that all of you, even us older people, will never know about.* We were always warned about them. *Dirty little boys who know nothing but walk the streets for a buck.* And spit, I added, they all knew nothing but spit Juicy Fruit in the streets.

Juicy Fruit, he must have been chewing that all day.

"You have to gather all your strength to push this cart. Move away. I'll show you." His laughter lightened up his face.

I took a step back. I could feel my knees moving. How weak I was. How weak I had always been. And with Boy Spit, weaker.

"See?"

I wasn't paying attention. Under the lamp post light, his face got darker. A ghost would never look like him if it appeared. He was too dark. Perhaps darker than me.

The cart jerked forward. It was as big as a bed. I had seen children sleeping in it many times, using the bundles of newspapers as mattresses and pillows. The morning sun climbed the carts the way it did the houses here. It woke the children up the same way so they covered them with plywood at night, like a roof.

"There are three wheels under the cart. The one in the front you don't see."

"Three wheels."

"Come." He walked me to the front, throwing his hand to grab my wrist but ending up clutching the cool night air instead. He bent his back. He wasn't wearing a belt. His shorts, cut off, threadbare, must have been given to him, or something he found while milling around.

"I see that. Smaller than the other two," I managed to observe. Something I thought about before I said it.

"That's for directions. The middle wheel. That's how the cart turns."

His hair was long. Too long. It covered his ears and landed on his eyebrows. Longer than Pipo's. I could hardly see the scar on his forehead that I used to notice before. Maybe it was healed.

"Wanna push the cart with me?"

Again, I could feel my throat when I swallowed. I said yes to him. Mommy was probably looking for me already. I had not had dinner. The milkfish women were already walking the streets, with flat wicker baskets on their heads. In the air, the smell of food cooking from different houses.

When I looked back, the children had cleared.

"Come," he summoned me. For a minute, I wondered where. To the right was where I had always gone. The right, was it? He turned his cart around. Did I say it? Did he know that I had not turned and walked left of my house since what happened at Boy Manicure's?

We walked through the streets. I pushed the cart with him but I knew he was the one moving it forward. I couldn't look at him, afraid that if I did, a jeepney would hit me. Drivers screamed at him a couple of times but he didn't pay attention. The lights of the jeepneys were as colorful as their painted bodies. They were always packed with passengers. Always full, never hungry, was painted on one hood.

Putang-inang mga batang kalyeng 'to. ANO BA? I had never been cursed at by a jeepney driver in my life. I immediately ran to the other side of the cart, that of the sidewalk curb.

Boy Spit moved over and gave way. I could tell he was going to laugh.

"Sometimes I don't listen to traffic," he said instead. "They would never hit me, these drivers. If they did, I would probably escape without bruises. But they won't. Their passengers won't. So they don't touch us. They see us, they only scream. They yell. They curse. *Putang-ina,* but I don't pay attention." He could probably tell that I was so aware of everything around me. "Push. We're turning. Push the handle down, then to the left. That's it. You see?"

You see? I said to myself. You can do it.

We rolled past familiar surroundings. Past Aling Tina's tailor shop where there was another huge mannequin at the window. Past Mr. Chua's store where an old man made the best sugarcoated boiled yams and bananas in big see-through jars. Past D'MacArthur Bakery where the round breads had shrunk through the years and the price remained the same. Past the house that got caught in a fire and was never rebuilt. In the dark, they looked the same, except I could see more of what was behind the windows, shadows moving past curtains.

The color of paint might be different but in the other streets, houses all looked alike. Streets were the same narrow size as ours. Even the way children looked never really changed much. There were also big windows in houses. Always with faces on bent elbows watching endlessly on the sills, also staring at the moon perhaps, or the cats. Always the same voices of the night. The same smell of food. In every street corner, the familiar look of hang-around men playing chess or checkers and drinking San Miguel, different faces but the same old bubbly breath.

"You, you, upstairs, upstairs." A woman suddenly appeared at a window and started whistling at her children to go back into the house. *Ano ba?* I looked up at her. She was a fat woman with curly hair. Pssst-tsst. Mommy's whistle was better, clearer.

I didn't ask Boy Spit where we were going. I continued pushing the cart as if it would direct me where he wanted to go. The weight of the cart I could feel on my upper arms. My shoulders tensed the longer I pushed. I slowly learned that by leaning forward a little bit, pushing became easier to do. Boy Spit's posture proved that this was something he had been doing for some time. His swift jerks and turns. His watchful glances at whatever might get in his way. Because in the night, you never know when a black cat will run in your way.

The breath of night was all over us but it was his breathing that I paid attention to, almost not feeling my own. I could actually hear it, the quick sighs, the sniffing, the sneeze. I counted them, too. How can anyone sneeze four times? And not cover his nose?

Not once did he ever try to look at me again. He was shying away perhaps, noticing that I myself had not said much the whole time. And I knew boys weren't supposed to do this. If I were Big Boy Jun, my arms would be all over him. I would be punching him on his sides, squeezing his arms. I would be laughing, spitting all over his face, pulling and ripping his already holed T-shirt. Our eyes would lock many times, and I wouldn't give it any other meaning.

But I couldn't even look at him.

My feet against asphalt at night. I was beginning to feel the ground we were walking on, with the occasional pebbles getting caught in my slippers. My slippers flip-flopped on the ground as if they were ready to snap at any time. On the other hand, Boy Spit's slippers had safety pins fastening the torn rubber to each other. They looked like they were made for walking hours of endless streets.

"Look!" He startled me.

Suddenly, outside a narrow street, a wide opening. I could already tell there was something else there by the way the sudden quiet approached us. *Hurry.*

I pushed harder than I had been. We walked through empty lots. There weren't houses anymore. Just vacant spaces with tall aluminum fences and barbed wires covering them.

And there was grass. For a moment, you'd think they were people, constantly moving, a dance at night. Arms, fingers swaying. But that wasn't possible. It was too late in the night.

Railroad, I thought. So this was where it was.

"It's ten o'clock. Won't your mother look for you?"

Why would he ask that now? "No," I said. I knew she probably was but it was too late to worry about that. "Of course not." I wanted to be there, as if we were the only ones left in the world.

He stopped pushing the cart. I couldn't do it by myself so I stopped, too, and stood behind the handle. He walked toward the overgrowth of grass.

"Where are you going?" I didn't want to be left there alone.

"Come with me."

I followed him through a clearing. Walking on pebbles and stones is difficult, especially if you can't see much of what is there. It smelled of leaves all around us the farther we went. Boy Spit ripped a blade of grass and put it in his mouth.

"What is here?" I asked again. I couldn't seem to forget that we were walking farther away from where I lived. I never thought I would go this far and I had no idea where he was taking me.

He didn't answer me. The moonlight was a halo on his head. He continued walking as if he had been there before, and many times. He would not even stop for a minute and wonder where we were. Eventually, he found a trail of stones where grass was more cleared.

The surrounding grass was up to my waist, some even taller. I had heard of this place as a little child when old people in our street would talk about how our neighborhood was before the city was built. All grass, nothing more, they would say. Tall grass, taller than any one of you. And a scattering of huts. You could breathe, certainly you could, unlike now. There were ponds between the grass, little ones with tilapia and catfish swimming in them. We made our own food. I could see that now.

Grass here moved a certain way, producing some kind of sound that calmed me as I walked through it, even if the sharp leaves sometimes brushed against my skin. They were singing as we walked, a tune that only grass could make. There was always something about the sound of the night. Sometimes it was hard to tell where the sounds really came from. Insects, trees, wind, in unison.

Many stories were created about this place. The abandoned grass, it's called. Nobody ever lived here. This was where the first train station in the city used to be. People hid here during the war. Never go there, was the message I learned. Dangerous. But while walking, I wondered where the tracks were. I couldn't see anything but swaying grass. At night, the sounds they made were long conversations on curfew nights.

Above us, above everything here, the watchful eye of the moon, so huge, so round and bright you could see the scars on its face. Even the moon is not perfect, look at the signs of misery on its face, Ninang Rola used to say while she pointed at the moon. The stones we walked on glistened with the light. The tips of the grass sparkled as if it had recently rained.

Boy Spit finally stopped. He picked up a piece of wood he found on the tracks and began poking the ground with it.

"What are you doing?"

"Looking for something," he quickly responded, then he sat down when he found what he was looking for. "Come, see this."

There was long, rusty metal on the ground. "What?"

"Railroad tracks. Haven't you heard of this before?"

"Y-yes," I said and joined him by sitting down. The tracks snaked through the grass. Not much of it could be seen. Stones and soil piled over. Grass curled and covered.

Where I sat, I felt the roughness of rust. "How did you find this place?"

"I get around." He stood up and balanced himself on one track. "I know every corner of this city. I know everything that happens here."

I didn't say anything else. I picked up stones and tossed them into the grass one by one. With moonlight, I could see the little hairs on my legs. After all this waiting to be with Boy Spit, here I was sitting not knowing what to say. Up close, I realized he was slightly bigger than me. The signs of hard work were all over his limbs. Even at night, he smelled of the sun.

"Have you heard of the cave?" He broke the silence.

"The what?"

"Cave?"

"No. What cave?" I didn't know what he was talking about. There weren't caves in big cities. I was old enough to know that.

"Are you hungry?"

"No, not really." Although I could feel my stomach grumbling.

"I am. I haven't eaten all day."

He looked like he hardly ate at all.

"You want to see the cave?" he asked. "Maybe not?"

He made me nervous not knowing what he wanted to say. I looked away from him. He laughed quietly. He sat down beside me.

"You are all right, you know?"

I turned my face to look at him. He had a smile on. The wind was blowing his hair off his forehead. The long scar appeared. Three stitches above his eyebrows.

"You want to see the cave?" he asked again.

"I don't know what the cave is."

"It's very brave of you to come out so late in the night."

"What time is it?"

"An hour before curfew. You're sure nobody is looking for you?"

"Yes." How many times did he have to ask that?

"Are you afraid of time? Why do you ask when nobody cares where you are?"

"I just wanted to know what time it was because it's getting really dark. Besides, you keep on bringing up—"

"You're funny." He stood up on the rail and jumped to the ground.

I wasn't being funny. The fact was I was getting nervous

being in a place I had never been in before. And no, I wasn't particularly afraid of whether Mommy was looking for me or not. She was probably in bed already, unmindful that I was missing in the bedroom.

"You're also very quiet."

So he noticed. He came closer to me. He looked at my face, so near I couldn't look at him. He giggled like a little child then covered his mouth. The wind blew his hair back to cover his forehead again.

"Let me leave the cart here, go home. Then we'll go to the cave."

The cave. "Sure," I answered.

He pulled my wrist. *Hurry.*

I looked behind us. Where the cart stood under the shadow of the tree it almost completely disappeared. "Nobody will take your cart?" I asked, when I was really worried about myself. I had been warned about that place since I was very young. The slums. Never go there. *Peligroso.* A bite of a rat, soiled and smelly. I could hear echoes of older voices, life-old warnings.

"No, it will be safe there."

Way past the gathering of grass, we sauntered through darkness toward an area with twinkling lights ahead of us. His grasp on my wrist was reassuring. He pointed to where he lived. I gulped.

"People there are nice, most outsiders wouldn't think that," was Boy Spit's response to my silence. "You get used to the smell."

The images slowly became apparent the closer we went. Already, I could tell the houses weren't like ours. They were very low, cardboard, and roofed by aluminum siding that Mommy used to dry our white clothes on. They were shoe boxes, just dropped to stay permanently where they landed, jutting out unevenly. At least our houses were neatly lined up.

The doors didn't particularly face the makeshift street. Up close, I could tell that most of the houses didn't even have doors. If you could call them doors, most of them being pieces of plywood leaning on human-size holes.

The whole area was damp and dark and bristled with noise. Light came from low trees, guava trees turned into lamp poles. There was no curfew here, I thought. Nobody's afraid here. There were men playing bingo with twisted bottlecaps, lit by burning wood beside them. They were a dirtier version of the *sangganos* where I lived, their shirts rolled up above their stomach. Women, with dormant babies tied around their backs, were hanging clothes on lines that webbed the entire area.

I felt as if they were all watching me, even if they didn't pay us any mind.

The ground was browned by soft soil, pebbles, and a cluttering of garbage. Puddles were like huge marble holes decorating the whole landscape. Right through the area were crisscrossing wood planks dumped there for walking. The man-made street sloped downward.

I kept on holding my breath. The odor was unexplainable. When I looked around, I could smell each image that I saw: rotting food, piles of month-old garbage, the schools of flies. It felt as if we were in the middle of a giant sewer. I could smell the mosquitoes coming toward us. I could smell everybody's stinking breath each time I looked at their faces.

"This third one," he said. Boy Spit pointed to the shanty that was the smallest of the row. "I made that myself," he proudly added.

It didn't look like it was something made by somebody his age.

"After years of selling newspapers, I was able to buy the concrete blocks I used for the walls. Cement is expensive. Those tires on the roof, I found them. They threw them, these jeepney drivers. But not bad, right?" He looked back. I wasn't paying attention. I was wondering how anyone could get in.

"Watch your step." The plank he walked on suddenly slipped, exposing a deep trench underneath. "I know it's dark but you have to make sure you're stepping on something solid. Come, let me hold you."

He took my wrist again. I followed wherever he stepped. Mosquitoes buzzed around us.

"Hey you, you idiot. Go to bed," yelled one of the drunkards playing bingo. "Idiot. Boy Idiot."

Boy Idiot? Boy Spit. I began to wonder again what his real name was.

"Shut up, you fuck!" He gave the man the finger. Then he said to me in a low voice, "Those bastards, they always pick on boys like me. I don't give them the time of day." His grasp on my wrist tightened. Across the plank, he said, "Turn left."

Left. Not the third shanty. The fifth one, in fact.

"I thought it was that?" I pointed to the *third* shanty.

"Those first two don't count. Can't you tell they don't count by the way they look?"

They were all the same shape, I thought, they all looked alike. Although I wondered about what he meant, I believed him.

He pulled aside the big plywood board that covered the door of his house. "In." I took two steps up the block of stones outside.

I was the first one to sit. Maybe he asked me to do that, I couldn't really tell. I knew that I was sitting on hard cement when I thought there would be planks. A gas lamp sat in the corner where there were piles of aluminum plates. He faced me when he sat down. "Are you okay?"

Curious was what I was. I had forgotten about time. About where I came from. As small as the space was, I felt there was much room to breathe. It felt safe inside, even if I knew everything around us could mean danger, judging by their odor.

He had calendars all over the walls, thumbtacked and neatly distributed.

"Those? I got those from a store on your street. Tarina All-Around. What do you think? Nice, huh? I put them there myself. That one I liked most, Donalduck. Funny, huh? I built this myself." He spread his arms. "Took me a while but you know, if you try hard enough . . ."

Are you okay? he asked again, noticing my silence. But my eyes were talking, if he didn't know, observing everything in this space. The little gas stove in the corner. Pots of different sizes. One for rice, I could tell, with burnt rice stuck on the side. Plastic drinking glass. There was no bed, no pillows. A reed mat was rolled, standing and leaning against the wall. One small chair, handmade, put together by strings. And in one corner, the darkest side, a luggage, a big one, enough to fit him in.

When I finally noticed him again, he was sitting beside me handing me food from his hands. His cheeks ballooned with whatever he put in there. Fish, it smelled of. He dug something out of the rice pot.

"Milkfish?" he offered. "I liked this cooked, burnt. But at night, who can tell? You want?"

No, I shook my head. Although I was hungry minutes before then. "A lot of little bones. Hard to eat at night."

"After a while, you eat them, too, the bones. Know that?"

Milkfish, of course, was my favorite fish. He ate it in chunks, pulling bones from his mouth every second, but swallowing most of them. He alternated fish and rice, cold rice as hard as little stones. He rolled them in his hands into his mouth, almost not chewing.

"You always eat with your hands?"

He laughed, spitting bits of rice all over me. I didn't wipe my face. I only stared at him.

"I really like you. You're funny," he said with a mouthful of soft laughs. "I think we must go to the cave."

He likes me, I thought. His saying that made me smile.

He got up and dangled the pot into the corner of the room. He poured water that he kept in a plastic container into it. Then he washed his face. He picked up a towel hanging on a nail on his way back to me, dabbing his face dry.

"Curfew." He leaned over.

"What?'

"Curfew, it's curfew now."

I stood up. I had never seen curfew. How does one know?

"Let's go." He walked toward the door and slowly pushed at the wood leaning across. He provided a hole wide enough for both of us to go through.

Outside, as if so many hours had passed, it was empty, quiet. The drunkards were gone. And the woman hanging clothes. Air was swiftly pushing the clothesline. A garbage basket was rolling on the ground. Chairs were toppled where the drunkards once were. And everywhere, the feel of curfew was strange. So this is it, I said to myself. Darkness. Silence. But not as frightening as what people had made it out to be.

"Sometimes police cars drive around. You know, arrest anybody who's out in the streets. We're so used to them. Here, we break all rules." Boy Spit seemed to be reading my mind. "You look like you have never been out at this time of the night by the way you hold yourself like that."

I didn't notice what I was doing. Quickly looking at myself, I realized my hands were crossed and my legs knocked against each other while I walked.

"Funny." He shook his head and rubbed his hair.

It wasn't hard to get out of the slums. His house was so close to the entrance. There were cement pipes piled up where the first shanty was. And when I turned back, I counted five, five shanties, even if for him two of them didn't count. I remembered the fifth one was his.

"Always remember, mine is the third." He reminded me while he grabbed my wrist again and pulled me out. He held me the whole time, swinging my arm every now and then.

Soon we were back in the grass. The moon had climbed up the sky so high, it completely lit the place. I was thinking of the cave. How caves would look like without mountains, without rock formations, rivers, and tall, old, weblike trees.

The wind of curfew enveloped us. This was what we were all warned about. Don't go out. Go to sleep. Don't even look out the window. Curfew *na*. Curfew *na*. But there was nothing there but silence. Deep inside, I knew silence had so much to hide. Was there more to this than what I could see with my own eyes?

"Slow down," he whispered. "We're not very far."

I walked so carefully that I could feel my own feet breaking stalks of grass. My legs were gaining strength. My pace was steady, and unafraid. All I was thinking about was curfew, of how I had broken the rule but somehow felt so safe.

"Down." Boy Spit suddenly ducked and motioned me to do the same. We hadn't gone very far. In fact, we had passed this place earlier. There weren't any caves in sight.

He slouched, pressing his finger over his lips to keep me quiet. I had not said anything the whole time. By doing that, he was keeping himself from saying anything else. "Listen . . ."

"To what?" I whispered as well. I could hear the cracking of grass and soil underfoot, the sound of the night I had noticed earlier, but there was nothing else.

Then he started to walk sitting down. I wanted to walk

on fours but I soon realized it wasn't the thing to do considering the sharpness of grass.

"Try to minimize noise." He hushed me when I almost slipped over a big stone.

Another kind of noise became apparent. The same kind of noise we made walking through grass except we were not doing it, because we were just sitting there for a while.

"We're here."

"The cave?"

He pointed to our front. At first, I didn't see anything but grass. But the more I focused, the more I noticed colors forming behind them. Clothes moving. There were other people there.

We walked a little closer. Voices tumbled in the air, not conversations, but quick repetitive sounds.

"Come. This is where I always go. Come. Here we can see clearly."

I followed him. Where he went he found a piece of wood. He handed it to me and gestured me to kneel on it. He got one for himself. It wasn't until I saw him doing it that I knelt down myself.

He took my hand again, which I willingly accepted by pressing my fingers on his palms.

"Look," he whispered, "do you see?" There was an opening in the middle where very tall grass was arching over making it look like a cave, huge and bending. I slowly moved between stalks trying to get a good glimpse of the people there. The more I stared, the clearer the images became.

There was a circle joined together by arms. It was hard

to recognize faces but after a while, I could tell they were all boys, older than me but not by much. Their backs were bare. Shadows followed the ribbed contours of their bodies. Their belts unbuckled. Pants almost down. They were circling this one boy in the middle who was absorbing all the attention around him. I couldn't see him very well. They were all the same height, it was hard to see each individual face. Cautiously they started to spread apart in twos, threes. The boy in the middle remained with whoever stayed with him.

Boy Spit looked at me and tightened his grasp. I knelt hard as rock, my heart beating so fast. I didn't let go of his hand. I felt warmth inside me, something that I knew was coming from his having constantly held me. I wanted to keep it in there though there was another feeling I couldn't understand. Fear, perhaps, but not of being caught by police cars patrolling the streets. Somehow I knew I would get back home. Boy Spit would find our way back. It was the fear of what I was seeing, of what the moon was slowly revealing with its light by moving each blade of grass apart so I could see more every minute that I stared into them. These faces, one by one, unfamiliar ones. It's curfew, how could they all be out? Why did they choose to come here? Thoughts ran through my mind. I thought how when no one was allowed to leave their houses, something like this could happen. While I had broken the rule just now, they had probably done it many times.

The boy in the middle.

The curfew moon climbed the sky, lighting the cave. The other boys came together again, holding him tightly.

Lips were meeting lips. Hands joining. Giggles. They all seemed to know how to move parts of their bodies, although they looked young. The sensation I felt was unfamiliar and I wanted to feel it more. The boy in the middle lifted his face to stare at the moon. His face was as bright as the many years I had stared into it. I couldn't help but wonder how he managed to get there, and why after everything that had happened to him, he would do this. He had broken many rules but this one he had kept so well. I nervously took Boy Spit's hands and wrapped them with mine. "Gringo," Boy Spit said quietly into my ear, "isn't that Pipo?"

SUNRISE, SUNSET

The lamp post in the corner shed its light.

I covered my face and looked through my fingers, hearing the loudness of the siren noise more when my palm touched my face. The red brightness circled and peeled the darkness around it. Doors and gates opened, footsteps thumped on the asphalt street. Bathrobes and nightgowns swished. Flashlights jumped all over. Lights were turned on in every house. More noise stepped out of houses, saying the same things over and over again.

All ran to the same direction, to the left from where I stood.

"Gringo." I heard Mommy's call. I paused and decided for a moment against following the crowd. *Gringo, come back in here.* I had not walked that part of our street for such a long time. As soon as I heard his name mentioned again, I slowly walked out of our gate. "You listen to me, get back here!" Mommy called again but I continued walking, leaving the door ajar, leaving her.

The air of curfew drifted past my face. That kind of air that we only wished for as children during the early nights of brownouts while telling ghost stories to each other. But no ghosts here, not when the police were around. Outside were recently opened eyes and the smell of mouths at twilight. All as restless as they could get. Worried, even. Not so much for what had happened but for what could happen to them.

Arms tightened, I pushed myself through a small opening to get to the front of the crowd. Whatever it was that compelled me to do this hit my face as soon as I saw myself standing in front of Boy Manicure's house again. The strange feel of the night crawled on my skin. Rubbing my palms against my arms again and again didn't do me any good.

The police were getting ready to cordon off the beauty parlor at the sight of people slowly crowding around their big police cars parked in the middle of our street. They never came to our street for any other reason than to pick up Sgt. Dimaculangan across from our house during the day. I had often observed them from a distance, especially the way they carried themselves as if nobody could ever hurt them. At night, sirens had occasionally lingered about but never stopped here. Nothing serious here to make them come.

"Hey you, get off!" one policeman shouted. Children

climbing the hood to get a better view of the house. On the roof, they were higher than everyone else.

Quick swing of flashlights striped their faces.

Fat Boy Max quickly slid down the hood, falling knee first on the ground. He quickly ran away. Another boy followed him, jumping on the hood and leaving a dent on it. *Ay putang bata,* said one neighbor. The cursed boy also rapidly took off when the policeman tried to chase him. Both of the boys disappeared in the night. Or so the police thought. They cluttered the guava trees not so far away, arms around thick branches.

The door was open, jambs fallen.

I could see furniture turned over, picture frames tilting on one side, the aquarium broken. The policemen were walking inside and trying to avoid stepping on the broken glass; the others were pushing us out as our curiosity pulled us closer to the house. The fish were nowhere in the aquarium. The window looked like someone had jumped through it and left it to look like an open mouth of a big fish with hungry sharp teeth. Its sharpness, broken in big and small pieces, was visible on the ground and all over the floor inside the house, deflecting the brightness of the siren light. I was pushed closer to his house. The smell of acetone and nail polish escaped from inside.

It must have begun with what our neighbors said.

They filled the little space in front of me, blocking my view. A red shirt. Burnt skin. Dial soap. Long hair with lice. A curious old woman whom I had always seen walking in the procession in a black dress. "*Dios ko, Dios ko,* what happened?" I was quickly pushed to the back but I managed to stumble my way back to the front again.

"My God! Death," the woman in black screamed again. "Death has fallen."

"Is he dead?" I heard a man chuckle. "Is he dead?"

Is he dead? I asked myself. What was so funny about someone's death? I looked around. The siren light took snapshots of everybody's face. Some were looking into the beauty parlor, searching for something, or someone. Some might have already found what they were looking for by the way they focused their eyes on something without blinking.

I could tell by watching their lips, they didn't have the taste of fear.

"What's that?" I saw a finger pointing over my ears, brushing my hair slightly. I tilted my head to the left.

"Can you see anything? Anything at all?" said one voice.

"It's red all over the walls." I heard another sleepy voice.

"Stupid. That's the siren light," interjected another. Quickly, giggles and curses.

"It's the spirit of your mother begging for food." A joke howled at the moon.

"No. It's manicure painted all over the wall," another voice giggled.

"Be quiet, all of you," scolded the elderly Mrs.-from-across-the-street. She looked very old in an embroidered white blanket that she lifted so it wouldn't touch the ground. She stood where the lamp post lit the ground

The neighbors hushed not because of her but because Sgt. Dimaculangan was coming from inside. Eyes rushed to him. Voices were left where I stood still, landing on my skin like blood-starved mosquitoes. His nameplate glistened and hurt my eyes.

The police pushed the people back farther with their clubs. I began to sink into the crowd again.

"Don't push yourselves here," shouted one policeman standing in front of Boy Manicure's house. The broken blue beauty parlor sign swung above him. The edge touched his head. He shook his hand over his head, accidentally pulling the sign off, showering himself with bits of cement and nails. I heard quiet laughter again. The blue sign bounced on the ground, landing at the foot of the Mrs.-from-across-the-street.

BOY'S BEAUTY PARLOR, MANICURE, PEDICURE, HAIR.

"Make way. Make way," the policemen ordered everybody. The ambulance stopped. The emergency men came out from the back and went into the house with a stretcher. We were pushed farther back for the ambulance to park. Children climbed the police cars again. I fell on the ground. All I could see were legs with nowhere to go. I crawled my way out of the crowd. The rough asphalt scratched my knees. After rubbing it a few times I saw a thin streak of blood on my palms. I stood up and wiped my hands on my shirt and continued watching from the sides.

"Oh my God. What's that for?" someone screamed.

"Calm down, everybody, please calm down." Sgt. Dimaculangan raised his hands. He wiped his forehead with the back of his wrist. He looked dignified in his uniform, although he couldn't hide the fact that he was nervous. Sweat glistened on his cheeks. His long sleeves were wet. "The beauty parlor was robbed tonight and—" He hesitated to say it but it seemed as if we all knew what he was about to say. He looked around, spreading his arms then putting his hands together again.

Calming down meant whispering questions, stating one's curiosity in low voices. Around me I heard people say that they were awakened by the sound of shattering glass, that the police were called too late to do anything, that they heard the sound but didn't have a telephone to call, that whoever was responsible for this incident must have gotten away already.

A hand lightly fell on my shoulder.

"Gringo, Gringo, what's wrong here?" Sergio Putita asked nervously, holding on to the edges of his thick bathrobe. He lived in the farthest corner of our street.

"I don't know. I'm not sure. He's *dead.*"

"Dead?" Sergio Putita looked at me.

I said it so well. Dead. Dead. Boy Manicure is dead. Maybe it was what I wanted.

"How can this happen at curfew?" asked a woman who was carrying a bag. Everybody swallowed her question realizing that it *was* still curfew and we were all out. I looked at her. It was English-speaking Titay's mother. "These things are not supposed to happen at curfew."

"I've never seen so many people out at this time," Sergio Putita whispered in my ear. Then he waved hesitantly at English-speaking Titay when she looked over to us.

Curfew is not what you think, I whispered. The thought of the railroad came back to me. Curfew was supposed to keep most of us inside our houses at night, to send the children to bed early. All crimes were committed indoors. Hushed at midnight. And outdoors, at the railroad, curfew came in the shape of a full moon over boys touching each other.

A bright eye, watching, always watching, like our window during the day.

"Have you ever been in there?" asked Sergio Putita.

I looked at him, catching a glimpse of Pipo on the other side. Mommy was there, one arm bracing herself, the other covering her mouth, exactly how I imagined she would look like. Pipo was just staring, arms on his sides. His face was awake but without expression. He was only slightly lit, for they stood in the dimmest part of the street.

"Common sense," one woman said. "It is common sense that he's dead. This is exactly what God wishes for people like him."

"Don't play with God. This is what happens when you play with God."

"You're absolutely right. *Nasa Biblia 'yan.*" All of it, in the Bible, another one commented.

The minutes of mumbling carried Boy Manicure out of his house. A piece of thin white linen outlined his body with spots of blood all over it. I could see the shape of his face through the sheet. The same face that had frightened everyone for so long didn't do anything less at this moment.

"Blood. Blood," someone screamed from behind me.

Sangre, I thought. "Blood meant death," someone responded to my mind. And death was dripping on both sides of the stretcher where his arms were. There was too much of it. It seemed to be coming from different parts of his body. Night flies hovered over him, following him out.

I bit my jaw when I saw him. I could hear his voice.

A woman began to throw up behind me. I moved away so she wouldn't splatter all over my back. The crowd where I stood followed the emergency men. I covered my eyes again and looked through my fingers. My hands started to shake. My heart was exploding right through my chest. I had never seen death so close. I couldn't imagine him dying like this. I thought about punishment. Maybe our neighbors were right. Maybe he did deserve it.

"Oh my, *Dios mío*. Oh my, *Dios mío,*" Sergio Putita panicked, covering his face. "I can't stand this." He pushed his way to the back.

"What are you doing?" a man yelled at him.

"Blood. There's blood," Sergio Putita answered back.

The emergency men opened the back door of the ambulance and carefully carried the stretcher into the big car. Inside were women in white. One woman looked pale as if she had just awakened from a long nap. Her eyes found their way to me; they glistened in the redness of the siren light. And the door of the car closed in front of them. Roaring noises broke out as soon as the ambulance drove away. The younger people chased the ambulance. Others stood still, waited, then started bursting forth with comments they had held inside.

"Go home. All of you, go back. Tomorrow, we'll tell you what happened," Sgt. Dimaculangan announced. His voice of authority stopped everyone from talking for a few seconds.

"Sergeant, what happened here? What happened here? Is he really dead?"

"Sergeant, you have to tell us now. We can't just go home not knowing what happened. Is there a killer on the loose? Are we safe?"

How could anyone ask that question? Only birds felt safe in this city. Only because they could easily fly away.

Then everybody screamed again. I stood there while people ran back to their houses in panic. Men and women tripped all over the streets. Sleepy little children were pulled away from the crowd. One drunkard was singing while he staggered and bumped into people. Another man punched his face, throwing him to the ground. He slumped and crawled.

Mommy came toward me, clutched my wrist as soon as she got close enough. "There you are. You should never separate from us on times like this." Then she pulled me home, holding Pipo with her other hand, who had grown almost as tall as she. Even their shadows at night were of the same length. "Why are you so interested in all this?"

I only looked at her. Maybe my eyes could tell her what she should have known a long time ago, then she wouldn't have to ask questions like that. "Go inside," Mommy ordered, locking the iron grill gate behind her. "Both of you."

Mommy walked in. Pipo and I followed. As soon as we got in, our eyes crossed. The expression on his face, it was familiar, fearful. We stopped there and for the longest time looked at each other. I could tell how afraid he was, those same watery eyes when Daddy Groovie was about to hit him with his *yantok*. The eyes that spoke, "No . . . stop." The same trembling lips like when Daddy Groovie was leaving at the airport and he was trying to say something but could not. He turned his head in the dimly lit room. He shivered as he walked away. I wanted to run and hold him. But that was something I had never been taught to do. I had seen people hold each other in the movies but I never knew how to do that for Pipo. We never held each other; we never knew what that meant. So slowly he approached the stairs, the same walk when he left Boy Manicure's house, legs apart as if torn, head bowed. I stood there listening to his footsteps on the stairs, very slowly, each minute recounting what happened in the bathroom that one summer night.

The sounds of animals were all over.

Six o'clock roosters crowed endlessly while digging dirt, dogs barked at every house and ran around in circles as if trying to catch their tails, stray cats leapt over the rooftops, chasing after each other, scratching the aluminum gutters, jumping to the trees down to the street, and soon rubbing themselves against strangers around, only to be kicked away, and birds, hundreds of them, above us, fled in droves.

"Where are you going now?" Mommy saw me walking

out the door. From the corner of my eyes, I saw her morning figure: an old sundress, a bucket of Sunday laundry and wooden clogs. "Come back here."

"I'll be back," was all I could say. I didn't know why she was concerned, or why it mattered to her. With all the time she spent washing clothes and cleaning, how would she know what was happening around her?

Police cars arrived in our street late morning. Some of them stopped in front of Boy Manicure's beauty parlor. The others drove through our street over and over again.

Faces were everywhere. Our street was jammed with the traffic of curious feet. Older women with older women. Drunkards with their beer drinking friends, who weren't drinking now. Children with children. Men carried their cockfighters and blew out smoke to the cocks' faces while they listened to the talk.

"Do you know this person?" one tall and big policeman asked a woman beside him, while he took out his notebook and prepared to write notes. I knew where she lived but I didn't know who she was. Many times people who lived in our street identified each other by the number at the top of their doors. It was a good idea but I could never remember their numbers, either. I could only remember the colors of their doors.

Everybody circled around them. I stood between an old man and another man who was slightly younger but just as tall. I didn't know who they were but somehow I saw a red and peeling yellow door by looking at them.

"Yes. Of course. Everybody here knows him. Right?" The

woman being asked looked at everyone, even me, trying to gain approval. When they all nodded, she continued, "He doesn't have enemies here. Don't even think about it. People in this street are very friendly people. You can ask Sgt. Dimaculangan. We are all friendly people. We wouldn't harm a fly."

Flies were very hard to harm, I thought. They always came in swarms.

"Nobody here can possibly kill him. No one—" She put her arms around herself.

"Mrs. . . . ?" the policeman interrupted.

"DelMundo. Corazon DelMundo." She lay her arms on her belly, which protruded out of her light green gabardine pants. She didn't seem to care even if an unbuttoned part of her blouse showed off her navel.

"Mrs. DelMundo, I wasn't putting anyone here on trial. I only wanted to find out if you knew him." The policeman moved his hands while explaining himself. He gave off the smell of Brut pomade, like the bill collectors that came here at noon.

"*Shempre.*" Of course, Mrs. DelMundo said again, her voice so coarse it matched the unironed blouse that was clinging to her body. "Like I said, everybody here knew him. Who wouldn't . . ."

The people around looked at each other, finishing her sentence in their minds, controlling the laughter that was about to burst through the fingers over their mouths.

"Nobody here hates him, let's put it that way." A man joined in the conversation, putting his arm around Mrs. DelMundo.

"You are—what's your name?" the policeman asked the man, ready to write his name on his notebook.

"Mr. DelMundo from the corner of the street," he said in a very boastful manner. I already knew what he was going to say next. Mrs. DelMundo gave her husband warning looks to shut him up. But once again, everybody nodded in unison. The husband rubbed his hands on his wife's back. The bones on her back were like two pieces of square stones. I finally remembered who they were. I had seen them around. The couple was from the faint yellow house across Tarina All-Around store. They always had Virgen Maria in their house especially when they couldn't find anyone to house her. She gave us crackers with little bits of omelet after the recitation of the rosary. Their house, like many people's, was decorated around their religion. They themselves were walking statues of saints.

"They'll never find out who did this, huh?" The man in yellow started talking again. Little folds drooped down his cheeks.

"I'd heard about the nightclubs for people like him," remarked Mr. Sing-sing from Tarina All-Around.

"What about those nightclubs, Mr. Sing-sing?" asked a woman who was carrying a child. She pulled her child up and rested the child's head on her shoulder.

"Well, that's where people like Boy Manicure go," Mr. Sing-sing responded, lighting up a Marlboro cigarette. He continued talking while smoke came out of his mouth, then out of his nose. He spoke like he had a bad cold.

"What's that got to do with what happened last night?"

asked the woman. Her child began pulling her hair. The woman slapped the child's face and pushed her head down on her shoulders with her hand. The child stared at me.

"You see, you don't know the whereabouts of Boy Manicure. That's what I'm saying," Mr. Sing-sing continued. "He could have owed someone money and the person came to collect, or it could be one of those, you know, take-care-of hustlers."

"Take-care-of *what*?" Mr. DelMundo asked. "How do you know about this anyway, Mr. Sing-sing? Sounds like you're talking from personal experience, huh?"

"Hey!" Mr. Sing-sing retorted, clutching his fist, ready to punch Mr. DelMundo.

I stepped back when I saw him roll up his sleeves. The man in yellow put his finger between his lips and whistled. Another cheered. I moved farther back.

"I bet a hundred for Mr. Sing-sing," shouted the man in yellow.

"One-fifty for Mr. DelMundo," shouted another man.

These were things they would say if this were a cockfight. Betting on their cocks while blowing smoke on their beaks. They would scream amounts of money that they didn't have.

The restless child who was staring at me lifted her head up and shook her head and wiggled her hair. Her mother slapped her face again.

"Stop this. Stop this nonsense." Mrs. DelMundo pulled her husband's arm away. "You stupid bastards! This is no time for play."

Mr. Sing-sing started to punch the air around him, like

a boxer in a ring. He was a very thin old man that looked like he was about to fall apart just by stretching his arms like that.

"O, O, Mr. Sing-sing is ready," the man in yellow hooted. They all laughed at the sight of Mr. Sing-sing rotating where he stood, still punching air and puffing smoke. "He's going to prove that he's a real man."

Real man. Real man. I heard him in Daddy Groovie's voice. Those words cracked in my ears like the lightning above us. The men bowed their heads and covered their ears. Everybody looked up. I saw lightning being eaten by the clouds and slowly disappearing. The clouds were very heavy, so heavy that I could feel it inside me, weighing me down. *Real man.* I swallowed spit when I left them. They were exactly as I expected them to be. All of them, the men of our street. They would say anything to assert their manhood, anything to show the thickness of their skin.

The sounds of animals were all over, and the voices of these men, I couldn't tell them apart.

And the women? Their voices, how would they be?

I turned around and followed the woman with a child going to a group of women who were starting to gather in another corner. The child waved at me, snot dripping from her nose. She poked her fingers into it.

There were fewer people outside. I could still sense eyes watching from the windows. If they weren't outside, people would be hushed inside, listening intently, watching restlessly.

Silence was beginning to take over the streets again.

"O, Gringo?" one of the women saw me and greeted. "Your mother home?"

"Yes," I said. "She's doing laundry."

"Your mother is always working," said the elderly Mrs.-from-across-the-street. In the light, she seemed older, the lines all over her body cast thin shadows. She was holding a closed umbrella, ready for the rain. She said something else to me but I had already lent my ears to the other older woman who was talking.

"But you know that his hands were chopped off," said the other older woman with big breasts that covered her stomach and flabby arms that looked like they were glued to the sides of her body. Her one arm was as thick as my thigh. "I can't imagine how that was done to him. I can't imagine. How can you chop off somebody's wrist? Was he drugged before it happened? We didn't hear any screams."

"That's because you live so far away," was someone's answer.

"How about his neighbors, did they hear anything?" asked the older woman.

"Not screams. They heard shattering glass. That's when someone called the police," said another woman in the group.

"Ayyy. *Imposible.* Somebody could have helped him. He must have screamed," said the Mrs.-from-across-the-street, covering her face with her shaking hands.

"Teodora, people scream in this street all the time, you never come to help. Oh, there's Lourdes. Aling Lourdes!

Aling Lourdes, come here and join us." The old woman started waving at Aling Lourdes.

Aling Lourdes lived right across from Boy Manicure's beauty parlor. She was thin and looked very mean, so I never said a word to her. I moved away when she stood beside me. She seemed very disturbed. Her eyes sagged.

"Oy, Oy?" Her voice was coming from her nose.

"Aling Lourdes, tell them you didn't hear any screams last night. Tell them."

Aling Lourdes started to wipe her eyes. The woman beside her put her arms around her shoulders. "I have been thinking a lot about this now. I think I *did* hear screams last night. I thought I didn't. I have lived across from Boy Manicure's for years. That *bakla* has been screaming all his life. I didn't think of it as anything."

I quivered when I heard what she said. That *bakla* has been screaming all his life, echoed in my ears.

"You heard screams?" another woman asked her.

"I—I think so but . . . but would you do anything if you were me?"

"No. But you know in the old days, they used to do that, cut fingers of thieves and all that. Or heads even. Wrists I don't know. I never heard of such a thing."

"But it's the seventies. This doesn't happen in the seventies. Too modern, the people around, and Martial Law?"

"Well, somebody must hate him much to do that. What do you think?"

"I don't hate him," said another woman who was quiet

for a while. My head was getting dizzy from looking at each one of them speaking.

"I don't either," the older woman said. "People lead certain lives. They pay for the lives they lead. I'm sure Boy Manicure paid for his."

"Did they find his . . . his hands?"

"I don't know. I heard they were missing. That's really disgusting. Really disgusting. What would they do with his hands?"

"Pray to God. God will save us."

Hands. Blood. God. The women wove those words together, the same way they hung their clothes on the lines. Mixing words like shirts of different colors, inseparable. Exactly the way they laid them out to dry on corrugated aluminum. The way they went to church every Sunday, veiled with holiness, only to come home screaming in the Spanish curses nobody could understand. I thought of umbrellas, how these women carried them in both rain and sun, always finding ways to cover themselves. The more I listened, the more I understood what had happened to Boy Manicure.

The heaviness of the sky walked me out of our street. I had long memorized how to get to the railroad. The signs were all there to lead me. The voices of our neighbors followed me. When I found the footpath, I sat on the rails. I put my fingers on it but it didn't seem warm the way it usually was. Above me, the skies were crowned by thick clouds, with very dark edges, moving very fast, light specks here and there.

The grass was swaying in different directions. The wind seemed to be screaming. Everything was angry.

I stood up again and walked on the rail. I heard a sound not far away. I looked around but all I could see were grass and skies and the blurry facade of slums.

The sound continued from behind. I decided to walk there. I picked up a few stones from the ground in case the sound turned out to be a wild dog. I tiptoed to the source of the sound.

"Sergio Putita?" I recognized his back.

His head was on his knees, his arms wrapped around his head. I could see his shoulders making little movements while he sobbed.

"What happened?" I asked again. I knelt in front of him. The pebbles were sharp, so I decided to squat.

He raised his head. He had bruises all over his face. There were lumps on his jaws. "Somebody hit you?"

"Can't you tell?"

"What happened?" All my life I had not asked that question when I saw a bruised face. I always knew what had happened. But I had never seen or heard of Sergio Putita being hurt by anyone.

"My father," he wiped his nose, "he beat me."

Father, I thought. "Why?"

"Well, he said that I would turn out to be like Boy Manicure if I didn't start changing now. He burned everything I had, then started beating me up." He began to sob again, much louder though, pushing his nose to his knees. The wind ruffled his hair.

I knelt on the ground. The pebbles scratched my knees

but I didn't move. I just watched him, wanting to touch his head, to hold him, to talk to him in ways I never did with my own brother. "I'm sorry that he hurt you. He didn't have to do this to you."

"I'm scared," he cried. His voice rasped, slipping out of his arms. He wouldn't lift his head.

"It's scary in our street," I said shakingly. "So many people around watching, everybody saying that they knew nothing about what happened. They said they all liked Boy Manicure but nobody liked him, I know. Not any one of them."

He raised his head and wiped his eyes. "I don't know what Boy Manicure has done to them. They kept on talking about how God did this and that. This is his way of teaching us a lesson."

By getting someone killed, I thought. I swallowed air and spit when I looked at his face, his punished face.

"Papa said the same to me. He even read from the Bible in front of my face. He said someday someone will cut my wrists, too. He was very angry especially when I told him this is the way I am. Gringo, what does he think I can do?"

I held my wrists at the thought. I stopped listening to him. Our neighbors. They could have heard Boy Manicure screaming but they never came. He could have screamed when his wrists were being cut off. They just listened.

Sergio Putita stopped sobbing and looked at me. "The police came to our house today," he said. "They asked if I had ever been to Boy Manicure's."

"W-why?" I could feel air getting caught in my throat, water in my eyes. "Why?"

"They just wanted to know if I had been going there before he was killed."

"What do you mean?"

"I don't know. I didn't understand them. They talked to my father. And when they left, my father just started pulling my hair and throwing me all over the floor."

"Have you been there?"

"No. What would I do there?" He started to cry again.

I stood up nervously. "When did the police go to your house?"

"J-just right before I came here," he answered.

"Pipo," I whispered to myself. I could feel my knees weakening as I slowly walked away from Sergio Putita. "Pipo—"

"Where are you going? Where are you going?"

I didn't answer him. I felt a sprinkle of rain on my head. I looked up. Lightning divided the sky like a huge white root that suddenly appeared above us. The wind rapidly pushed the heavy dark clouds.

"GRINGO—"

I walked on the footpath, ignoring Sergio Putita's call, forgetting that he was still sitting on the rail. I didn't look back at him. From afar, I could see that it was already raining on the other side, slowly coming toward me. I cupped my palms and continued walking, getting closer to the rain. Soon it drummed on my shoulders, on my legs, circled my feet, filled and splattered over my cupped palms. Mud began to form on the ground. My slippers sank.

I let the earth pull me in.

Boy Manicure's death frightened me. I wondered if

Sergio Putita's father was right. Would he grow up and be killed, too? Would Pipo? Would I? Did Boy Manicure get what he deserved, like what the neighbors said? When I saw his blood all over the stretcher, I thought of Pipo, his blood on the floor in the bathroom. Maybe it was punishment for what he did to my brother. Was he killed because of what he did or was it because of who he was? Was he killed because nobody liked him? I remembered when children used to make fun of Pipo and call him the same names they called Boy Manicure. Would they do the same thing to Pipo?

Lightning struck like an angry thought, quick and violent. It poured even harder.

It would have been better if it rained when Boy Manicure got killed. That way people could say they didn't hear anything and it would be believable. I imagined him sitting on his sofa. He could have just finished feeding his fish, naked, the way I saw him last. He could have been putting fish bones in cat bowls. Or maybe he was lying on his bed, waiting for curfew with eyes open. And that was when a man walked into his house, maybe from the back patio. Boy Manicure could have heard the noise and gone downstairs. The lights were off but the lamp post from outside had allowed some light to come in. Across these little lines of light on the floor and walls, he could have seen a shadow. He could have asked him what he was doing, who he was, why he was there. The man could have hit him right there, called him *bakla* many times. The neighbors could have heard the screaming but they pretended to be sleeping on their beds.

Cries were the music of curfew nights. They lulled them more to sleep.

Boy Manicure could have stuck his head out the window and screamed for help while the man pulled him inside and started to punch his face. His voice could have traveled in the air. The neighbors could have heard him again. They could have heard the aquarium shattering, the chairs being thrown all over. They could have heard his loudest screams.

Then I thought of Pipo. He could have been screaming, too, when he was at Boy Manicure's house. They might have heard him, too. But nobody paid any attention. When I got there, it was too late. Pipo was already hurt.

When they found Boy Manicure, he was already dead.

Lightning struck again. My hair lay flatly on my face. My clothes became a thinner part of my skin. I could see my skin through my white T-shirt. The wind took me to its arms, carried me out of the railroad. My legs had splatters of mud all over them. I held my shorts because the weight of rainwater was pulling them down. I plodded through the mud, sinking each time I put down my feet.

When I got back to our street, the skies thundered. The streets were almost empty. The wind was very strong, pushing its way toward people's windows, slamming the walls.

"Go home. Go home." I heard a voice but I paced my walk, dipping my feet in puddles. Even in the rain, I could hear whispers, people talking amongst themselves.

Somehow, I felt they were talking about me now. Not Boy Manicure anymore.

"Go home, Gringo. Your mother is looking for you," said the Mrs.-from-across-the-street. I looked at her. She gestured me to go home. There were other people there, staring at me as I walked. Then they looked at each other, and started talking and shaking their heads. One woman made a sign of the cross, whispering names of saints perhaps. They gathered around and talked more, each time turning their heads to look at me. The rain muffled their voices, although by the way their eyes moved, I knew they were talking about me. "Go home . . ."

I didn't know what it was but I felt something was very, very wrong.

I held the grill of our gate tightly as if I was about to pull it right out. I stood in the rain, knowing it might be the last time this rain would come to me. Right through the holes on the roof gutters, rain came down like waterfalls. I felt it land on my head in big splashes of water. I turned my head, opened my mouth, let it inside me. Inside me. I opened my eyes, let it pass through my eyelids, inside where I could see it in my sleep.

Tears fell down my face. In the rain, it was safe to cry because nobody could tell. It began to thunder making it safe to scream. I held myself and felt that there was so much inside this little body of mine that could be washed away by rain. But everything stayed inside as if they were the reasons why I lived.

I sat there like a piece of stone, unmoved.

"Gringo." I heard a voice from above me. "GRINGO."

I looked up and saw my mother's head out the window. "Gringo, come up now!" I had never felt so heavy. I couldn't even get up anymore. I was prepared for anything now.

I had grown veins on my skin, thick ones.

I dripped on our floor when I walked in. The door was left open. Pipo was sitting quietly downstairs, with the same fearful look on his face. He watched me walk upstairs, leaving a trail of rain on the steps.

"Close the door," Mommy said, her voice was soft yet had a sense of impending anger. "Close the door behind you, Gringo." She was sitting on the edge of the bed. She threw a towel at me.

Wiping my face, I stood in front of her.

I felt the door opening again. Pipo walked in the room and sat on the opposite end of the bed.

She stared at me for the longest time. She had never looked at me like that before. She probably noticed that I had grown, that I looked different from what came out of her body twelve years ago. She probably realized that she had stopped noticing me as soon as she brought me to this world.

"Have you ever been to Boy Manicure's?"

I didn't respond. Why was she asking me that? I thought about what Sergio Putita told me earlier. My eyes lingered about the room, looking for an answer.

"Tell me, Gringo. Have you ever been to Boy Manicure's?" She stood up and took something out of the cabinet. She held the *yantok*, which I had not seen since Daddy Groovie left. She whacked it and hit the floor. I jumped upon hearing the familiar sound. My mind was cluttered with thoughts. I wanted her to lower her voice so that nobody could hear her but she continued, her voice turning into a hammer that pounded me deeper into silence. I began to shiver. My teeth cluttered. I thought everybody could hear her, even if the rain was screaming loudly. Mommy took something out of a bag and showed it to me.

"Do you see this?"

It was my Jockeys.

She turned the garter over and showed me my name which she herself had written so that my Jockeys wouldn't get mixed up with Pipo's. She tightened her jaws. "Your name! Gringo!"

I didn't understand what she meant. I noticed that Pipo started to cry. My eyes blurred my vision. Water clogged my ears. My hands shook like the earth once it had become afraid. I looked toward Pipo and saw his hands about to cover his face. I heard his voice, becoming louder and louder. "Leave him alone, Ma."

I stood there, my hands shook.

She walked closer, lifted my chin up with her fingers, looked directly into my eyes. Looking into an older person's eyes meant telling the truth, everything that could possibly be told.

"The police was here today while you were gone, Gringo. They found your Jockeys in his house. GRINGO, answer me, what was this doing in Boy Manicure's house?" She pushed my Jockeys to my chest. They instantly got wet. She shook me until I backed up.

My Jockeys slid down my arms into my hands. They still felt soft. Used. Never washed. I looked at it.

"You never helped me. You never loved me," Pipo yelled at her from the corner. I knew he didn't want me to speak. I didn't know what to say. I wondered how my Jockeys ended up at Boy Manicure's. I knew Pipo had always worn my Jockeys, though I never said anything about it. I didn't think it would matter. "You should have done this yourself." Pipo's voice was angry. He picked up the *yantok* that Mommy had dropped on the floor. I watched him the whole time as he stepped on the other end of the *yantok*, twisting it into a curve. He angrily pushed the ends close together. He broke it into small pieces. Then smaller. He started pounding them on the floor, yelling at the little pieces. He cried louder and louder. When he tired, he crawled around to pick up the scattered pieces. He gathered them into a mound, and weakly sat in front of them. How much I had wanted to tell Mommy to hold him and tell him that nothing bad would ever happen to him anymore.

I saw the faces of our neighbors again, heard their whispers, talking about Pipo this time, looking at him, chasing him with their thoughts while he sat there, completely drowning in his own silence.

Mommy looked at him, then at me, then at herself. I knew she couldn't see me anymore, her eyes full of tears she had held over the years. It was the first time I saw tears in her eyes. Now there was too much of them, she couldn't control their coming. I didn't move toward her to hold her and comfort her the way I always wanted to. She quickly wiped her face, turned to me again, put her hands together between her thighs and asked softly, "Gringo, tell me, were you at Boy Manicure's?"

I looked at Pipo one last time, sitting there, broken into pieces like Daddy Groovie's *yantok*, fallen, pale. My brother, I thought. When I opened my mouth, words freely flew out like flies, like birds after a quick pick of leftover bread on the streets, like stray cats leaping out of rooftops, all these things I had kept inside me flew out, in one sound, "Yes, Mommy, I was."

Silence escaped out of our walls again so that I could only hear my own breathing. I stopped crying. Pipo stared at me for a long time but I didn't meet his eyes. I bowed my head. Mommy froze where she was, holding herself, hand over her mouth. The wind pounded against our window; what came into the room slightly brushed my skin, making me shiver. I continued to drip on the floor.

It was the season of rain.

Woodside, D'Merica 11377

"Can't go anywhere. People who run away always end up in the same place. That's why the world is round so you have no place to go. Who would have known everything would come to this? I only drained my body thinking about everything, worrying about you, Gringo, Pipo. My tongue dried of spit talking to myself every day, asking, Why, why? Why here? Why now? *Dios ko,* only to find myself sitting here with you again. Still I don't understand how everything can arrive to this. *Hay naku!* Believe me, all the time away from you was spent putting all the pieces together, finding an ultimate answer to questions that have been bothering me for years, but look at me, even now, now that I'm back, I don't have anything. Nothing to answer why things happen the way they do. I ask the Lord to guide me, but I'm not sure if he's listening to me anymore."

I wasn't really sure why Ninang Rola came back. Even that day, when I sat outside the bedroom, on the stairs, pressing my ears against the wall even if I could hear everything with the door ajar, I wondered why she was here again, or who she came back for. It was Mommy I had been waiting for to speak; every word she said was so important to me.

"Is this what the Lord wants, Estrella? Is this his plan for us?" I imagined Ninang Rola's arms around Mommy's while they lay on the bed, her fingers in Mommy's long hair, grouping the strands, pulling them softly into little curls. It was as if she had sensed what had happened here while she was gone. When she returned she knew she would have to stay with us again. She brought back all her luggage, took the folding cot out of the storage under the stairs, washed the webs off, left it under the sun to dry. Soon her presence was back: the smell of food all day, the mosquito nets at night covering the entire living room, the creaking of the cot on which she slept in the quiet of the night, and the words, the never-ending words. And she had been spending a few hours every day holding me, examining my eyes. I could feel her touch, her reassuring way of rubbing my skin. I listened to everything she said although I didn't say much, only nodding my head in agreement even if half the time my thoughts were somewhere else. She had not asked me what had happened, nobody ever did.

Her face, the same aging face I had always seen, always so close to my breathing space.

"So many things I can never explain to myself. I have made many sacrifices in life, only for more sacrifices to come facing me afterwards." Mommy's voice was shaky, perhaps from not having said much for weeks. She had waited for this moment. Before Ninang Rola came back, she had been watching Pipo and me closely, the way drunken men train their cockfighters by examining their every move, feather after feather, measuring the depth of their soil diggings with Popsicle sticks. Her eyes were all over the house, knowing exactly what Pipo and I were going to do next. What are you doing, was her frequent question, the only thing she really said, other than the common, let's eat, go to bed. Even if she wasn't there, I could hear her in my mind. Her voice was frail, and had gotten weaker each passing day. Sometimes, she stood, hands crossed at the window, studying the wind, whispering to herself, calling Ninang Rola's name, perhaps that's why when Ninang Rola came back, she brought color to Mommy's face. Slowly, Mommy's voice also came back. "You know how I brought Pipo into this world. I didn't ask for him but you were the one who told me, God gave him to me, and therefore, I shouldn't take his life. I was ready to drink roots to put an end to him. Now, I wonder whether that would have been a better decision."

"You know when you got pregnant and I told Germano where you were, I always thought I was doing the right thing. And no, I never regretted having done such. I know families belong together, even the unborn. You are all here for a reason. I never had a family. I only had you. So I sent Germano to get you, to convince you to marry him. A child needs a father. If you look at your boys, you know you made the right decision."

I felt feeble sitting there, knees as weak as Ninang

Rola's. I couldn't get up even if I tried. The curling corners of the yellowing wallpapers tickled my brows. The heads of the nails poked my cheek. Dust occasionally blew from the landing behind me. I bent my legs and put my arms around them. Every moment was so important. The idea of them not knowing I was there made every single word they said worth listening to. Earlier, they sent both Pipo and me on errands. *Pipo, go get some* kangkong *and* galunggong *from the market. Gringo, did you check the can for rice? Why don't you go get three kilos from Tarina All-Around?* I quickly slipped back into the house, leaving a trail of rice grains on the floor. *I had to come back.* Pipo had not returned. I imagined him reading comics at the market. They rented them out, twenty cents a minute, if you sat there and stayed.

"I married him because of Pipo. Whenever I looked at Germano every morning since, I repeated these words to myself: I will learn to love him. I have been trying for so many, many years, Rola. The same thoughts keep on coming back to me, like the hands of the clock, hitting the same numbers each time, over and over again, only for me to make the same mistakes each time, the same lies, the same lies, again and again . . ." Mommy stopped, started sobbing. *Ayoko na! Tama na!* This has to stop. In the dark side of the stairs, I held myself tightly, felt the warmth of my arms. I wondered what Mommy would think if she found out I was sitting there. Would she look at me and tell me the same things she had just said? Would she walk past, as if I was so hidden in the shadow of the plywood walls she couldn't see me? "Rola, you're wrong. You are so wrong. You can never learn to love anyone, not with constant reminders, not with *your* daily prayers."

Ninang Rola remained silent. I knew she was agreeing with Mommy. She had once told me: You can't make up a story you don't believe, nobody will. You can't force people to believe what you don't. That's just the way it is.

"Whenever he touched me, my pores tightened, my throat clogged. I ended up gasping for air. Every time he touched me, my insides got all intertwined, as if my heart was going to burst out of my chest. So I kept on saying to myself, this is the way it is, this is my fate. I have to stay here. I have to *be* here. Endure all this. I wanted to leave so badly. If you weren't here, if not for the children, I would not be here anymore."

"Es-tre-lla . . ."

"I have tried and God knows how much. I stayed here, didn't I? I lived here? Rola, I didn't have to do any of that. Rola, are you listening to me? I didn't have to do that. But I did. Then I bore another child. When that happened, I didn't know what to do anymore. I knew I had to stay. Then what you used to say became even clearer, we don't have to want what we have, we'll just have to live with it. Our life isn't ours. My life is not mine anymore. When the children were born, I gave it to them. My Gringo, my little Gringo, I didn't ask for him, either. Are you listening, Rola? I didn't ask for him, either!"

My grasp of my legs slipped, my palms suddenly wet. *She never asked for me.* My breathing slowed down. *She never asked for me, either.* My chest, tight. I could feel how cold the wall was. Cold, in the summer heat. I bit my teeth. My lips, heavy. I shut my eyes, tried to keep the tears in.

"*Puñeta ka, babae ka?* How in the world can you say anything like that?" Ninang Rola raised her voice so loud it shook my head off the wall. "Those are your sons! You bore them for months, you gave them their lives. I raised them like mine, too. My own children. Look at me, without anyone to carry my blood. *They* are the ones who will, although I never gave birth to them. How can you say that? What made you think you are worse off than anybody else? Huh? Look around you. Look. Why do say such things, Estrella? *Santíssimo Rosario,* Estrella? And Gringo? You were married already when he came, how can you say that . . . lightning can hit you saying that!"

The mattress coils shrieked. She moved away from the bed. *That bed, that bed.* The warm air around them spoke. Mommy's footsteps approached the window. The sound of her tears followed her around. I heard the window shutters sliding closed. The thought of the nights came back to me. The sound of a bird, the cockfight, the rain. The chilling cry that lulled me to sleep. I could hear Mommy asking Daddy Groovie to stop, *stop, stop, I don't want any more.* That was how I was brought into the world.

The same way Pipo was.

"Sometimes . . . some . . . times," Mommy seemed farther away, her voice softer, "I feel that this is somebody else's life. That I had become someone else when Germano took me to that motel. I was changing all the time. From giving birth to Pipo, to Gringo, and each day I watched them grow up. They are constant reminders of what is wrong. It's hard to keep on seeing them. But somehow I have learned to accept it. Rola, I don't see myself as unluckier than any strange face out there, no, you are wrong when you say that.

"I wanted Germano to leave so badly, the States would change him, I know. He had to get away from here. He had to start anew. He could never be a better father here. Not with me around him all the time, reminding him of what he cannot possibly become. If you read his letter, you would know that he has found his direction. He misses his boys. I haven't told him what happened to Gringo. I don't think I can. I won't. Writing him is as much a struggle to begin with. Let it all be forgotten."

"How can anybody forget anything like that? *You* never forgot."

I could hear the wind blowing into the fall of silence inside. The sudden quiet of spaces between them that always took them back many years. "Nobody forgets," Mommy responded in a soft voice, soft enough to be carried by the wind to where I was, words dark as dust. "But didn't you just say one can always forgive. It's hard to learn how to, but maybe it is possible. Maybe Gringo can, too."

Maybe *Pipo* could. Maybe without the eyes of the people following him around, he could finally heal. Without the weight of shame in his life, he could move on.

"Everything repeats, you know." Ninang Rola lowered her tone so that Mommy's sniffing could be heard. "*Sangre de familia,* Estrella. I can't bear to think about what happened to my poor Gringo. It destroys me inside that that *demonio*

Boy Manicure could do something so evil. I can't even bear to ask Gringo about it. O, Estrella, see how everything repeats? This cycle has to be stopped now. Gringo needs you more than anything else right now. And Pipo, he has been waiting for you for so long."

"Please . . . please, Rola . . ." Mommy burst. She flooded the room with her cries. I could see Ninang Rola pulling Mommy close to her and resting her head on her chest. *It's always best to cry close to a woman's heart.* "I don't . . . know w-what to do," Mommy continued, her voice marred by tears coming into her mouth. *Spit out your tears, never let it back inside you.*

Tears tasted like water with salt crystals one gargled with every morning and every night before going to bed. I wiped my face before they slid down into my lips. I covered my mouth so they wouldn't hear my heavy breathing. I ground my teeth to keep myself together.

"Show them what's been missing here for a long time."

"How do I do that, Rola?"

"You had always known—"

"So easy for you to say that, Rola."

"No matter what you say, you have gotten this far. You don't want your children to grow up not knowing how much you love them. It's not too late, no, *hija*?"

"Where does someone like me begin?"

"Let me give you something. I have always wanted to give this to you."

"A small box? Looks old. What is it, Rola?"

"I should have given this to you a long time ago. Open it."

A sound of cellophane unwrinkling. "What is this?"

"I kept it all these years. Your firstborn's umbilical cord. I kept it. It's your turn to keep it now, the only thing that connects you to Pipo. So you may always remember—always, from the very beginning."

Everything began with open eyes.

Mommy had never looked as much into my eyes before. Anyone who did always meant something more than just looking at you. The way Ninang Rola would say, Your droopy eyes, have you been thinking much again, huh? Mommy's way of staring was one that didn't make her say anything, that made her gulp and take a deep sigh. Are you all right? she would ask hours later after she had walked away from me. How are you feeling today, Gringo? Once, she touched my hair and smiled, then shook my shoulders: So big now, she commented, shoulders wide.

From my bed, I watched her at night. Her eyes dazed into the dark while she turned restlessly on her bed. She lifted herself up to look at me, not knowing that in the darkness, I was watching her, too. Then she stared out again. From her bed, her gaze took her outside the window, into the lamp post light, to circle with fireflies.

Late Sunday morning, after circling the middle of the bedroom repeatedly, Mommy looked at Pipo and me. "The park, we're going to the park. After lunch."

"The park?" I asked. Why? I wanted to know, but as soon as the early afternoon sun showered the bedroom with light and I saw her dressing up, I went to change, too. Pipo ran to the other room to get dressed. "Wear the nice shirt I bought you last, the blue-striped one," she told him. Not your father's hang-around T-shirt that's so big on you, her lips seemed to say while they followed Pipo next door.

Pipo came out of the room wearing exactly what Mommy had asked. She didn't tell me what to wear so I put on the shirt she had bought me at the same time. She always bought us shirts that halfway matched. This one differed in the colors of the strips. I had yellow. He had red. Both shirts, background blue. Blue, I remembered, was the color of the plastic tent at the outside market from where we had bought them.

Mommy took a quick glance at me when she finished combing her hair. She let go of her hair, its tips touching the middle of her back. She slowly approached me with a powder puff and started making quick dabs of Johnson's Baby Powder on my neck. "Hot outside, you know?" Some of it dotted my T-shirt. She continued, "This way, you don't sweat too much. I know how you are."

Pipo laughed quietly where he stood. I had not seen him do that in a long time.

The sky towered above us, clear as our street that day. Sunday, of course, was always the day of silence. I was once again afraid to walk outside for the fear of prying eyes. Mommy must have known because she quickly held both our hands as soon as we left our house. There were neighbors outside, fanning themselves. They waved their hands and Mommy nodded her head to acknowledge them. *Magandang umaga, Aling Estrella.*

They looked at me again, a look full of pity and shame.

"More beautiful than the morning is seeing the three of you together," commented Mrs. Dimaculangan from across the street. I didn't look at her and I was glad we didn't stop.

The jeepney street was almost empty. It looked emptier without the newspaper boys chasing the smoke. Inside the jeepney we took, I sat without being squished by passengers. Mommy dropped coins in the driver's palms when he reached out. *To the park.*

"Why are we going there?" Pipo asked. I caught him wiggling out of Mommy's grasp only to have her tighten it more.

"We haven't done this for some time," she responded. I could have told her I was too young to remember the last time I went there. Going to the park took much preparation. I had seen our neighbors do it: fold blankets, pack food in picnic baskets, bring water in plastic containers, slice white bread with egg salad, put red-salted eggs and tomatoes in Tupperware.

We didn't have anything at all. Our hands were only full of each other's.

The park was an hour jeepney ride away, which easily passed because of what there was to see on the way. In the late afternoon, there were less people there. Perhaps the reason why we didn't bring food to eat.

The sky was moving, waves of orange and blue.

Mommy sat us on a cement bench, her in the middle. "Look around you. Take as much of this air in. Leave it inside your body for a minute. This country smells differently. You don't know that because you're too young to know the difference. Someday, you will wonder how everything smells here. In the States, there will be nothing like this."

Pipo and I both looked at her. She steadied her gaze on the bay.

"Your father has rented a house in Woodside. We must get ready to leave."

She put her arms around our heads, her fingers traveled through our hair. It felt different from Ninang Rola's, as if her hand didn't belong there.

A balloon man walked by, looking at us. *Loboooo.* A cotton candy man followed, holding a pink one that was bigger than his head.

Our heads were talking to each other. What she just said played in my head over and over again. I waited for her to say more but we sat there not saying anything at all. We stared at the sky, the bay that overlooked the park. There were little boats that floated far away. On the shore of rocks beyond the concrete fence were children splashing themselves with water. Their giggles played with the sound of water rippling. Birds walked on water.

I was trying to smell the air. It was different here, not like the morning smoke from the jeepney streets. The air seemed thicker, wet. Would the States be any different?

Mommy rested my head on her shoulders then kissed my forehead. She did the same thing to Pipo. This time when she took his hands, Pipo willingly gave in. I could hear his heavy breath.

He had been waiting for this moment for years.

We sat there for hours. The moon was lighting the whole park when Mommy shook me up and decided it was time to go. I had closed my eyes for some time. For a moment, my eyelids were sticky. After rubbing them a few times, I caught Pipo's eyes still staring into the bay as if memorizing everything that was there. The shore was empty by then. The voice of the water was still. We slowly walked to the jeepney streets, where we got off. Mommy never tired of holding both of us. When I looked back, I saw a man and woman holding each other, kissing against the backdrop of a very red sky. Then a boy with a basket of preserved eggs walked by, quickly turning his head to look at me, screaming something I was too sleepy to hear.

"How about Gringo?" Pipo asked Mommy, while I sat on a high chair watching both of them in the kitchen. It looked odd seeing Pipo there with the counter only a few inches below his chest. And not being told to leave.

"Careful with that blood, you'd splatter it all over. Ooops. I'm telling you." Mommy was slicing a fresh cow's heart into cubes. There were dots of blood on the counter. "You will teach your brother when you learn, in due time," she told him, then turning toward me, winked.

I pressed my lips against each other. I blinked my eyes a few times. Why would I want to learn how to do any of that? The sight of blood didn't send my skin crawling the way it used to. There was a huge bowl of it on the counter with bubbles on the surface. I had always wondered why we ate pig's blood stew. Mommy had said once how it connected us to our roots. Many centuries ago our ancestral warriors cut their skin to seal their fates in a blood compact.

Without any sense of disgust, Pipo started peeling onions and garlic, then slammed them with the cooking rock.

"See these little cubes? All the meat should never be any bigger than this." Mommy struggled to pick up a small piece and moved it close to Pipo's face. "As small. It's easier to eat it this way."

"What's that?" Pipo caught Mommy pulling an irregularly shaped meat from a bowl of water.

"Pig ears."

"They don't look like ears."

"They've been shaved, and the outer skin removed." She pulled them up so that I could see them. They dripped all over the counter. Mommy cupped them with her hand. "Be careful when you handle this. It hears everything you say."

"So, Gringo, don't say a word. Shhhh." Pipo turned to me with a big smile on his face, then back to Mommy, not knowing how funny what he just said to me was. "You also chop them into cubes?"

"Yes, a little bit longer like this. See?" Mommy's response interrupted my thoughts. The volume of her voice was full so that she could be heard from the other end of the house. It was competing with the wheezing sound of heat.

The pig's ears dropped on the wooden board, bouncing like a piece of thick plastic. If they could only read my mind, they would wonder what was going on in the kitchen, why Mommy suddenly decided to teach Pipo how to cook, why I was asked to sit there and watch. Why all this? Do they cook this in the States? Do they eat blood?

"Once in a stew, nobody could tell any of them apart. They also all taste the same way, except that pig's ears are crunchier," continued Mommy, demonstrating how to properly slice the ears and which knife would be best to use. She gave one piece to Pipo and guided his hand until Pipo said that he could do it himself. He sliced it with an expertise of one who had it in his blood to do this. Mommy gingerly gathered the pig's ears with a spoon and threw them back in the bowl of water. She then took out another piece of meat from another bowl.

"What's that?" Pipo acted as if he never knew parts of a pig's body, bombarding Mommy with questions he probably had answers for. "Looks like a face towel?"

"Tripe," Mommy answered. She held it by the ends, sending ripples all over it. "Where are the garlic and onions?"

"Here." Pipo placed a mound on the arrangement Mommy prepared on the cutting board. There were little hills of pig parts, peppers, onions, garlic. A pot full of blood on another. A bottle of vinegar. A bowl of coconut milk. Salt. Mommy turned the stove on.

"Now listen to me, both of you, *this* is how we begin."

GARAGE SALE.

There was no garage on our street. Our neighbors parked their old cars outside, adding tightness to our already narrow street. Maybe that's why nobody understood. It was Ninang Rola's idea. She was in charge, she said. *Better let the old woman take care of this.* So she put a big placard on the window, tied the ends with straws. Very early in the morning.

The neighbors started knocking on the door. "What's that?"

"You're not renting out your rooms again, are you?"

"What garage?"

"I just don't understand Rola. The sign is so big but I don't understand what it means."

Ninang Rola's attempt on something Stateside came back into the house so that she could write the message over on the back.

EVERYTHING FOR SALE.

The word *everything* sent the signal out. Voices traveled so quickly that soon our neighbors were back knocking on our door again. The closest ones were the first ones there. "Reserve this for me and that." "How much is the cabinet? Is the Frigidaire to go, too?" "Estrella, *loca,* you're so lucky, in the States, everything will be new, not all the stupid, decrepit appliances you have. *May* washing machine *pa*!"

The cabinets would be the last ones to go, according to Ninang Rola. And the beds. "You don't want to sleep on the floor. Anything big like those need to stay and be taken once you are all gone. It's lucky that way." Luck, all we needed at that time. "The stove can go. And the Frigidaire. We can buy cooked meals for a few weeks. That will be okay, what do you think of that, Estrella? The money we need now, right? We must sell most of what you have?"

I didn't know what it was they were taking away from us, but it didn't feel right seeing our neighbors walk away with what I had gotten used to seeing all these years. I stayed in corners to make sure nobody came and asked me questions. I could tell by a quick look at their lips that they were asking about me. Ninang Rola was always ready to dismiss any questions from curious neighbors. "Everybody here is all right, nothing to worry about. Are you buying something? What? What?" When she meant, he's okay. Don't bother him. Meaning me.

I always felt everybody knew. I knew whenever they looked at me, they wondered what had happened, recreating it in their heads. There was always something in the way people looked, one could easily tell if there was more to it than just a passing glance. Especially when they talked about it in whispers, or when people stopped talking as soon as they saw my shadow approach. One of them had the nerve to walk out of our house and say, Poor boy, good thing justice is served.

Was it? Whose? Nobody knew who killed Boy Manicure. Nobody claimed seeing and hearing anything at all. "It's sacrilegious to bring up names of dead people," they'd say. Closed case.

Except mine, here was an opportunity to see me in full view, to imagine. At first it was hard to accept what I had done, the cost of my lie, people constantly looking at me, talking, but whenever I saw Pipo smiling, laughing, being his old self again, I thought maybe it was all worth it. I didn't have to sit Mommy down and tell her it wasn't me.

The neighbors came; one day, in fives, the next, in droves.

Everything for sale. Day by day, one piece would be removed from the house. Mommy tried to hold on to certain things only to have Ninang Rola grab them from her and say, Everything to go.

Everything, everything. Ninang walked around the house and tagged everything she could touch with masking tape and wrote prices on them with a black marker. "Ten pesos. Fifty pesos. Hundred pesos. Don't you wish you're getting dollars now? Soon, you'll hardly see peso bills in your pocket. Ayyy! Make sure you think about me whenever you pull out dollars from your wallets, huh, Pipo? Gringo? No checks. Cash, huh?"

We will always think about you, was Pipo's answer, then he turned to me. The way he looked at me now, as if he always wanted to hold me.

I had never seen her sew so much in her life. The Singer Machine was breathing day and night, one of the few belongings that they had decided not to sell. Mommy came home one day with rolls of white fabrics. Another day, khaki-colored ones. Then Ninang Rola bought the linings for the jackets. "It's cold when you get there." She would never stop telling us what to expect. "Rola, Rola, guess what I read this morning." *What?* "The cold weather is actually good for your skin. That's why those actresses always had ice compacts on their faces."

"I'm sure Groovie has been dipping his face in the snow, Estrella. Dolares is probably doing the same thing. She can use a good dipping, I'm sure. That family could be so ugly, let me tell you. I can see her taking a whole bucket of snow back to her house and throwing her face into it. I never met the woman, Estrella, but I can see her doing that. No wonder those *kanos* have such nice skin. The snow, *hija,* the snow."

Mommy measured Pipo and me with her old red tape that she kept in a small red box. Shoulders. Arms. Legs. Raise your arms up like that. Don't move. Okay, lower them now. Gringo, your arms are almost as long as Pipo's. Neck, eight inches? *Dios mío,* you're so thin. She listed down our measurements on a pad only to repeat them again. "In the States, when you get there, I want to make sure you look Stateside. Right?" I saw them on a hanger two weeks later: our *despedida* clothes. And embroidered on the front pockets of the jackets, our names.

One said Felipe. The other, Gregorio.

D*iario. Bulletin.*

Boy Spit's voice quickly pulled me out of our house. He was standing in the street, his back on the concrete-block fence. I edged closer. I thought I was looking at another person. He had no dirt on his face. His hair was newly cut and wet, well combed. His T-shirt had no holes, but wrinkled on the edges. He was wearing black shoes.

"A few more days?" He looked at the sign on our wall.

"Yes."

He puckered his lips, stared down for a while. He put

his hands in his pockets. He swallowed air then stuttered, "S-so w-when do you leave?"

"Three days." I didn't know what his real name was. I had never addressed him by his name. "Come in."

His shoes made knocking sounds on the ground when he followed me. I could tell he wasn't used to wearing them. He almost tripped before we went into the house.

"It's almost empty." His eyes darted from wall to wall. He touched the parts of the walls where the cabinets used to be. "No wallpaper?"

"The cabinets were too heavy to move when we wall-papered the house. But they are all gone, at least four men had to carry them out. Come upstairs, let me show you something." I heard voices in the kitchen so I knew no-body was in our bedroom.

He went straight to the window when we got there. Then he turned and looked at me. "I used to see you here all the time."

He knew I had been watching him all this time? I moved beside him, laying my hands on the sill. He smelled of Johnson's Baby Powder. I could see traces of it on his collar and sleeves.

"There's a lot you can see from here." I quickly scanned what surrounded us on eye level, our neighbors' roofs, their big windows through which you could always see what they were doing, the antennas felled by typhoons, the blur of tall buildings far, far away. There is much to see, I qui-etly repeated to myself.

"I'm sure," he echoed. "Sometimes when you look too much, you see more than you want."

I didn't respond to him because I knew what he meant. Our city was full of eyes looking, constantly judging everything they saw. Our street was part of that and, in each house, the windows, open, wide, never-blinking eyes.

"You're going to be happy where you're going."

"H-how do you know that?"

"I just know. It's different there, the States. Saw it on TV once when I was delivering newspapers."

It was then I realized I was leaving him. I immediately wondered what the future held for somebody like him. Would he be selling newspapers all his life? Would he get a chance to go to school?

"Here, we never know what's going to happen next. It's like the rain, you never know when it comes and hits us hard. Does it rain in the States? Probably not, right? Snow?"

"You will take care of yourself?" I turned to him, and before he could answer, took his hand and pulled him into the middle of our bedroom. Holding him made me feel as if my hands belonged somewhere close to him, where I could touch him whenever I wished, where I could smell him all the time. "Come, I have something for you." I pulled a shoe box from under the bed. "Take this."

"What?" he opened it. "Calendars?" He rummaged through the pile and pulled one out. "MikMouse!"

"I saved them for you." And I wanted him to keep them, for him to know that we had known each other once—the year, the month, the days.

"Umbrellas, so many?"

"I took all of them before Ninang Rola could sell them.

You can put them on your roof when it rains so it won't leak inside your house."

He pulled one of them. "Automatic, too?" The umbrella flew open and bounced around before it settled beside us. An open umbrella, I thought to myself, remembering what Ninang Rola had always warned me, but I left it there, for the breeze to push it around.

"It doesn't rain in the States. . . ." Boy Spit's lips started to shake, his eyes slowly pooled. Before I could say another word, he gingerly pulled me close to him and tightly held me. When he let me go, he cupped my face with both hands. I could see tears streaming down his cheeks, into his lips, and down to his chin, dripping on my arms. He moved his face close to mine until I could feel his tears sliding down my own. He kept our faces together for a while. He was breathing very, very fast. I could feel his heartbeat on my chest. I could hear him swallowing spit again and again. When he looked at me again, he slowly approached me with his lips, first on the cheeks, on the nose, then, the longest, on my lips, so tenderly as if I would break if he tried harder. I felt my body accept him so openly. That him being there, our skin touching, was always meant to be. I felt very light, the heaviness of everything inside slowly drifting down to my toes.

The breeze blew in, the umbrella began to tumble about.

"W-what's your name?" I finally asked.

"Fer. Fernando."

It was a very beautiful name, just like him under the

dim flicker of the fluorescent light, his face slightly lit by the window where I had watched him all these years, the most beautiful thing I had ever seen.

"Ninang Rola. Mommy. Upstairs, quick!" Pipo yelled from the top of the stairs. "Hurry. You have to see this."

"What is it?" Ninang Rola was in the kitchen, wiping her hands on the towel around her waist.

"You have to see this," Pipo shouted again, waving his hand this time, bending his knees and his back so that he could see her downstairs. "Mommy."

I was at the bottom of the stairs, deciding against going up.

"Hurry. Hurry." Pipo disappeared into the bedroom.

"GRINGO." His yelling of my name was so loud, it moved me a step up.

When I saw Ninang Rola and Mommy coming, I raced them upstairs. They looked at each other, wondering what Pipo was up to now.

I was standing in front of the window in a wide open gaze when both of them got there. The breeze was blowing into my face, into the already empty room. Pipo was closer to the window, his hands almost on the sill. The curtains were freely flowing above us.

Ninang Rola slowly walked past me, closer to where Pipo was. "Ahhhh."

"What . . . ?" Mommy asked softly, following Ninang Rola and stopping beside me.

"Mariposa," Ninang Rola said. "Mariposa."

A swarm of yellow was resting on the window grill. Motionless, they looked like buds of flowers that just grew out of the rusty grill overnight.

Ninang Rola moved closer, holding Pipo's shoulders as she approached.

"Why would they come here of all places?" she asked, sticking her head into the window gently so as not to scare them away.

"Yellow butterflies. The sign of flight . . ."

It was as if as soon as she had said that, they all started to flicker their wings in a simultaneous motion. One flew, then another. Soon all of them were hovering in front of us, while the curtains continued to ripple in the breeze.

"Mommy?" Pipo turned around and looked at her while she stood there agape. *Mommy?* Her eyes were layered with tears that wouldn't slide down her cheeks. Her fingers shakingly climbed over her chest to cover her lips. It was then that Ninang Rola also turned around, but she only stood there and watched Mommy as well. The many years of being here sank into her cheeks, then into her neck, creating hollows on her skin. It wasn't Ninang Rola anymore, I knew. Not the one who trusted me with the story of their lives.

The darkness on her face, as if she had fallen at the foot of God.

"Ma, don't anymore," Pipo begged. Because by the look on Mommy's face, he could tell that she had once again flown into her own world but had locked herself in it, trembling in the heat of the sun.

Dawn. A heavy hand shook my shoulders. A soft voice, almost from a dream. "*Gising. Gising.* Six o'clock."

I lifted myself up. I was alone in the big bed in the middle of the room. "Get up. You must get ready. Pipo is already showering downstairs."

The only light in the bedroom was what dawn brought in. I could hardly see Ninang Rola but her voice told me she was right next to me, sitting perhaps.

"Six o'clock?" I repeated. No roosters were crowing. I turned sideways to face her. "Are you sure?"

"Get up." Then she walked out of the room, letting in the light from downstairs when she opened the door. She left it ajar so that a long streak of light swung across the room. I pulled myself up and sat down, staring at my shorts for a while. I jumped out of the bed in panic and opened the door widely so that I lit up a great part of the mattress. Right in the middle of it was a round stain. When I touched myself, I was wet, so wet in fact, pee was still sliding down my legs.

"Gringo," Ninang called out again, "Pipo's finished, it's your turn."

I stood there, my legs spread out. I grabbed a towel and wrapped it around myself. I threw pillows on the stain so nobody would notice until it dried. I wiped myself while walking down, rubbing my eyes at the same time.

Downstairs, our luggage was lined up against the already empty walls, our names written on squares of masking tape. "Woodside, Nuyork," I whispered to myself, "11377." Those were the first things I saw in the light. I said those words over and over as I lingered downstairs. Woodside, that was the place in the States. *D'merica,* Daddy Groovie would say in his letters. His last one told us we would love D'merica, he would take us places we could never imagine ever existed, buy us food we have never eaten. When I woke up the next day, that was where I would be. It would be Monday again, except, it would be cold, very cold.

Salted fish. *Longganisa.* Fried rice. I smelled our last breakfast. The sound of frying led me to the bathroom, where Pipo was just stepping out, a turban of towel wrapped around his head, another around his body.

"Miss World," I said in a sing-song tone that only he could hear.

Unibers, he corrected me. Boasting a smile, he walked upstairs, his hands in an eternal posture of display. Twisted, turning elbows. Much like a mannequin, I thought, much like one, or in fact, much better. I watched him until he disappeared into the darkness of the stairs only for him to run back down. He grabbed my hands and danced with me in circles. "Da-da-da-da-rin," he sang something familiar but I wasn't sure what it was. I laughed. We were like two little boys again, going around in circles, jumping and laughing. "Da-da-da-rin-dum-dum-doo." We laughed so hard he was holding his stomach when he walked upstairs, his turban of towel falling all over his face.

The inside of the bathroom was different without the huge plastic pails that used to line up in there. I quickly threw water on myself, splashing all over my feet that measured at least four tiles on the floor. I had learned to bathe standing up. I was told that that was the way they did it in the States. Learning early wouldn't hurt. They even sat down on the toilet seat. I tried doing that here but my buttocks almost plunged into the bowl so I squatted again. Someday, maybe I would learn to sit down. I wrapped a towel around my waist. Another over my shoulder. This bathroom. A few more years, I would be able to touch both walls by merely stretching out my arms. The bulb swung above me, moving my shadow on the floor, reading my mind, "But you wouldn't be here long enough to know that."

"It's going to rain again." Ninang Rola handed me my departure clothes when I stepped out of the bathroom. "Dress up quickly, We'll leave immediately after breakfast."

I glanced at the table with plates neatly arranged over it, food steaming. I couldn't feel hunger. I dried myself with a towel and splattered Johnson's Baby Powder all over my face and neck.

"Ninang Rola!" Pipo stampeded down the stairs. "Ninang Rola!"

She came running to meet him. "What?"

"Mommy? Where's Mommy?"

I looked around me. I had not seen Mommy since I got up. I realized she wasn't in the room when I woke up. "She wasn't in the bedroom this morning."

"Where did she go? We're leaving soon. Huh?"

Ninang Rola lowered her body to Pipo's height. She smiled at him and flattened his hair. "Look at this. Wet. Go upstairs and finish. Don't be worrying about her. She has to say goodbye to some relatives. She'll meet us at the airport."

"She'll meet us there." Pipo threw his voice into the air that smelled of food.

"Yes. Go. And you, Gringo, hurry, too." She tapped my back. "She'll meet us there." It was her comforting voice, just the right tone to send Pipo running back upstairs, water all over. She quickly turned and walked past me to the dining table to rearrange the placemats and the plates.

There was something in the way she had set the table. Everything on it cast a very unfamiliar shadow, even her own was different, too. Forks and spoons neatly placed beside the plates. Coffee in a porcelain pot we had not used for such a long time. A mound of fried rice sat perfectly in a big bowl, strips of omelets over it.

The steam hovered over the food like spirits—dancing, inviting.

When we started eating, she simply stared at both of us, somehow managing to see us with one glance. I waited for her to say grace but she didn't; she didn't cross her body, either. She hardly scooped anything into her mouth. She held the spoon, rested it on the plate, then folded her hands over the table. Plate, empty. But her glassful of water she had been gulping for hours. "Here, more." She pushed the plate of *longganisa* to me. "Eat more. Eat. There's nothing like that in the States." She was holding her breath, biting her lip. Every time she let air out, her upper body drooped. Pipo was the first one to get up. Ninang Rola asked him to leave the plate when she saw him pick it up. His plate was clean again, as always, licked clean. Mine, unfinished rice, half-eaten sausage. But I decided to get up anyway.

And when we stood up, she ran to us and pulled us close to her, so quickly that it took me a while to realize that I was being taken by her. Her smell was a combination of all the mornings I had woken up to over the years. I could hear everything she had told me without her opening her mouth. Pipo stood there and held her, too, leaning his head on her shoulder.

"You will do well where you're going. You'll do very well. Something about our people. We're like grass. Grass. We grow everywhere." She let out a very nervous voice.

I saw the wide open grass of the railroad. The dance of grass, the dance of people. They were just like people, she was right, growing everywhere, without anybody to care for them. Grass. And Pipo, in the middle of it, me on the side with Boy Spit, and curfew hovering over us.

"You have managed all these years. It was never very easy here. I know. For both of you, life has not been easy. But you will make it there. Nothing can ever stop you now. That is the nature of our people. Nothing ever stops us from moving. Where we plant our seed, we will grow. No matter how hard it is, we will."

Just when she looked at me as if to ask me again if I understood, a man came through the door. "Rola! The jeepney is here. Are you ready?"

"Oh, Mang Tano. Of course, we're ready. We were just waiting for you." She let both of us go, tapping our backs, slightly pushing us forward like little children who had no directions in mind. "Go help Mang Tano take the boxes to the jeepney. Put them in the back." She wiped the tears on her eyebags.

"Wait," I said. Pipo did as asked, yanking a box out of the house with all his force. I ran upstairs to the bedroom, stopping at the threshold. I could hear the heavy sigh of the morning, a clear signal of a coming rain. I walked to the window. The lights of our neighbors' were still out. There were shadows in some of the yellow-lit ones. But most of them were dark, window shutters closed. It would be better this way, they would never know when we left. For them, one day, we "were just gone."

"Gringo, come down." Outside, Ninang Rola saw me and waved for me to go out.

I took one last look at our bedroom. The bed lay quietly there, spreading the smell I had left. The cabinets. Everything else was gone. The walls were bare except for the cardboard picture of Jesus with a glowing heart. He watched me quietly walk out of the room. I pulled down the seams of my jacket to free it of wrinkles. Looking down, I could see my own name, nicely embroidered in Mommy's familiar handwriting.

Every step I made were the last sounds I would hear in our house. I memorized everything, like a Kodak would, putting everything where they rightfully belonged in my heart. The bedroom. The kitchen. The bathroom.

The house. The wallpapered house.

"Gringo, hurry," Ninang Rola yelled again. The jeepney outside was already coughing smoke into the dimly lit street.

I ran into the jeepney and sat beside Pipo who was counting the boxes inside. "Something is missing. One. Two. Isn't something missing?"

"They're all there," reassured Ninang Rola. "Roll down the curtains. It's going to rain."

The unrolled plastic curtains darkened the space inside.

Mang Tano started driving, making us grab the edges of our seats. Ninang Rola sat beside me, close to the driver's seat, then began talking to him. I decided not to listen. I kept on looking into her eyes but she kept on avoiding mine. Instead, she carried on with her conversation by facing Mang Tano's pomaded hair. Slowly, the rain pounded on the roof. First, as gently as finger drumbeats. Then, as hard as a boxer's fists. Either way, the rain made me nervous. Outside, I could tell it was going to flood again. I couldn't see much of anything. The rain cast darkness all over. Rain. Luck. Not seeing much might mean a lot of luck.

Pipo was holding his breath every time I looked at him. I wanted to reassure him, but nothing could be more powerful than Ninang Rola's words. Everything she had said for the past hours had left a mark inside me. She could be right. Sleep through the trip, when you wake up, Daddy Groovie will be there, but don't forget to change your watches, it's thirteen behind where you're going. Pipo wasn't thinking of that. Not thirteen hours. Not even a whole hour trip on the jeepney changed the expression on his face. The rain drumming above us didn't remove his squint. That gaze into the plastic curtains like there was something there to study. The familiar stare of Mommy.

The jeepney glided through quickly flooding streets and roads. What jeepneys were able to weather was certainly reflected by those who drove them. Most drivers drove as if they had no passengers. In this rain, Mang Tano had managed to keep the jeepney from rocking too much. It also began to clear outside when he said, "We're getting there soon. Keep yourselves dry." Dry wasn't the word to describe us. Our newly sewn clothes looked like they were about to be laid flat on corrugated aluminum.

Pipo was the first one to jump out of the jeepney when we got to the airport. "To where? What door?" His face searched, capturing the entire cluster of buildings with one look. "Which?"

Buses. Jeepneys. People. Wet slippery sidewalks. More people. The sun inching slowly to us.

Ninang Rola pointed to a glass gate where a lot of people were pulling boxes then throwing them into carts. She instructed Mang Tano where to check our luggage and boxes, then turned to catch Pipo who had soon disappeared through the gates. "Where did he go?"

I pointed where I saw him last but Ninang Rola didn't pay attention to me. She repeated her instructions to Mang Tano and quickly grabbed my wrist to pull me inside. I had been in there before, what was to be seen wasn't something that surprised me. But where was Pipo?

When my eyes adjusted, I caught him wandering around. "Over there, there he is." He rambled around a woman and looked at her face. He opened his mouth and scratched his head at the same time, then he pulled his hands together and nervously roamed again.

"Pipo, where are you going?" screamed Ninang Rola who wouldn't let go of my hands. "Pipo!"

He didn't hear her. Then, he stood in front of another woman. There were other children with her, throwing him strange looks. One little girl ran behind the woman, away from Pipo.

I followed his jacket, making sure I didn't lose sight of him. He ran around aimlessly, sneaking his way through crowds and luggage that lay all over the floor. He pulled his sleeves down, turning his face everywhere. Before we could catch up with him, he was already running back to us, panting, wiping his nose with his collar.

"Stop running. Stop," said Ninang Rola, letting go of my hands, bending her back forward to catch Pipo's shoulders. "What do you think you're doing? Are you trying to get lost? We don't have much time."

His arms swayed, telling us something he couldn't say. When his feet finally settled in one place, he said, "I don't see Mommy anywhere."

"Look what you're doing to your jacket. Don't wipe your nose on it! Stop that!" She pulled Pipo's hands off, and held them down.

"Where is Mommy?" Pipo started shaking, his face turning red. "Where is Mommy?"

Ninang turned to me. "Here, take this envelope. Your tickets are in there. Don't lose this, Gringo." Then she grabbed me and held me again, kissing me on both sides of my cheeks. I could feel that her lips were shaking like mine.

"Where is Mommy, Ninang Rola? How come she's not here?"

She looked at him, his face lined with tears. "Pipo, Pipo . . . my young boy. You will take care of yourself in the States." She smoothed his pants that were already wrinkled by the rain. "I know you will turn out to be good. You will take care of Gringo. Promise me that. Promise your Ninang Rola, Pipo?"

"You told me Mommy was going to be here. You told me . . . you told me." His voice was cracking in the air. "You lied to us. Where is she? Why isn't she here! Where did she go? How can she do this?" Then he ran off again.

Amid noise, I could only hear his voice going *Ma, Ma, Ma*. He stopped a woman who was walking through one gate. I tightened my grip, wishing somehow that he was right, but as soon as the woman turned around to find out what he wanted, Pipo screamed at her, "No, you're not!" In full view, it was clear that she wasn't: skin too dark, hair too short, and too heavy. I could have told him that. There were many women around. I wondered if Pipo would run to all of them. I found myself looking at them, too. "But not any one of them looks like Mommy at all." My thoughts came out of my mouth.

Pipo came running back to us again. "Ninang Rola!"

Ninang Rola pulled him to her chest, resting her chin over his head while he pounded on her. "Stop, Pipo, please." Then Pipo hardened, his whole body so solid it would crumble. She then took my hand and moved me close to her as well. For a moment, she didn't speak, opening her lips to try but nothing came out but more deep breaths. She only grabbed us tightly as if by letting loose of one finger, she would lose us forever. That was when she said it, and I knew she had waited for so many years, not wanting to accept it to herself, but finally in those last moments together, she let go of it: "Your mother belongs here. This is her only place in the world."

And that was all I needed to hear. I blocked out everything else she tried to say. For the first time, I understood her, without ever wondering for a moment what she was trying to tell us. *Your mother belongs here.* I took Pipo's hands, peeled him away from Ninang Rola. She wouldn't let go of us at first, her hands wrapped around us like cellophane stuck to my skin. Pipo was still very stiff. I removed her hands again. "We're going," I said softly, pushing the envelope up in front of me so that it wouldn't slip.

She gently pushed us away, saying something I couldn't hear. Maybe she was telling us to go as well, pointing to the gate we had been standing in front of for some time.

Your mother belongs here.

This is her place in the world.

Her last words, uttered with much remorse. Her face told me so: broken, aged by the many years she had tried to keep us together. The eyes of surrender. The loss of faith. Her religion finally slipped off her lips, down to the ground where she had once walked on her knees. *Santíssimo Rosario,* she would say, I knew she would, and it wouldn't mean anything to me. How many beads of rosary could bring us together now? How many more could have saved Pipo from Boy Manicure? Maybe what it all meant, by not having Mommy there, was that somehow Ninang Rola got to keep her. But I didn't ask, maybe someday I would learn to understand.

I lifted my feet, as heavy as they seemed then, still hearing Pipo's quiet cries. In front of us was a crowd of people rushing through the gates, brandishing their tickets. They all couldn't wait to leave. I imagined watching Daddy Groovie walk through them, turning back every minute to look at Mommy. I imagined Mommy watching him, her jaws so tight she would break her teeth. I put my arms around Pipo's waist. Soon there were people behind us. Everything slowed down. Faces. Eyes. Breathing. Even my own legs seemed to be taking their time. Or my own thoughts. In Ninang Rola's eyes, we were already gone in the crowd. I remembered what she had said earlier, finally understood why she said so: If you have any questions, always ask the women in blue, the stew-ward. And they were at the gate, with their welcoming smiles. I continued to look ahead but made sure not to lose grasp of Pipo. I could hear his breathing slowing into sobs. "M-mommy," he mumbled again. His arms were down on his front, immobile. I held my brother more tightly. I had never held him like this before. I didn't want anyone to touch him again, or harm him. Inside, I would carry the weight of what I knew, everything I knew about him, no matter how heavy it was. I didn't know why he would let me do this or lead him like that, this person who would always be older than I. Perhaps it was the look on his face, that look that made him know what we were leaving behind. I had the look all over mine, too. The face of the no-turning-back. Not a quick glance. Not a spit of goodbye.

ACKNOWLEDGMENTS

Maraming salamat to the early readers/editors of this book: Curtis Chin, Noel A. Jackman, Leslie Lum, Marie G. Lee, Berry A. Realuyo, Randy D. Suba, Victor Tolentino, Barbara Tran, and everyone at the Asian American Writers' Workshop, NY—salamat; and a special salamat to Grace Suh, for "talking."

Maraming salamat to a great writer and editor: Rahna Reiko Rizzuto.

Maraming salamat to Wendy Schmalz for taking the book when I wanted to let go, for hurling it to the literary world—with uncompromising strength; and to Amy Scheibe for pulling the novel out of its dark box, and giving it colors, support, and faith. For both of you, the grace in which you handled this novel is more than I can ask for. Salamat.

To the cities where the book was conceived, written, and finished: New York City, Jersey City—thank you, Madrid, Barcelona—muchíssima gracias, and Manila: for the pain, and the inspiration—maraming salamat.

Maraming-maraming salamat sa aking pamilya: Daddy, Mommy, Ate Berry, Bong at Bobot at Auntie Mely, at lalo na, Bogs, Nicole at Kiko—dahil sa inyong pagmamahal, pagmamahalaga, at walang patid na paghawak ng aking mga kamay, narito ako. Mahal ko kayong lahat!

At sa mga Pilipinong bahagi ng aking mga ala-ala, at sa *bansa ng payong* na hanggang ngayo'y nagdudulot ng hiwaga, sa init at bagyo, para sa inyo ang aklat na ito . . .

The Umbrella Country

Bino A. Realuyo

A Reader's Guide

A Conversation with Bino Realuyo

Q: Although completely set in the Philippines, there seems to be an underlying relationship with the United States running throughout the book. Why is this?

BR: I wanted to write about America without setting the book in the United States. I think the borders of world literature are slowly diminishing as a result of the globalization of culture, commerce and technology. The "American dream" is as strongly felt in the streets of Manila as it is in New York City. While it works to the advantage of some, it breaks the hearts of many.

Q: Why did you feel the need to write about America?

BR: This country saved me and my family from poverty. If I hadn't come to the United States, I wouldn't have all the advantages I have now and I most likely wouldn't be writing. I would be more concerned as we were then about putting food on the table and would be expected to labor for little money. Literature is a luxury for most Filipinos, whether it is reading or writing. So growing up, we always had this dream of going to America, where those who went before us were doing so much better than those of us left behind.

Q: The narrative structure changes in different chapters, sometimes linear, sometimes conversational. Why is this so?

BR: During the writing of this novel, I read a lot of contemporary literature. I knew even then that I didn't want to write conventional narratives. I wanted a variation on storytelling on many different levels, without losing the sensory and emotional content of the novel. I like the idea of trying to do something different by writing a book without following a particular standard. This was very liberating.

Q: The chapters read like interwoven stories, with distinct beginnings and ends. Why did you choose to tell the story this way?

BR: I wondered at first how Gringo would have dealt with his remembrance of his past. I thought his memories might have come at different times. I don't think memory flows smoothly. I think it's more uneven, like the way I have shaped the book, with each chapter like a sudden rush of thought, it began, it ended, then followed by another influx of memory. It takes the reader through a different kind of remembering, with each chapter having equal emotional impact.

Q: You also write poetry. How does this affect your fiction?

BR: They complement one another. When I began the novel I was trying to finish my poetry collection. Actually, I got bored with the restraints of the collection and needed a diversion. Before I knew it, I couldn't leave the novel and felt the need to finish it. I have learned that fiction gives me the space to experiment with language, while my poems are quite formal. I think poetry can be very restrictive because a poet must deliver the message of the work in so few pages. Because of the length of a novel, there is a lot of room for creativity. The only relationship between the two for me is that I am working within the confines of the same landscape of images, my body of work being all about the Philippines.

Q: As a Filipino-American, do you find much representation of your culture in books?

BR: There has been a Filipino presence in American literature for a very long time. Filipinos first started writing in English a hundred years ago when the United States took over the Philippines in 1898. And because of immigration to the United States, there has been a steady increase in Filipino-American literature. Many non-Filipinos write about the

Philippines and our experiences, but we are slowly reclaiming our voices, our stories, our truths.

Q: Daddy Groovie, Gringo, and Boy Spit are all very colorful names, as are the others in *The Umbrella Country.* How carefully do you choose the names for your characters?

BR: I revere names, that they mark people, so I am very careful to attach meaning to all names. In the Philippines, the name of a child often reflects changes in the political climate. There was a period when everyone had multiple Spanish names, like Maria Consuelo Veronica de Los Santos Buenaventura. During the American Period, Anglo names were suddenly adopted everywhere. Then to reclaim some of the past, we started giving our children combinations of Spanish and Anglo names. This has caused a lot of confusion, as many people now have complicated names, or similar names, so if we don't know someone's name, we give them nicknames based on how they look or what they do—like Boy Manicure, Boy Spit, or Sergio Putita.

Q: You seem to have written a classic coming-of-age story—would you agree?

BR: I don't want the book to be read only as a coming-of-age story of the two brothers. I think there is much more in the novel than watching Gringo and Pipo deal with their lives. I am also trying to explore the strange and very complex nature of family bonds amid poverty and sometimes violent circumstances, while telling the quiet story of the Philippines during its most turbulent period. So I guess it's also a sort of coming-of-age for the country and all the characters, not just the boys, as we are never too old to grow.

Q: There seems to be a trend toward young, immigrant fiction. Do you see yourself as part of this movement?

BR: I think literature in other countries has always been the domain of the economic elite because they are the ones who have the luxury to send their children to good schools at home and abroad to study literature. The Philippines is no different—the literati there is dominated by people who were schooled in the United States. I think immigration of people from the lower economic bracket has given birth to a new form of world literature—the literature of the educated poor. I am very excited to be part of this emerging generation who understands what being hungry means because they have either experienced it firsthand or have once lived so close to it.

Q: There are shadowy characters in the novel—specifically Estrella and Boy Manicure. Why did you choose not to develop them more?

BR: Well, I chose to sketch Estrella simply because Gringo didn't know her. Returning to the past was a way for him to find her, to get to know her, only to realize memory isn't enough, and perhaps can never be enough. For Boy Manicure I wanted to create a gay character who exists only in the perception of the people around him, based on the stereotypes and homophobic ideas of the society he lives in. Because no one really knows him, everybody fears him, so they must make him an outcast. Very few people are strong enough to withstand that pressure. Boy Manicure is no exception.

Q: Does much of your fiction originate from your personal experiences?

BR: Yes, but I use my entire family's life, not just mine. I draw much inspiration from the rich and complex histories of my family, beginning from the root—my father, who was imprisoned by the Japanese in the concentration camps during World War II, then my mother, then my whole family—we all have special relationships to the Philippines. However, these stories do not come without a price. They may be rich sources for future literary works, but writing about them is very painful and difficult.

Q: Your female characters are very believable, and you seem to love writing about them. Why?

BR: When I was growing up my father wasn't around much and when he got sick and was taken to the United States, the only people around me were my mother and my oldest sister, so I was basically raised by women. Because of the lack of male figures, I used to always think I knew exactly how to be a woman but had no idea what it was like to be a man. This might have affected my character and sensitivity to women's issues—a lot of my poems are written in a woman's voice.

Q: When Gringo refuses to look at his mother at the airport, he seems to be turning his back on the past, as though he'll never return. Have you ever gone home?

BR: For many, many years I would go to sleep and end up in Manila, as if in my psyche I needed to be taken home to face my past again. The reality of it was I had no desire to go home. Home for me goes beyond native origins; home is where you find your heart, your soul. That for me is the United States. Writing is my dialogue with the Philippines. I am not sure when this conversation will end, or if it will. But I know that someday I will have to confront my country by going home. By then, I hope to be armed with a great deal of understanding of myself and my past.

Reading Group Questions and Topics for Discussion

1. Why do you think the author titled the novel *The Umbrella Country*? What metaphors were used in the novel for the author to decide on this title?
2. Gringo's family lived during Martial Law, one of the most repressive eras in Philippine history. How do you think the political situation of the times affected the characters' view of the world around them?
3. The novel offers an intense look at family life in the Philippines prior to immigration to the United States. Are these desires and dreams typical of future immigrants? Should countries in the "first world" keep their borders open to less developed countries? How are attitudes toward immigration changing in the United States and the world?
4. The novel begins with the line, "It was the season of sun." Many chapters begin and end with images of the changing weather. How was climate used to describe situations and sentiments of the characters?
5. What anxieties would Gringo and Pipo experience growing up without their mother? More and more, we are seeing single parent households; how is society dealing with these changing family structures? How do you think our definitions of "family" will change in the coming century?
6. Ninang Rola mentioned the United States when she was telling Gringo about the women's liberation in the Philippines. How do you think the women's movement in the United States affects the movements in other countries? How do you feel about social movements in other countries emulating American ones?
7. Sexuality and identity are important themes of the book. How did these differ between the male and female characters of the novel?

8. The novel deals extensively with the adverse effect of homophobia on its young characters. How do you think attitudes about gays and lesbians have changed over the years? How does religion affect these attitudes?

9. Names tell much about a family's history. How did the author use names to reflect the characters, histories, and attitudes of the people? Share the origins of your family name and stories behind it.

10. One of the most important passages in the novel is what Ninang Rola has said a few times, "Certain things are better kept than said." Do you agree with this statement? What are the ironies built around this statement in the novel?

11. In the chapter "Querida Means 'Dear,' " the author gives a look at the life of "other women" in the Philippines. How is this different in your country?

12. How would you compare and contrast the way Gringo and Pipo dealt with the world around them? Are there patterns that foretell the kind of future the brothers will have?

13. The family in the novel eventually immigrated to the United States. How is your idea of immigrants affected by reading this novel? How is this novel different from other immigrant stories you have read?

14. Explore the character of Boy Manicure. What do you think is his most significant contribution to the novel? Would the novel be any different without him?

15. Do you think Ninang Rola made the right decision when she encouraged Germano to find and marry Estrella? Ninang Rola compares the situation to a "rock on a ring, never to be separated again." What are the positive and negative attributes to her statement?

16. In one of the most memorable episodes in the novel, Pipo pushed Gringo away, saying "Run, Gringo, run," only to get himself hit by Daddy Groovie. What does this tell us about the character of Pipo, his inner strengths and weaknesses?

17. If you were to write a sequel to the novel, how would it begin?
18. Estrella is perhaps the most complex character in the novel. If you were Estrella, would you have stayed behind?

BINO A. REALUYO was born and raised in Manila, Philippines, and studied international relations in the United States and South America. He has finished a poetry collection, *In Spite of Open Eyes,* and is the editor of *The NuyorAsian Anthology: Asian American Writings on New York City.*

Bino's poetry and fiction have regularly appeared in *The Kenyon Review, Manoa, New Letters, Puerto Del Sol, The Asian Pacific American Journal,* and *The Literary Review.* He has done readings across the country, and was an invited poet at the Geraldine Dodge Foundation Poetry Festival in 1996 and a guest lecturer for literature at Yale University. He has received a Pushcart Prize nomination and the 1998 Lucille Medwick Memorial Award from the Poetry Society of America.

Bino works full time in the field of literacy and technology and also teaches survival English part-time to immigrant sweatshop workers. He is at work on a new novel and a second poetry collection. He lives in Manhattan. *The Umbrella Country* is his first novel.

[illegible] was born and raised in Manila, Philippines and studied international relations in the United States and South America. He has published a poetry collection, [illegible] and is the editor of *The [illegible]*.

[illegible]'s poetry and fiction have regularly appeared in *The [illegible]*, [illegible], *The [illegible]* [illegible], and *The [illegible] Review*. He has done readings across the country and was an invited poet at the [illegible] Poetry Festival in [illegible] and a guest lecturer in literature at [illegible]. He has received a [illegible] and the [illegible] Award from the Poetry Society of America.

[illegible] works full-time in the field of [illegible] and has taught [illegible] English [illegible] to immigrants [illegible] writers. He is at work on a new novel and a second poetry collection. He lives in [illegible].